MAGIC AMBUSH

MAGIC AMBUSH

THE EVERMORES CHRONICLES™ BOOK 2

MARTHA CARR
MICHAEL ANDERLE

DISRUPTIVE IMAGINATION

LMBPN Publishing
PMB 196, 2540 South Maryland Pkwy
Las Vegas, NV 89109

Version 1.01, December 2021
ebook ISBN: 978-1-68500-604-4
Print ISBN: 978-1-68500-605-1

THE MAGIC AMBUSH TEAM

Thanks to our JIT Readers

Dave Hicks
Diane L. Smith
Zacc Pelter
Jackey Hankard-Brodie

Editor

SkyHunter Editing Team

CHAPTER ONE

The ground was shaking. Leaves trembled on the trees that lined the sides of the hidden valley. The stream's water frothed and lapped against the base of the crystal that sat at the center of it all. The gem-like monolith glowed with magic as well as the bright light of a Texas dawn.

Under one of the trees, Fran Berryman sat with her phone in one hand and a ball of light magic cupped in the other, just in case. She didn't expect to be part of the action, but it was always best to be on the safe side.

"You could've dressed a little more subtly," Singar said. The Willen was half Fran's height and had a rat-like face. She was sitting with her back against the tree, a laptop on her knees, and assorted sensors plugged into the computer.

Some were purely technological, designed to measure infrared light, unusual sound waves, or vibrations in the ground. Others were more esoteric, crystals and runic cards attached to the ends of data cables to pull in information about any magic around them. Singar pointed at one of those crystals across the valley, calibrating it against the magic given off by one of the Evermores waiting in ambush around the crystal.

"I like these clothes." Fran ran a hand down her sequined t-shirt and embroidered jeans. "At least I left my roller skates at home."

"They wouldn't have done you much good here." Singar nodded at the rough ground running down to the stream, then straightened her baggy camo print shirt. "But that outfit is going to draw the target's attention the minute it appears."

"I'll be fine." Fran smiled. "The Source isn't interested in me. It's after the kemana crystal, remember? Winslow told us."

"Yeah, but did you notice how he didn't tell us why?"

"I'm sure he'll tell us later."

"I think you're trusting these people too much, just because they've got the same magic as you."

"Because I'm one of them." Fran toyed with one of the sequins. "I know this is, like, a weird thing to say, but now I know that I'm an Evermore, that I've got these strange powers in common with them, I want to—"

"Hold that thought," Singar said as something started *beeping* excitedly on her computer. "We've got trouble incoming."

Across the valley, the Evermores were bracing themselves. In their sturdy boots and worn jeans, they would've appeared to most people like another group of hikers out enjoying the wilds, not a group of centuries-old magicals bracing themselves for battle. Then again, most people wouldn't have been able to find this valley. Past a certain point, disguises didn't matter.

Winslow, the leader of the Evermore group, raised his arms and started to chant. The others joined in and as they did so magic flowed from their hands, weaving a net in the air. It shone with power but a subtly different sort than the kemana crystal. The Evermores' magic lay in light and sound, and that was what they'd woven their trap from.

The ground shook more violently, and the stream lapped across its banks as if the water was trying to escape. Then there was a roar and the ground burst open close to the crystal. Dirt flew through the air, and a creature emerged, water flowing past it down into the hole.

The Source was a being of pure power, its constantly changing body made up of magical energy. Its legs were those of a bear one moment and a giant chicken the next. Mole-like paws the size of digger scoops became razor-sharp claws became clusters of tentacles that waved like they were stroking the air. Its head was a lion one moment and a pointed selection of crystal shards the next, but it always looked fearsome. It stepped out of its hole and ran one of its shifting limbs down the crystal.

The Evermores' chanting rose in volume and the net they'd been weaving closed in around the Source. It finally noticed them and howled, a distorted, discordant noise like a tornado blowing through a trumpet shop.

Fran held her phone steady, filming the Source as it turned to face the Evermores. "Wow. That thing is, like, so weird, and so amazing!"

"It's certainly different." Singar adjusted one of her sensors, her eyes never leaving the computer screen as she watched the data rolling in. "We need them to keep it there for a while if we're going to get enough data to redesign the trap."

"They might catch it. Then they won't need our containment unit."

"Let's hope not, for the sake of our profit line."

The Evermores closed in on the Source, hands still raised. The net grew more tangled the closer they got, but Fran found it hard to make out the details. There was so much light, sound, and magic from the Source and the Evermores that it all turned into a jumble. She had to keep filming. They could make sense of it later.

Then something changed. Wings spread wide from the Source's back, and the Evermores went flying. Strands of magical net evaporated as the whole thing burst apart.

Winslow landed on his feet, as graceful and steady as a martial arts master in a kung fu movie. He charged straight back in at the Source, hands waving through the air, spinning a circle of light. The Source turned to face him. He flung the light at it, but whatever he'd been trying to do, it didn't work.

The Source absorbed the attack, then opened its mouth and spat a beam of sound so powerful that Fran saw it rippling in the air. Winslow dodged around it and grabbed hold of the Source's arm. His magic flowed, shaking the Source with a deep and powerful sound wave, but it flung him off. This time he splashed down on his back in the middle of the stream.

Winslow's attack might not have beaten the Source, but it had given the other Evermores time to recover. They were back on their feet with magic in their hands. Enfield ran over to the fallen Winslow and gave him a potion from a pouch, while the others used blasts of sound magic to push the Source away from the crystal. They were moving out in a loose circle, trying to surround the Source as they steered it, maneuvering toward an open patch of ground on Fran's and Singar's side of the stream.

"That's not going to work," Singar muttered as she stared at her screen.

"How can you tell?" Fran tried to glance at the readings while keeping her phone pointed toward the Source, but it was hard to take in both things at once.

"The power levels. These guys are potent, but they're not as coordinated as their poses pretend, and that thing's an absolute beast. No way will they overcome it."

"I don't know. They're winning right now, maybe—"

The Source lunged at one of the Evermores. As it moved, its body changed again, becoming a narrow, focused shape like the head of a gigantic arrow. It cut straight through the magic the group had been weaving and sliced into the shoulder of the Evermore, who yelled in pain as she fell.

The Source landed past her, and its shape changed again. Now it was a thing from nightmares, a hound the size of a tow truck with blazing eyes and pointed teeth. The savage claws of its six legs tore up the dirt as it ran up the slope, straight at Fran and Singar.

"We have to help!" Fran dropped her phone, raised her hands, and opened her mouth wide. She yelped, and her magic added to the sound, turning it into a concussive blast that hit the Source right on its snout.

The Source flicked its head, shaking off the pain, and kept running. Fran threw another blast of sound magic and another. The third hit the Source in its shoulder, and it started to limp. Then its legs became wheels, and it moved steadily again, faster now, a snarling dog riding the bulbous tires of a monster truck.

Fran stood her ground. She was sure that was what you were supposed to do in a fight, especially when your friends were in trouble. If the Evermores weren't quite her friends yet, they were relatives.

She gathered all the power she could muster, shaking the earth in front of her, turning it from solid ground into loose dust that anything the size and weight of the Source would surely sink into.

Wings sprouted from the Source's back again. It soared over the broken ground. Fran had a fraction of a second to stare in terrified awe as it sailed right across her trap. Then Singar slammed into her, knocking her out of the Source's path.

The Source flew past them and hit the ground on all four wheels. Singar had pulled a switchblade from the folds of her skin. She rammed it into the closest tire. However, it was nowhere near enough to stop the Source. The knife was wrenched out of Singar's hand and flung down into the dirt as the Source kept moving, rolling on up the hillside.

The Evermores ran after it, hands and voices raised as they summoned their magic. Winslow was in the lead, dripping from the stream.

"Weave a new net," he shouted. "Pen it before it can get away."

It was too late. The Source leaped into the air. Its front turned into the head of a giant drill, and it slammed into the ground. Rocks and dirt flew as it burrowed into the earth, vanishing into the darkness.

Enfield ran to the edge of the hole and peered down the tunnel the Source had left in its wake.

"Should we follow it?" he asked. "Try to catch it while it's wounded?"

"We wouldn't catch it," Winslow said. "We barely scratched it, again." He picked up the switchblade and handed it to Singar. "I'm afraid that weapons like this won't do much damage against a being of pure power."

"Maybe not, but it'll think twice about messing with me again." Singar folded the knife and carefully wrapped it in a clear plastic bag. "Besides, I'm mostly after the blood sample. The more data we have, the better we can adapt the containment unit ready for next time."

"I admire your diligence." Winslow smiled. "Fran has done well in recruiting staff for her company. I should warn you against assuming that the Source will learn from what you just did or that it thinks in any way. It's a beast of pure instinct, not of reason."

"Then I'll keep sticking it with knives until its instincts tell it to lay off." Singar put the knife in her backpack, then picked up the laptop with its attached sensors. "Oh dung, the screen's cracked. Let's hope that was the only thing that got damaged."

Down by the stream, a pair of Evermores used sound waves to collapse the tunnel that the Source had arrived from, while Enfield did the same for its escape route. The idyllic forest kemana, a place of magical refreshment and thriving life in the middle of the desert, wasn't quite back to how it had been, but it was close enough.

"Back to your office?" Winslow asked as he summoned a portal, a glowing ring through which they could step from Earth to Oriceran. Through it, the wall of a dusty basement was visible.

"We have some other sensors to gather first," Singar said. "We'll meet you there."

"I'll leave the portal open."

"That's okay." Fran pulled out a handheld mirror with runes and circuitry attached to the back. "We have ours." She tucked it away again for safekeeping

The Evermores stepped through the portal, which closed neatly behind them. For the first time since they'd arrived that morning, the valley seemed peaceful.

Singar stowed away the sensors attached to the computer while Fran gathered others they'd set around the valley. She picked up her phone, which was dusty but intact. Then she pulled out the mirror. Before she could activate it, Singar laid a hand on Fran's forearm.

"I'm serious about what I said earlier," the Willen said. "Whatever Winslow is to you, he's not being completely honest with us. He's bad news for the company, and I'm not sure he's planning to pay us."

"It'll be fine." Fran offered her friend a reassuring smile. "We're not doing this part for the money, remember."

Singar wrinkled her nose. "I hope that wasn't supposed to sound like a good thing."

CHAPTER TWO

In a gloom-laden world of nightmares and anguish, the Darkness Between Dreams sat watching its creatures at play beneath a scab red sky. The nightmare hounds chased each other across a landscape as twisted and unforgiving as the Darkness Between Dreams' mind. This was a bleak and terrible place. That was why the Darkness loved it and why it wanted more of reality to be like this. More space for the dark and twisted. More room for the Darkness's people.

"Soon," the Darkness said. It stroked the head of one of its hounds with a tentacle. "Soon we'll break the barriers, and you can go through. Soon the Earth will be ours." The Darkness sighed, a sound like the gurgling of pipes in a broken-down factory. "First, I have to gather my resources. I have to understand what we're facing."

The hound's needle-like teeth sank into the Darkness' tentacle. The Darkness laughed and shook off the dog. The beast flew into a circle of other nightmare creatures, and they tore at each other with teeth and claws. It was enough to make the Darkness Between Dreams swell with pride.

The Darkness extended a tentacle and drew a circle in the air. Magic flowed and formed a portal. If only it were this easy to make a way through for the hounds and all the other nightmare creatures. However, the Darkness needed to pave the way for them first, to make a world they could live in. For itself, the portal was enough.

The Darkness stepped through into a top-floor office in a tower block on Oriceran. The office was large and decorated with the quality that extraordinary wealth could buy.

A vast desk of imported red hardwood and a firmly upholstered chair custom made to fit its owner dominated the workspace. A pair of abstract paintings on the walls, both the work of critically acclaimed artists, provided splashes of color. Across the room from the desk were floor-length windows that looked out from the twentieth floor across the irregular, improvised urban sprawl of Mana Valley.

The portal closed. The Darkness Between Dreams went to the back of the room and opened a wardrobe hidden in the wall. It pulled out a skin suit, a thing made with as much magical as technological skill, designed and refined by witches, beauticians, and plastic surgeons. The Darkness stepped into it, its body flowing to fit the human form, and carefully closed the opening up the front. When it looked in the mirror mounted to the wardrobe door, it wasn't the Darkness Between Dreams anymore. Instead, tech entrepreneur and Mana Valley celebrity Howard Phillips smiled back from the polished glass.

Phillips selected a suit from the wide selection on the rack, all handmade to his measurements by the finest gnome tailors. He'd barely pulled his pants on when there was a knock on the office door. "Come in, Julia."

The door opened and Julia Lacy, his personal assistant, walked in. She blushed and averted her eyes when she saw him standing there bare-chested. One hand pushed back a strand of blonde hair that had broken loose from her ponytail.

"I'm sorry, Mr. Phillips, I can come back when you've dressed."

"Really, Julia, do you think I'm going to get embarrassed about this?" He slid a tentacle out through the wrist of the suit and waved it in front of his chest. "This isn't even me naked."

Julia laughed. "Of course not. Sorry, Mr. Phillips, it's a habit, I suppose."

"Never let habit get in the way of your work. That's not how we win in Mana Valley."

Julia sat in front of the vast desk and laid a tablet on her knee.

"Would you like to go over today's schedule?"

"I need to talk to you and Handar first." Phillips buttoned up his shirt, watching himself in the mirror the whole time. He liked this body, partly because it reflected the extent of his power in this place, but he could never quite get used to it. Wizards had such a strange form with only four limbs and two eyes. That was no way to design a body.

Julia's fingers tapped on her tablet. A minute later, as Phillips was doing up his tie, the door opened again. Handar Ennis walked in.

The contrast between Phillips' bodyguard and his PA

was dramatic. Handar was a towering slab of Kilomea muscle, Julia a slender, diminutive woman. Handar was intimidatingly ugly, with his wrinkled brow and tusks, while Julia was, as others reliably informed Phillips, what humans considered quite pretty.

Handar solved his problems with muscle and intimidation, while Julia used knowledge, magic, and more subtle forms of persuasion. That contrast was why Phillips found it valuable to have them both around. That and their willingness to work with a nightmare beast set on conquering the world. Not everybody could get on board with that part.

"Sit down, Handar," Phillips said. "I don't need guarding here."

The Kilomea scowled but sat next to Julia. The seat creaked under his bulk but didn't bend or break. Phillips bought his furniture to last. If it couldn't withstand a heavy body, what use would it be once this whole valley was a mass of blood and shadows and tentacular beasts?

Fully dressed, Phillips closed the wardrobe and made his way to another wall section. A brief wave and a touch of magic opened it to reveal a safe. He entered the key code, opened the door, and took out an ancient sheet of parchment.

"The prophecy our late gnomish friend found." He laid it carefully on the table and sat. "Very inconsiderate of him to die before he could bring it to me, or perhaps share what else he knew about his sources."

"One of the Tess prophecies, ain't it?" Handar growled.

"It seems that way. Like so much information around those ancient manuscripts, it's incomplete."

Julia leaned forward in her chair, far more interested in the document than Handar was. She peered at the writing, trying to decipher an ancient text in an obscure script, written with all the cryptic evasions that made prophecy such a nightmare to untangle.

"Is there something you'd like us to do?" she asked. "A clue to where the rest of the document is, perhaps?"

"Nothing so helpful, but there's something in here I want you to pursue."

Phillips tapped a finger against a line on the manuscript. The appendage bent at an unnatural angle as the tentacle inside the skin suit briefly twisted to its usual patterns before snapping back to something more human.

"These Evermores," he said. "They're supposed to guard the magic on Earth. I want to know more about them."

"You think we could seize control of Earth's magic, boss?" Handar asked. "Make 'em all do your bidding in return for their power?"

"We can't leap straight to the takeover, Handar. We have to lay some groundwork first, and I think these Evermores could be a valuable source of power in their own right."

Julia looked over some notes on her tablet. "The prophecy implies that they have powerful magic and control over an even more powerful magic source. Are you thinking that we might ally with them, gain access to this source of power?"

Phillips shook his head.

"I've been dealing with magicals for millennia, and I've started to understand groups like this one. They're people with a mission, a great sense of their righteousness. They'll have some moral direction or code of honor that means they have to keep protecting the Earth. You can't success-fully stay hidden this long without the certainty that brings. When they find out about me, they'll want to stop me, not to help."

"So they're an obstacle to be overcome?"

"Or an opportunity."

Phillips got up from his desk and walked over to the window. He stood there with his hands behind his back, gazing out. The other two, experienced in their employer's moods, went to stand either side of him.

Beyond the window, Mana Valley sprawled in the sunshine beaming down between the mountain lines that ran to north and south. On either side of the River Almane, tower blocks reached into the sky. Some were modern, slick fingers of concrete and glass. Others were older, the homes of ancient wizarding orders, polished buildings of marble with shining turrets and wide balconies. Others combined the two styles, tradition and modernity melding like the magic and technology for which the valley was renowned.

Around them, the city sprawled for miles in every direction. There were apartment blocks, factories, ware-houses, mounds full of gnome and Willen tunnels. There were roads, railways, and power lines. In the foothills were the grand arches of dwarf strongholds and the scree slopes made of rubble from their mines. Vast lizards flew along-side flocks of birds, and an elf flew past on a giant butter-fly, a spectacular way to stay clear of the commuter traffic.

"Mana Valley is the key," Phillips said. "There's so much power here, applied in so many ingenious new ways. It's the point where Earthly technology and Oriceran magic achieve their greatest coming together. It's a key point around which the universe turns. That makes it a weak point too, one that we can exploit.

"To do that, I need power of my own. Coming here sets certain limits upon me. I'm not everything that I would be in my realm. If I can consume the power of others, unique and ancient power, then I can do what I need to do. I can crack open the walls between realities, turn this whole place into one giant portal, and use it to channel my power and my minions onto the Earth."

"You're going to suck the power from these Evermores?" Handar asked.

"Yes. For that, I need to find them. I'm going to be working some magic of my own, but I need you two to set your minions on the task. Call back whatever hirelings or summonings you sent out to find that portal mirror and set them on this instead."

Julia and Handar exchanged a look.

"There's a problem there, boss," Handar said. "Those guys, they ain't come back."

Phillips stepped back and stood facing his employees, arms folded across his chest. "What do you mean, they haven't come back? Are they dead, ran off, arrested?"

"We don't know," Julia said. "After the first few magic mirrors they found turned out not to be the target, we both told our people not to report back until they found the right one. Now they're not answering us."

"Hm." Phillips stroked his chin, a human gesture he'd seen on television and found oddly satisfying. "So somebody else is standing in the way of my plans. I wonder if they know what they're doing or if they got lucky... Well, it doesn't matter. Find some new hirelings, summon some new spirits, do whatever you need to do. Find me these Evermores."

"Yes, sir," they chorused.

Julia headed out the door, but Handar lingered, frowning as he looked out the window once more.

"Is there something else you wanted to discuss?" Phillips asked. "I have a meeting with the senior management team."

"That mirror," Handar said. "You was going to try to get to the netherworld, to summon an army of the dead."

"Yes, I know my plans."

"Ain't we doing that no more? I liked the idea of working with dead people."

"Oh, it's still on my agenda." Phillips nodded at the door, which was open a crack. Handar closed it. "It's not a priority now and not one that I want to push around Julia."

"Why? She went along with it before."

"She'll do as she's told, but I've been reviewing her human resources file. There are certain...sensitivities, losses in her past. Dealing with the netherworld might bring those up and destabilize her.

"We'll pursue that avenue quietly for now, without her direct involvement. When the time comes, she can come to terms with the results. Until then, I want her in top form. No need to bring up the netherworld around her again. Understood?"

"Yes, boss."

"Good. Now go find me these Evermores."

CHAPTER THREE

Fran skated slowly along the sidewalk so her colleagues could keep up. That wasn't much of a challenge with Elethin Tannerin, whose long legs and elven stride meant that she could move quickly even in a pencil skirt, but Bart Trumbling only had a gnome's legs and an old gnome's legs at that. Letting him keep up meant making slow progress.

Elethin glanced at her watch and tutted.

"We're going to be late," she said. "People at this level don't appreciate being made to wait. They're all either very busy or the sort of people who would rather be skiing than in a meeting."

"You could've gone without me," Fran said. "Then I could've stuck around in the workshop to look at the Source data with Singar and Smokey, instead of rushing straight from the portal to this."

"We couldn't do this without you. You're the CEO of Mana Wave Industries. Big investors need to meet you in person to evaluate you and what the company offers. The company's face is a critical part of its sales pitch."

"Surely they only care about the money we could make. This is all about figures, right, Bart?"

"I'd like to agree with you," Bart said. "It would certainly make my job easier as Director of Finance. The fact is, even the most modern investment funds don't work by pure, cold logic and spreadsheets. The human factor matters and part of the human factor means showing that we're treating them seriously. That's where you come in."

Fran sighed. This wasn't what she'd expected when she decided to set up her own magitech company. It was all going to be about experiments with circuitry and spells, about making new machines that did things no one had ever done before or did them better than anyone else could.

It was going to be her in a lab, surrounded by heaps of machinery, reinventing the world. Instead, there were all these meetings and emails, so many emails that they tempted her to invent a spell code that would answer them for her.

"Who is it today?" she asked.

"Elizabeth Dooley." Elethin opened her phone and brought up a file, reading the screen without slowing her pace. "Head of Dooley Holdings. They have operations here and on Earth. They've backed most of the biggest tech innovators of the past twenty years, both magical and mundane.

"She's renowned for her ability to pick a winner. Get her on board, and half the hedge funds in the valley will be hammering at our door, looking for a chance to invest."

"They'd better not hammer too hard. Our door has rusty hinges."

Fran had expected Dooley Holdings to be based in one of the slick modern tower blocks down by the river. Instead, their route carried them to one of the older buildings, half wizard's tower and half anthill with giant termites crawling over the outside carrying out maintenance work. A gnome receptionist directed them to an elevator at the back of the lobby, powered by a pair of six-foot stick insects in a giant hamster wheel. The turning wheel pulled on a rope that lifted the wooden elevator through five floors to the hallway outside a meeting room.

"I feel like I've shrunk to the size of a fly," Fran said. "Is there a giant spider somewhere that's going to catch us in its web?"

"Don't make any comments about this place unless Dooley asks you to," Elethin said. "Her family made their fortune retraining transport and agricultural insects for construction and industry. She's very proud of that background. That's why she always invites potential investments here so she can show off what the Dooleys made."

"Got it. No spider jokes." Fran nodded. "I will be the embodiment of seriousness."

"Good. The quirky, roller-skating CEO is great for grabbing headlines and getting us into the room, but once we're there, you need to show what you're capable of. Right, Bart?"

"Oh, absolutely." Bart ran a comb through his tousled mess of white hair. "This is the big leagues now, and it's the funding we need to step things up at Mana Wave. With her backing, we could buy some of those new three-dimensional printing machines that Singar's so excited about, not to mention the enchanted processors Smokey has been demanding. It would be a huge advantage for us all." He smiled at Fran. "I know you've got this."

"Thanks, Bart." Fran grinned. "All right, let's do it."

She pushed the door of the meeting room open and rolled in. The others walked in behind her.

The meeting room was much more modern than the building around it. Only monitors decorated the walls, two of them showing figures from stock markets across two worlds, the rest currently blank. A meeting table stretched down the room's length with metal chairs on either side of it. A woman in a suit sat at the opposite end of the table. Two dwarves with open laptops occupied the seats to her left. She stood to greet them.

"Bartholomew." She shook Bart's hand. "It's been a long time."

"So long that I wasn't sure you'd remember me."

"This must be Fran Berryman, the remarkable young woman everybody has been telling me so much about." Dooley looked down at Fran's roller skates. "My, you're even wearing those away from the cameras."

"Oh, totally, I love…I mean, it's important to display a consistent image." Fran shook Elizabeth's hand. "It's great to meet you. This place is, like, totally cool, but in an ordinary business way, nothing weird just really awesome and, um, oh yeah, this is Elethin Tannerin, our Director of Public Relations."

"I imagine that's a challenging role at a firm like yours."

"Oh yeah, totally, Elethin has to—"

"Not at all," Elethin said. "You'd be amazed at how smoothly Fran has Mana Wave running."

"Your Director of Software Development was arrested

by the Silver Griffins while running naked down the street."

"An unfortunate misunderstanding and a reflection of the passion that we at Mana Wave Industries bring to everything we do."

Dooley chuckled. "Not the worst pitch I've ever heard. Speaking of which, the floor is yours."

She sat and watched them expectantly.

Bart took a laptop from his briefcase and plugged it into a data cable that snaked out of the table. An image appeared on one of the blank screens, a slide reading "Mana Wave Industries" with their temporary logo in one corner. Fran suddenly remembered the big load of notes Bart had sent her to prepare for this meeting that she'd almost entirely failed to read. She was sure it would be fine. After all, this was her company. No one knew it better than she did.

"Okay, so, this is us." Fran smiled. She'd insisted on the next slide, a picture of their small team in their basement office, smiling and waving at the camera. It was a picture that helped her to relax and put a human face on the company. Or, more accurately, a magical face. "Mana Wave Industries is a new company developing magical solutions for the modern age. Our approach brings together the best of Earth technology and Oriceran magic to develop outside-the-box answers for problems people didn't realize they had, for a dazzling synergy of the best of two worlds."

She was particularly proud of wielding the word "synergy," which she'd learned from Gruffbar. She felt it gave the presentation a professional feel.

"This is our central product." She motioned, and Bart

moved them to the next slide, which showed a gray box with crystals along the top and wires dangling from one side. "It doesn't look like much, but the Mana Wave Deluxe Battery is the future of power sources. It stores electricity and magical power, combining them to provide a superior energy flow for any magical technology. By integrating it into our other devices, we intend to grab the attention of a wide range of market sectors while demonstrating the efficacy of our design."

It was all coming back to her now. Why had she ever worried? She knew the presentation back to front.

"How does it work?" one of Dooley's dwarves asked without looking up from his screen.

"Oh, that's the cool part!" Fran rolled over to one end of the screen and pointed at one of the battery's crystals. "This here is, like, a whole new sort of—"

Elethin coughed. The sound was small yet still sharp enough to bring Fran up short. Then she remembered the practice run they'd done to prepare her for moments like this.

"That's proprietary information." She leaned into "proprietary," another of those grand words that made her sound all business-like. "Obviously, in the interests of our investors, we can't reveal details of our intellectual property at this time."

Dooley nodded. It was a small nod, but one that made Fran feel she must be on the right track.

"We have one contract already, for a piece of technology powered by this battery, which we'll be delivering to the—" She caught Elethin's expression before the elf needed to clear her throat. "The people we totally can't talk about, because I agreed to a, like, really thorough non-disclosure agreement, but that contract is legit and real, honestly. Once we deliver we'll be able to talk about it, and show people what we made, and you're going to be so impressed."

"I'll be the judge of what impresses me," Dooley said sternly.

"Oh, yes, sorry, I didn't mean to..." Fran's voice trailed off. She was losing this. She skated from side to side, trying to gather her thoughts, but it was hard with these smartly dressed people staring at her in this intimidating board-room. Now a giant ant was crawling past the window, and she knew she shouldn't talk about that, but she really, really, *really* wanted to ask how they trained them, and now that was all she could think about, and...

"Bart, you tell them about the finances." Fran hurriedly took a seat.

"Okay." Bart skipped a bunch of slides until he reached the financial graphs, then started talking about buy-in, overheads, and return on investment. That got the attention of the second dwarf, who stared at the slides intently while Fran sat drawing deep breaths and trying to remember what she had to say next. There was something about the flexibility that came with a small operation in its early stages, about lean processes and agile working practices and...

"Thank you, Bartholomew," Dooley said as Bart shifted from one slide to the next. "I think I've seen enough."

Fran glanced at the others. If Dooley had seen enough, that was a good thing, right? It meant that she'd heard enough to persuade her.

Elethin was as smilingly calm as ever, but the look on Bart's face said that this wasn't what they'd wanted. Fran huddled forward in her chair.

"First, I want to say thank you for coming here today," Dooley said. "It's always a pleasure to hear about up-and-coming businesses, and yours is certainly interesting.

"For my fund to invest, interesting isn't enough. I need to be sure that you have the stability, the solidity, and the firm leadership to navigate the difficult waters of establishing yourselves. What I see from you here has potential, but people with potential come to me for money every day, and potential isn't enough. I'm sorry to say that what you're offering doesn't fit the Dooley Holdings investment strategy."

She gave a small nod, and one of the dwarves got out of his seat. "Diri will see you out."

Bart disconnected his computer and put it back into his briefcase. Trying hard not to let his dejection show, he followed the dwarf out of the room, with Elethin not far behind and Fran bringing up the rear.

"Ms. Berryman?" Dooley called as Fran reached the doorway.

Fran turned hopefully. Had Dooley changed her mind?

"Magical pheromones," Dooley said. "I can't tell you the details, but we use magical pheromones to train the insects. I saw you watching the ant through the window, and it struck me that you're the sort of person who would want to know."

Fran smiled. It was something at least, and she appreciated the act of kindness. "Thank you."

"You really do have potential, but you're going to need

to treat this whole business more seriously if you want to succeed. Take my advice, leave the roller skates at the door next time, and the sparkly t-shirt with them."

"Thank you." Fran turned and skated off down the corridor.

CHAPTER FOUR

After the disappointment of the meeting with Dooley, Bart decided to splurge on a taxi to carry the three of them back to Mana Wave Industries' headquarters. They ended up catching a flying cab and rode in a basket hanging from a griffin's claws, which deposited them outside the front door of the Worn Threads carpet store. All sorts of magical creatures were adapting to the modern business environment of Mana Valley, and that included flying creatures doing deliveries and transport.

As she walked into Worn Threads, Fran waved at Raulo and Gail standing behind the counter and made her way to the door at the back. She didn't know where other startups found their homes, but she thought Mana Wave was probably the only one where another business sold carpets upstairs. Except maybe if there was a carpet startup, but she couldn't work out what that would be for. Cleaning maybe?

Through the door and down the stairs, she emerged into the large basement. It was a lot less dusty than it had been a few days before with fewer spiderwebs hanging everywhere. The old mirror-making machines still lined the back, and the dust sheet covering a gigantic display mirror filled one wall.

The team from Mana Wave Industries had set up two distinct working areas within the basement. In one corner was the office, a set of desks where Bart, Elethin, and the dwarf lawyer Gruffbar could do their work.

In another corner was the workshop, with prototypes lying out on the workbenches, tools lined up neatly on a table to one side, and crates of components next to that. It also contained computers used for coding and design work. This was Singar's and Smokey's realm, home to the creative side of the business, where they made the technology.

Fran had space on both sides of the room so she could alternate her work as CEO with helping to design and create their magical technology. Although the office was closer to the stairs, today she skated straight past it to get to the workshop. After the frustration and failure of seeking investment, she needed to do something practical, something that would make her feel like she could get things right.

Smokey was at his computer, analyzing the data from the encounter with the Source. He was currently a cat. Fran couldn't help thinking that it would be easier to type if he shifted into his other form, that of a particularly hairy dwarf. He claimed he found it easier to think while in feline form.

The CEO on roller skates wasn't going to argue with anybody else's whims. Across from him, Singar was working on the components for their prototype containment unit. So many of their hopes rested on the technology. She wasn't alone.

"Hi, Winslow!" Fran said brightly. "And Enfield. What are you guys doing here?"

"Helping Ms. Twitchtail with her work," Winslow said. "We have more experience with the Source than any other magicals do, so we can provide invaluable insights and ensure that you quickly and effectively complete the unit."

"Helping, right," Singar muttered. "They're fiddling with things they don't understand." She smacked Enfield's hand away from the rune-etched mirror at the base of the device. "Seriously, touch it again, and I'll get you with the soldering iron."

"This is ridiculous," Enfield said. "We have a higher cause, and we need your device to fulfill it. We're only trying to help."

He crossed his arms, and the muscles under his tight t-shirt shifted. As Evermores went, he was the most pleasing to look at. Fran wouldn't have objected if he wanted to stand around the office flexing his abs. It was when he tried to flex his authority that the problems came.

"It's great that you guys want to help, but this is our business, it's our prototype, and you need to let us get on with our work," Fran reminded them.

"Exactly." Singar glared at the Evermores. "Keep your hands to yourselves."

Fran examined the prototype. Its fundamentals hadn't changed much from the last time they'd used it. The mirror at the bottom had runes etched along its edges. Above that was a collapsible framework of metal rods, painted black, with crystals and electronics dangling off their joints. The battery pack, which used the technology she'd so proudly showed to Dooley, was wired onto one edge of the mirror.

"Is it working yet?" she asked.

"Not yet." Singar took an etching tool from her toolkit and started fixing one of the runes, where the glass had melted and reformed under the pressure of magical power. "The strain of capturing those goons put more pressure on the system than we thought. I don't want to run a live test until we've got it running at least as efficiently as before."

"More efficiently," Smokey interjected. "Looking at this data, we need ten times the containment field we had last time around."

"That shouldn't be a problem." Fran detached the battery unit to look inside. "It's working on feedback, remember. The stronger the magical inside, the stronger the containment field."

"Sure, and that's great in theory. It only works if the hardware can support that level of magic."

"Which is where things went wrong before." Singar moved on to the next rune. "Your battery and feedback loop gave us enough power to hold them all, but the framework couldn't take it."

"Oh, I hadn't thought about that." Fran peered at the layers of magical and technological materials in the battery pack. "How about if we set an upper limit on the feedback?"

"Then we couldn't hold this monster you're so excited about." Smokey tapped his screen, where her video of the Source was showing next to data from magical sensors. "It's insane. Where did you find it?"

He looked at the Evermores. Enfield watched Winslow from the corner of his eye, deferring to his superior's twenty-six thousand years of experience.

"The Source has been with us for generations," Winslow said. "It was safely contained and can be contained again once we get it back to its holding place. The difficulty is getting it there, a challenge that I'm confident you young people can meet."

"'It's been with us for generations' doesn't answer my question."

"I thought your interest was in the future, not the past."

"Knowing where this comes from will help me understand how it works. We can't do our best job when we don't have the full information, and when I do a job, I always do the best."

"An admirable attitude."

"Hey guys, I have an idea!" Fran looked up, grinning. "What if we replace the rods with a magical alloy? Some dwarf forges are producing amazing things now with enchantments mixed into the metal."

"We've tried toughening up the frame, remember?" Singar shook her head.

"Then not a tougher alloy, but one that will transfer the power more quickly."

"Won't that add to the strain?"

"No." Smokey jumped from his stool onto the workbench, landing smoothly on all four paws to examine the parts more closely. "If the power flows more quickly, we reduce buildups, which will alleviate the pressure, in theory at least…"

The three of them fell to talking enthusiastically about

the technicalities of metals and magic, bouncing ideas back and forth.

"You see," Winslow said during a break in the breathless chatter. "This is why I have faith in you to deliver the containment unit for us."

"Not for you." Gruffbar had come over to see what all the talk was about. Now he looked up at the Evermores. "We have a contractual obligation to make the prototype for the FBI. Once that's done, we can make something for you."

"Master Steelstrike, I understand that you have concerns about the finances and reputation of your company, but trust me, providing us with what we need won't do you any harm."

"Absolutely. Once we've fulfilled our contract."

Winslow's placid smile stiffened.

"Perhaps you don't appreciate what's at stake here. This is the Source, a creature of vast, chaotic power. For the safety of the whole world, we need to contain it."

Gruffbar snorted. "Everyone thinks their problem is the biggest in the world, but right now our problem is staying afloat, and that means fulfilling our contracts."

"Contracts are such small things in the span of centuries. We shouldn't let them hold us back."

"Lives are small things in the span of centuries. I've seen them lost over a packet of chips and a few poorly chosen words, but they still matter."

"I'm not quite sure what your point is."

"That reminding me how much bigger the world is won't impress me. Things that seem small to you matter to the rest of us. Things like Fran's dreams for this business."

At the mention of her name, Fran looked up from a pile of components.

"What's the matter, guys?" she asked.

"Your colleague is in some denial about the situation here," Winslow said. "There are bigger things at stake than some matter of business, no matter who it's with. Prophecy tells us that letting the Source run free will lead to disaster, and we must do everything we can to stop it. That means we need your trap."

"Prophecy." Gruffbar snorted. "I'm a lawyer, not a seer, but I'll tell you this much for prophecy. It's baloney."

"Excuse me?"

"Prophecies are cryptic and ambiguous, every one of them open to interpretation. Even if you had the most solid prophecy in the world, different people would still use it in different ways to justify what they want to do. That's how prophecies get used, as an excuse for every side to do what it wants to do already.

"Want to save the world? Prophecy told me how. Want to conquer it? Prophecy guided me to triumph. As reasons go, that's no better than 'because I wanted to.'

"Prophecies sound impressive, and they're a great excuse to do what you want. They don't impress me. I have free will, and I intend to use it, not to have my fate dictated by somebody who died centuries ago."

"Very grand, Master Steelstrike, but it doesn't change the fact that the Source is out there, and we need to contain it."

"That doesn't change the fact that we have a contract to fulfill."

"This is absurd. Fran, you'll give us a containment unit first, won't you?"

"Um, I think, that is…"

"Fran, we can't give it to them. You know that. It's your company at stake here."

"Yes, but, well…"

"You're an Evermore. Your duty is to the Evermores. You will build the device for us."

Fran frowned, then shook her head. "No, I don't think that's how this works. Whoever's kid I was, I chose to make this company. That's what matters to me. I've already messed up taking care of the company once today. I'm not doing it again."

Gruffbar watched Winslow's reaction. The Evermore had lived for thousands of years, but no one had defied him often in that time. He was used to being around people who did whatever he told them to.

Now that he was in different company, he was treading more softly, but he'd gone too far in his moment of frustration. He knew it too. He was backing off a little, giving Fran space, carefully considering his next words. Gruffbar was very curious to hear what they would be.

He didn't get to find out because Fran had her own ideas.

"There's an easy solution," she said. "We'll make two prototypes at once, one to the standards the FBI set, and the other for the Evermores, specially designed to contain the Source. That way, everybody gets what they need, and the FBI gets theirs at the same time as the Evermores, so they're still first; just joint first, is all. We meet our contract and save the world." She beamed at them all, caught up in the excitement of the moment. "Perfect, right? I'm, like, thinking outside the synergy box, being all lean and agile and business-like."

Gruffbar couldn't help laughing. "It's certainly not what anyone was expecting. Won't it mean that both prototypes take longer?"

"Most of our time's currently spent on problem-solving and working out the tech," Singar pointed out. "Doubling down on the same components won't make much difference."

"The control code should work for both," Smokey added.

"See?" Fran turned back to her work. "Everybody can have what they want. Someone grab another mirror, and Singar, give Bart the brief on what we need for the new alloy rods. He's best at haggling over prices. We're not building one prototype. We're building two, and better than ever!"

As the technical team got back to work, Gruffbar and Winslow exchanged a look, evaluating the other.

"Looks like prophecy might get fulfilled after all," Gruffbar said.

Winslow offered a small smile. "It tends to do that."

CHAPTER FIVE

Fran woke to the sound of tapping on her window. She reluctantly pulled the duvet from over her head and peered blearily at the world.

"What's happening?" she mumbled and looked at the crow perched on the window sill. "Is there some emergency, or have you ruined my sleep so I'll give you birdseed? Because that's not going to fly."

Her phone started *beeping*, the sound of her morning alarm.

"Oh!" Fran switched off the alarm and went to open the window. "You were getting me up for my working day, huh? In that case, thank you very much."

The crow hopped onto Fran's shoulder and sat there, cleaning its feathers, a black and sinister presence against her pink pajamas.

Fran yawned, stretched, slipped her feet into her fluffy bunny slippers, and headed out of her room. Her mind was on coffee and breakfast while she tried to remember what she was doing with her day. There was a meeting with an investor, sorting out the workspace, and tests to run on the containment units.

She didn't mind being busy, but it was starting to feel like her life was out of control, constantly rushing to do things that other people had scheduled. What happened to running her company, her time, and above all her creative work? At least she could have a bowl of cereal and watch some cartoons first to get her ready for the day.

Then she saw the pile of blankets on the sofa and remembered that her apartment wasn't her own anymore. "Morning, Mom."

"Good morning, Francesca." Irene Berryman stood amid the clutter of modified magitech devices in the kitchen with a mug in her hand and a bewildered expression. "Is there something wrong with your coffee maker? I've pressed this button five times, and all it's giving me is this strange purple liquid."

"You have it on the squirtle setting." Fran shuffled over and took two clean mugs from the cupboard. One of them had a picture of a smiling kitten, the other a unicorn flying over a skyscraper. "Here, let me show you."

"Squirtle? What's squirtle?"

"It's this new gnome thing. It's tasty. You should try it."

"I don't think so, dear. I'm happy with my coffee."

"Then you need this setting." Fran turned a dial on the machine, which gave a strained sound and leaked a little steam.

"Is it supposed to do that, Francesca?"

"No, but it's okay. It won't do any harm."

"If it keeps doing it, you'll peel the paint off the wall. You should stop that, or you could lose your deposit."

"Okay, Mom. I'll fix it later." Fran hit a button, and the machine filled the kitty cup with coffee. "Here you go."

She turned to hand the coffee to her mom, but the kitchen was so small and cramped that they almost knocked into each other. Irene took the mug, smiled stiffly, and backed out.

"I'm sure you could do better than this, dear," she said. "Remember that job in Portland?"

"I don't want to work in Portland, Mom. I want to work in Mana Valley."

Fran took her coffee, a bowl of Chocolate Frosted Glitter Bombs, a carton of milk, and went to sit on the sofa. She had to push a heap of blankets and pillows around to make space, but that wasn't too bad. It made a nice sort of nest.

"Are you putting the news on?" Irene sat next to Fran and picked up the remote. "Good to see that you're staying informed about what's happening in the world."

"Actually, I was going to... You know you can look up the news on the Internet, right? Then you can read the stories that matter to you, instead of listening to ten minutes about some budgetary business in the elf lands before you get to the tech news."

"I suppose you can, but then you might miss out on something important. The presenters always seem so calm and confident that it makes the difficult bits easier to hear."

Irene turned on the wall screen, and a news anchor appeared, an elven man in a suit with a spiraling wire running from his old-fashioned earpiece. Those had become fashionable again on the news channels lately. Viewers apparently found the old-fashioned touch reassuring. Fran found it annoying. Why use old technology when you could have shiny new toys?

At least Irene put the sound down low, so they could hear the news without it screaming into their ears. If Fran didn't pay attention, she could almost pretend the reports were a segment from *Superhero Action Hour*, and the presenter was talking about the heroes beating the villains. The cartoons would kick in properly at any moment. It wasn't quite the start to the day she wanted, but it would do.

Josie's bedroom door opened and she emerged, already smartly dressed and ready to face the day.

"Good morning, Fran." Josie kissed her friend on top of her head. "Good morning, Ms. Berryman."

"I've told you already, Josie. You can call me Irene."

"I'll get used to that eventually. Just give me another —oh!"

Josie disappeared from view with a *thud*.

"Are you okay?" Fran turned to peer over the back of the sofa.

"I'm fine." Josie picked herself up off the floor. "Just tripped over this case."

"Sorry, Josie." Irene set her coffee down amid the clutter on the coffee table. "Let me move that out of your way."

She picked up the case and looked around, but there weren't many places to put luggage or anything not stuck to the walls.

"Fran, maybe I could put it under your bed, dear?"

"There isn't space under the bed, but you could leave it on there while I'm out at work."

That wouldn't help much in the mornings, but it might

at least give Josie more room while Fran was out, and that felt like a good thing to do. Fran was acutely aware that however much her friend insisted Irene's presence wasn't a problem, they were both sacrificing space and privacy for someone Josie barely knew.

While Irene wrestled her luggage into Fran's room, Josie sat on the sofa with her green tea and a bowl of soaked oats.

"What's going on in the world?" she asked.

"Something about magic disruption on Earth and a political thing between the dwarves." Fran picked a piece of soggy cereal out of her bowl and held it out for the crow. "I don't follow this show, but honestly, the characters are completely unconvincing. I mean, who calls a mining ruler King Deepdelver? At least try to give it some subtext."

They laughed, and Josie changed the channel to cartoons. A giant rabbit was fighting a robot in an exaggerated version of downtown Mana Valley, with lots of explosions and a bright pop music soundtrack.

"Space for one more?" Irene returned from her tidying mission.

"Sure, Mom." Fran shifted closer to Josie, making space for Irene. The sofa was technically only a two-seater, but none of them were very big so they could just about squeeze in. "Maybe we should get a chair."

"Where would we put it?" Josie asked.

"Um…" Fran looked around. "Maybe it could be on the wall and, like, fold away inside when it's not needed?"

"We don't have much spare wall."

"Ceiling then?"

"Genius. This is why you're going to rule Mana Valley."

Having eaten her breakfast with remarkable speed, Josie got up. "No offense, ladies, but I need to get out of here. I want to get in early and have a look at our product specs so I can make a good impression in this conference call."

"Good luck!" the Berrymans chorused in unison.

"Thank you." Josie grabbed her bag. "Have fun."

She headed out the door, leaving Fran and her mom alone. Fran shifted over so they each had space on the sofa and ate another spoonful of Chocolate Frosted Glitter Bombs. Nothing set her up for the day like sugar and artificial food colorings.

"I'm confused," Irene said. "Why is the rabbit fighting the robot?"

Fran ran through the plot of *Superhero Action Hour*, which took far longer than she expected. The background between Superbun and Dr. Roboticon alone took several minutes. Then she had to explain why the archangel wings were in storage in a Mana Valley office.

"Honestly, dear, I'm amazed at your ability to follow these things," Irene said. "Even when you were a little girl, you understood them far more easily than I did."

"I had an advantage. They designed them for little kids."

"True, but you're not little anymore. You're all grown up, running your own company, living here with your friend. I'm so proud of who you're becoming."

"Thanks, Mom. It's nice to have you here. We haven't hung out in far too long."

"I know, it's just... Well, you know I don't like to travel too much, and you've come all the way over to Oriceran. It makes it a bit tricky to fit around work."

"Aren't they missing you right now?"

"They've let me work from home for a few weeks. I told them it was a family emergency."

"Is it?" Fran looked at her mother, a little worried about where this was going. The crow hopped onto the coffee table and joined her in staring. Irene glared back at the bird.

"You, shoo." She made as if to kick the crow. "This is between my daughter and me." The crow hopped back. "I said shoo. Unless you really want to get into it with me right now..."

With a flutter of wings, the crow fled through Fran's room and away.

"Don't you like the crows?" Fran watched a black feather drift to the floor.

"They're fine. I just..." Irene sighed. "Never mind that. We were talking about my visit."

"You said it was an emergency."

"It certainly seemed like it at the time. You have to understand. I've been sheltering you from your Evermore background your whole life, not telling you where I came from or what that means.

"Then this business with the Source kicked off, and Winslow headed out into the world for the first time in years. I hoped you wouldn't get caught up in it, but then I heard they were heading this way. I wanted to be there for you, to explain some things first, to stop it from becoming stressful and difficult. Something tells me I haven't succeeded."

"Honestly, Mom, it's fine. You told me I'm an Evermore, which explained my powers. Maybe it'll give me some opportunities. Understanding my magic can help me with the tech we're making, and capturing the Source will give us new ways of testing it."

"That's all Winslow's asking you to do, help capture the Source?"

"Yes, Mom. What else would he ask for?"

"I don't know. Winslow and I go back a long way, but I hadn't seen him since before you were born. A lot can change in twenty-five years."

"The guy's twenty-six thousand years old. Is a couple of decades going to make a difference?"

"That's what I'm afraid of. Never mind that, look at the time. Don't you have a meeting this morning?"

"Yes, but—"

"Shouldn't you have a shower first and pick out a professional-looking outfit?"

"I guess, but—"

"So, you get cleaned up. I'll wash the dishes. Then I can help you pick out something to wear."

"You don't need to do the dishes. We have a machine for that. I say machine, but it's more a sort of magical cupboard."

"Does it work as well as this thing?" Irene pointed at the broken magical footrest lying in front of the couch. "Because I don't want to risk this lovely kitten mug on a machine that might break it."

"Kitty is pretty cool."

"I want to be useful, to say thank you for having me here."

"Fine, you can do the dishes." Fran handed Irene her bowl. "I really should get ready."

Only when she was cleaning her teeth did Fran realize

how quickly the conversation had shifted away from the Evermores. There was still so much she didn't know, like why her mom had left that home behind, what her role had been among the Evermores, and how much Fran's powers were like theirs. What might the Evermores want from Fran now that they were here, beyond building the containment unit?

There was no time to think about that now. She had a busy day ahead of her, meetings to prepare for, better devices to make. Tapping on the window told her that the crow was still out there, urging her on, ensuring she got where she needed to be on time.

Her mother's past could wait. Fran needed to focus on the future.

CHAPTER SIX

Fran walked into the Blazing Bean with her skates in her hand instead of wearing them. That seemed like a good way to show that she was the sort of sensible adult investors could work with.

The coffee shop was fairly quiet. A few skaters sat by the window, and a group of young witches experimented with illusions at a table to one side. Bart was sitting alone at a table near the back of the room, under one of the shop's many pop art posters. Fran waved to the skaters, who she'd chatted with a little at the local skate park, and made her way to the counter.

Behind the register, Cameron was leaning over his laptop, his blond hair sticking out like a crazed halo around his head, whistling while he typed something.

"Hi, Cam." Fran smiled as she approached. "Working on your thesis?"

He looked up with a distracted half-smile.

"Hi to you too." Sparkling blue eyes peered at her

through a pair of round glasses. "What can I get for you today?"

Fran looked at the blackboard behind the counter, which listed the day's cakes and all the many coffee options that the Blazing Bean's staff took such pride in.

"A large latte with chocolate and hazelnut syrups, please."

"Haven't you had that one before?" Cam started the grinder, filling the air with the machine's roar and the delicious smell of fresh coffee beans.

"I have? In that case, can I please have some chocolate sprinkles on top too? Those shouldn't be reserved only for cappuccinos. The other coffees will feel left out."

Cam grabbed a syrup bottle off the shelf. "Anything else?"

Fran perused the row of cakes. "A donut, please. The one with the glittery icing and the raspberry filling."

"I thought you might like that." He set her coffee on a tray and took out the treat. "There you go."

"Thanks, Cam." Fran paid, then lingered a moment longer. The investor wasn't here yet, and no other customers were waiting for service. She could afford to stop and chat with her favorite barista. "How are things going with you?"

"Oh, fine." He turned his attention to his laptop and gestured at something on the screen. "Trying to get on top of this paper, you know? Deadlines."

"Yeah, I get it. I have an investor meeting." When he didn't say any more, Fran picked up her tray, feeling disappointed in a way that she knew wasn't rational but still felt very real. "I'll see you later."

"Sure, see you."

She walked over to the table with Bart and set her tray down. Then she noticed his empty cup.

"Oh, I am such an idiot!" she exclaimed. "I forgot to get anything for you."

"Don't worry," Bart said. "I've had more than enough caffeine for now. Besides, the investor's here."

"Really?"

A dwarf in a suit was at the counter, giving Cam his order. Fran was painfully aware that once again, she hadn't read her briefing on the client. Instead, she'd spent her time working with Smokey and Singar on the containment unit, and now there wasn't time to ask Bart about him. She would have to improvise and hope for the best.

She settled into her seat, straightened her blouse, and tried to make herself look presentable. The blouse and slacks had been her mom's suggestion. The unicorn rainbow hair clip was her way of asserting her style.

"You look very pulled together," Bart said.

"Thanks." Fran drew deep breaths, trying to calm her rising tension. "I'm trying to be more professional."

"Well, it works."

The dwarf came over with a mug of black coffee in hand.

"Mr. Trumbling." The dwarf nodded at Bart.

"Mr. Bloodax, thank you for taking the time to talk to us." Bart gestured at Fran. "This is Mana Wave's founder and CEO, Fran Berryman."

"Ms. Berryman." Bloodax didn't hold out his hand, but the way he bowed his head held as much formality as any greeting could.

"Pleased to meet you, Mr. Bloodax," She tried to imitate the solemnity of that nod. "How are you today?"

"Busy, but who isn't?" He looked around. "I've never been in here before. It's very…bright."

"Isn't it fantastic? I come in here, like, all the time. It attracts the most interesting people, not at all like the…" Fran stopped herself before she said anything about the bland chain coffee shops that filled most of Mana Valley.

Those were probably the exact sorts of places that Bloodax normally did business, and she'd been on the verge of insulting him. She felt proud of herself for avoiding that. "Well, anyway, we're holding meetings here while we wait for work to finish on renovating our office. It's convenient to our HQ."

"Where is your HQ?"

"A few streets over. Nowhere you're likely to have been." She'd learned that "under a carpet store" didn't always strike the right professional note. "If you're busy, maybe we should start the presentation?"

Bart turned his laptop so that Bloodax could see the screen and they started going through the same slides they'd taken to Dooley Holdings. This time, sitting in a familiar, comfortable environment, chatting over coffee instead of standing up in a boardroom, Fran found it easier to stay calm and concentrate. She talked through her parts, and Bart covered the financials, setting out the funding that the company needed, what they would spend it on, and what they expected to deliver in return. Throughout, Bloodax listened and watched with a serious expression. He occasionally wrote things down in a small leather-bound notepad, using a fountain pen.

At the end of the presentation, Fran sat back, feeling very happy with how she'd done. She glanced at Bart, hoping to get some idea from his expression of how it had gone. He gave a shrug that was small even by gnome standards.

Bloodax looked up from his notes.

"What you're talking about here is certainly impressive, Ms. Berryman," he said. "If your technology provides even half of the power potential you've suggested, it could be transformational for several industries that the Bloodax clan is involved in. So my question to you is, can you show me this power in action?"

"Not yet," Fran admitted. "We have a prototype we're working on, using the power source."

"I'd be happy to observe a prototype in action, with one of our technical experts, to verify your claims. What does this test device do?"

"Sorry, but I can't talk about that, or show you the device before we've delivered it to the one client we have, or even tell you who that client is." Fran blushed. "That doesn't sound very convincing, does it?"

"It sounds like Mana Valley." Bloodax crossed something out in his notes. "It's the sort of risk that the magitech hedge funds take an interest in. The Bloodax clan has never worked that way. We invest in sure things, whether that was my great-great-great-grandfather buying new axes and armor to raid the goblin towns in the high hills or my great-grandfather investing our raiding wealth in iron mines. We're not about risks, Ms. Berryman, and until you have something concrete to show me, you are a risk."

"Oh." Fran sagged.

"Mr. Trumbling has my details. Feel free to call me when you have more to offer. I'm interested. I just can't help you now."

Bloodax finished the last of his coffee and slipped his notebook into his jacket pocket.

"One word of advice, though." He pointed with his pen. "Next time, don't wear a child's hair clip. It might come across as cute with other humans, but you're in magical business now, and magicals take their business seriously."

As he walked away, Fran grabbed her donut and stuffed half of it into her mouth in one go. It wasn't half as comforting as she'd hoped.

"Www a waan we," she said around the mouthful of donut.

"What was that?" Bart asked.

Fran swallowed, then spoke again.

"I said that went well. Only I didn't mean it. Because nothing went well." Sarcasm worked for Singar, but somehow it came out wrong when Fran tried it for herself.

"Actually, that wasn't bad. We'll need other investors later, and Bloodax wouldn't have said to contact him again if he didn't mean it."

"But we still don't have any money!"

"True, but Raulo and Gail are letting us use their basement free of charge for now, we got our furniture practically free from that office clearance, and I've found us some good deals on parts. We can get by a little longer."

"A little longer? Bart, I need to pay my rent, and I'm almost out of Chocolate Frosted Glitter Bombs."

Bart patted her on the shoulder. "This business is a marathon, not a sprint. We'll get there."

"Are you sure?"

"Absolutely. Ninety percent sure. Ninety-five, even."

"That's not as sure as I was hoping."

Bart put his laptop into his briefcase. "I have to get back to the office, but why don't you take a bit of time to yourself? Finish your donut, have a chat with Cam, go for a skate. That always clears your head. You'll feel better after, and we can start planning for the next investor."

"I suppose so."

Fran watched her mentor disappear out the door, then stuffed the rest of the donut into her mouth. Her fingers went to her hair clip, and she was on the verge of taking it out, but then a crow fluttered down onto the table and shook its head.

"You're right," Fran mumbled through her donut. "I should get a plain hair clip first."

She picked up her bag and skates and headed for the door. As she went past the counter, she looked over at Cam, hoping that he would stop her for a chat, to say something reassuring or tell her a joke, to lift her spirits with his smile, as he'd done before. He didn't look up from his laptop. She sighed and stomped out the door.

Behind the counter, Can watched Fran's departure from the corner of his eye. He felt bad, letting her leave in a sad mood like that, but he couldn't bring himself to start a conversation right now. Instead, he got back to making notes on what he'd seen of her and Bart's meeting.

Of course, he'd been taking notes on the Mana Wave Industries team long before they moved into their basement, but it had been the party to celebrate their new office that had aroused his suspicions. Before then, they'd been one more Mana Valley oddity, something he made notes on in case it connected to the great cause, the threat he knew was coming but that his family wouldn't take seriously.

Why would they listen to the magic-less dud and his wild conspiracy theories when they knew so much more about the magical world than he did? Why would they pay attention to the crazy talk of the family disappointment?

Still, he'd seen the signs. Something big was coming to Mana Valley, something dark and destructive. He'd found so many clues to it in so many different places, not least the piece of the Tess prophecies from the Dark Market.

While he was at the Mana Wave party, he'd seen strange magicals arrive to talk with Fran. Then he'd heard someone use the word "Evermores," something he'd only previously found in that prophecy. There was a connection here, and if Fran was part of it, he needed to be careful around her. She seemed so charming, so well-intentioned, so cute, but what if she was part of the threat coming to the Valley? What if she was one of these Evermores, or her technology was at risk of unleashing something terrible, or...

"Hey, buddy!"

Cam looked up with a start. He'd become so engrossed in his thoughts that he hadn't noticed the Kilomea waiting to order.

"Sorry." Cam hastily closed his laptop. "What can I get you?"

He made the Kilomea's coffee on autopilot, his mind

elsewhere. Once he'd finished serving, he didn't open the computer again. Instead, his attention drifted to the doorway and the memory of Fran walking out into the street. She was normally so cheerful, but today she'd looked like the weight of the world was dragging her down. Even if she might be a threat to existence, he wanted to comfort her, to let her know that it was going to be fine, that the difficult days would pass.

Then the door opened, and more customers came in, the beginning of the lunchtime rush. Cam set aside all those thoughts and got on with his job.

CHAPTER SEVEN

Fran skated down the street, singing a Weird Al song as she went. A pair of crows flew beside her, cawing in time to the tune. A winged chorus, not tuneful but dramatic. Who could ask for better backing singers?

Bart had been right. A few laps of the skate park had lifted her out of her low spirits, and a few more laps had put her in a positively good mood. Or possibly the sugar from the donut had kicked in. Either way, she felt ready to face the world and her work.

The sooner they finished the prototypes, the sooner they could show one to the FBI and maybe get more business from them. Then they could move on to other things, possibly ones they could share with the world, ones that could prove to people like Mr. Bloodax how brilliant their devices were. If she persisted, she was sure that things would work out in the end.

She stopped outside the door of Worn Threads and switched from her skates to a pair of striped sneakers. Raulo and Gail were happy to have her skate around the building, but getting up and down the stairs that way was a total nightmare.

"Hi, Fran." Gail waved from behind the counter as Fran walked in. "How are you doing today?"

"I'm good." Fran looked at the crochet Gail was working on. "Hey, that's the same blue as your hair."

"Isn't it cool? I'm making a hat so that when the weather gets colder, I can stay warm without hiding my color."

"That's so smart."

"Thank you, dear."

Fran crossed the shop and headed down the stairs to the basement. She expected to walk into the focused quiet that had marked the team's recent work, but instead, there was noise, disorder, and dust in the air. They'd unplugged the computers, moved the desks and workbenches into the middle of the room, and everybody was talking loudly over each other.

"We need to put the desks there for the power outlets." Bart pointed at where the desks had sat before.

"I told you already, we'll run in new lines," Singar said. "Have you even been listening?"

"The meeting room should be near the exit to hide the rest of the mess," Gruffbar said.

"I'm not using this thing, no matter what you say." Elethin held out a vacuum cleaner like it was a bomb about to go off. "I refuse to know how it works."

"Where's my nap basket gone?" Smokey perched on one of the desks, reaching for something down the back with one paw. "The blanket's down here, but where's the basket gone?"

They all kept talking, voices rising as they struggled to make themselves heard.

"Hey, guys?" Fran called.

No one paid her any attention.

She raised her voice and used her magic to give it extra volume.

"Hey, all of you!" This time they all shut up and turned to look at her. "What's going on?"

They looked at each other. There was an awkward pause.

"This place needs sorting out properly," Gruffbar said. "Bart thought we could surprise you by doing it before you got back."

"So, surprise?" Smokey waved a paw.

"Aw, you guys!" Fran ran over and hugged the two nearest people. Singar and Elethin both stood uncomfortably still, tolerating her appreciation. "That's so sweet. Thank you!" She looked around. "What's the plan?"

"There's the problem," Elethin said. "We don't have a plan."

"I do," Gruffbar said. "Office there, workshop there, meeting room near the front, space to expand production at the back."

"Sounds great," Fran said. "Let's do it!"

"We need to get the space ready first. Clean, dust, paint."

"They gave me this." Elethin waved the vacuum cleaner like it was something disgusting. "Just because I'm a woman, you think I'll do the cleaning."

"No, it's because you refused to carry the desks," Gruffbar said.

"That's manual labor. It's beneath me."

"But not below us?"

"You're a scruffy, bearded criminal who dresses in smelly biker leathers. It's the perfect job for you."

"I have an idea," Fran said. "Let's all do the dusting and cleaning together. You can use vacuum cleaners or dusters or magic or whatever you've got. We'll clean together, then we'll decorate together, and once we finish that, we'll sort out the furniture together."

"That doesn't sound like the most efficient way to work," Bart said.

"Maybe not, but it'll be great team building." Fran took the vacuum cleaner. She'd read about team building in a blog post, and it seemed like the sort of thing a CEO should encourage. "Come on, let's get down to it."

They spread out around the room, using whatever tools they had to clean it. Now that she had a chance to show off her magic, Elethin was happy to be involved, using gestures and incantations to sweep away spiderwebs and layers of dirt. Fran handed the vacuum cleaner to Gruffbar, who applied it with a dwarf's systematic industriousness.

Fran's sound magic helped shake the dust loose, while others applied cloths and dusters. Smokey found a way to be useful in cat form, squeezing into narrow spaces with a cloth between his teeth.

After an hour of vigorous cleaning, the air was still dusty, but the basement itself was the cleanest it had been in decades.

"We should get rid of those." Elethin pointed at the old mirror-making machines in the back of the room. "Ugly, rusty old things and they're taking up space."

"We should talk to Gail and Raulo about that first," Fran said. "After all, it's their basement."

"I want to hang onto the machines," Singar said. "We're using mirrors in our devices. Those could be useful for making custom mirrors later."

"You're looking for an excuse to play around with them," Smokey pointed out.

"Isn't that basically what our whole business is about?"

"Executive decision, the machines stay," Fran declared. "I can do things like that. I'm the CEO."

"Fine, but can we at least cover them up until Singar's renovated them?" Elethin asked. "Right now, they look like junk, and that won't help our public image if clients or investors come here. We should get rid of all those scrap carpets too so this place doesn't look like a dump."

"Ooh, or could we turn the scrap carpets into a cover for the machines? Like, a kind of patchwork thing. There are some lovely colored bits, and it would save us buying anything new."

"Yes, that could work."

Elethin waved, and pieces of carpet lifted from the pile. They headed toward the machines. Several of them hit Gruffbar in the head on the way past, even though he wasn't in their way.

"So sorry," Elethin said. "Terribly clumsy of me."

As they gathered by the machines, the edges of the carpets unraveled. Threads from the edge of one remnant interwove with ones from the next as they started to connect.

"I'm going to sort out the wiring." Singar picked up her

tool kit and a device with a laser on the top. "Can you lot do something about the walls and floors?"

"Here." Gruffbar dragged a plastic crate from the corner of the room. "I bought paints and brushes already. I just didn't think we'd get to them today."

"We've started, so we might as well do the whole job," Fran said. "Let's paint!"

They grabbed rollers, brushes, and cans of paint, and spread out around the room. There were a lot of walls to cover, as well as the ceiling. Fran wasn't a great artist, but fortunately, this wasn't that sort of painting. She set about it with enthusiasm, as well as a lot of splashing. Blobs of paint ended up on her clothes, her face, and all over the floor, but at least her wall was getting done if a bit patchy.

On the far side of the room, Gruffbar was systematically working across a wall, using long-handled rollers and a stepladder to reach the higher parts. There was a lot less mess where he was working. Bart was similarly effective but used magic to spread the paint around. Even Smokey shifted into dwarf form, put on some clothes, and picked up a brush to help.

The work wasn't only about decoration. There were practicalities to consider as well. Singar used her laser drill to make holes for electric and data cables, which ran all around the room and through holes in the ceiling.

"What are those for?" Fran asked at one point, looking at the wires dangling from above.

"We can lower them to plug machines in," Singar explained. "It means that we can hook up anywhere in the room, without running cables all over the floor where people might trip on them."

"What if the sockets bang against people's heads? Not everyone's as short as you and Bart."

"Not a problem." Singar pressed a button on a remote control and the cables *whirred* up into the ceiling. "They go up as well as down."

"Brilliant!"

While they were still painting, Elethin finished making the cover for the machines, a tasteful arrangement that looked like a deliberate work of art instead of carpet samples and offcuts. She moved on to making a floor covering, selecting different colored carpets for sections of the basement to create a sense of separate rooms, and weaving in resilient rolls of plastic flooring instead of carpet for the workshop.

Yet again, some of the flying flooring hit Gruffbar, who glared at Elethin but otherwise didn't react. A malicious smile twitched the elf's lips as she watched his rising annoyance.

By the middle of the afternoon, the whole place had been repainted and carpeted, but the work still wasn't complete. The furniture was all piled up on one side of the room, on the first sections of carpet that Elethin had laid down.

"Wow, this is impressive," Gail said when she brought them coffee and cookies. "I knew I heard thumping noises, but I thought that must be some sort of machine."

"That's us, a well-oiled decorating machine," Fran announced.

"Is the well-oiled decorating machine thirsty?"

"Ooh, yes. This is hard work."

While they ate and drank, they talked about how they

could lay out the space. Now that it was so clean and well-decorated, everything seemed different in Fran's mind's eye, and she was determined to get it right.

"You were talking about a meeting room," she said to Gruffbar. "How can we do that without walls?"

"Display boards," he said. "Freestanding ones. We set them up around a designated area, probably that patch of blue carpet by the stairs."

"That's why the blue is there," Elethin said. "A soothing color for calm meetings."

"Right, well, Bart thinks he can get us some cheap display boards, about six feet high. They'll do for walls. We still have spare chairs from that clearance, and there's a trestle table upstairs that Raulo says they don't use. It won't look one hundred percent moneyed professional, but it'll be a lot better than holding all our meetings in the Blazing Bean."

"What about the noise?" Elethin asked. "We don't want everyone who visits to hear our latest developments from the workshop or to have meetings disrupted by the ghastly roar of machinery."

"Ooh, I can solve that!" Fran waved. "I'm good at manipulating light and sound. I can cast a spell that will stop noise crossing in or out of that area, like a giant invisible wall."

"Then won't we need you to cast a spell every time we have meeting? That doesn't sound like a good use of the CEO's time."

"I'll set up a device to hold the spell," Singar said. "Something with a simple on-off switch. Just activate that every time you're about to have a meeting."

"It would be good to have some magitech on display around here," Elethin added. "That's the product we're selling ourselves on. It's good PR to show it off."

Another idea floated across Fran's mind.

"Could we have a reception area?" she asked. "Somewhere visitors go before they come into the meeting room? And give it, like, a display case along one side with lots of cool things we've all made, like my flying carpet and Singar's sign language machine. That way, everyone who comes in will get a big reminder of what we're about and what cool things we can make for them."

"I like it." Elethin nodded. "A trophy cabinet, except that all the trophies are things you made yourselves, instead of ones other people gave us. That has real swagger to it."

With the coffee break over, it was time to rearrange the furniture. Smokey stayed in his dwarf form to help carry desks and workbenches.

They set up an office space again, next to where the meeting room would go. Elethin hung one last piece of carpet on its wall, an abstract pattern made from small pieces that looked like it could be a real work of art. In the workshop area, Singar carefully arranged the boxes of supplies in order, put up hooks for their tools, and painted the tool's shape around each hanger to tell people what went where. She also hung a sign above them that read, TECHNICIANS ONLY. DO NOT TOUCH WITHOUT PERMISSION.

Singar commented, "You lot aren't total idiots, but I don't trust anyone except Fran and Smokey with my tools, and I barely trust them."

At last, they finished the work. A day before, the space

had been a barren, dusty basement with a few pieces of scavenged furniture. Now it looked like a real business was based there. The smell of fresh paint and a few drifting carpet fibers hardly detracted from it.

"It's nearly the end of the afternoon," Fran said. "Why don't we take the rest of the day off as a reward for getting this done?"

"I thought we were going to test the containment units," Smokey said.

"That can wait for tomorrow." Fran yawned and rubbed her eyes. One hand came away with a smear of paint from her cheek. "Today's been a long day, and we've all earned some time off. I'm going to go watch cartoons before my mom comes home and makes me sit through the news."

CHAPTER EIGHT

"That's it." Singar stepped back from the workbench. "Two fully functioning containment units."

Fran and Smokey stepped back too, admiring their handiwork. The containment units were very similar in design, with their mirror bases, frameworks of extending rods made from enchanted metals, and a plastic container for the battery pack and control unit attached to the side of each base. One had a new mirror instead of the slightly battered one they'd been working with from the start and white rods instead of black ones so they could easily tell them apart.

"You're sure this time?" Fran asked. "No more tweaks to the control software? No more alterations to the construction?"

"Software's all good," Smokey said. "Or at least as good as it can get until we've run some live tests."

"Same for the hardware," Singar said. "We'll have to make improvements, but we can't tell what they'll be until we've tried it all out."

"So now we need test subjects." Fran smiled sweetly at Smokey. "Would you mind climbing in so we can give it a go?"

"Once was enough for that," he said. "Besides, I need to monitor the results from the outside."

"Maybe we could ask Gruffbar…"

Fran looked across the basement. Aside from the enclosed reception area and meeting room, the place was still an open plan. The office and workshop's inhabitants could see each other across the gap between them. Gruffbar was at his computer, working on some corporate procedures, while Elethin and Bart went out in search of more investors.

"I heard that," Gruffbar said. "I'm not climbing inside your machine. I've spent decades avoiding a trip to prison. I'm not planning on being jailed by you lot."

"Not even if—"

"No."

"Fine, we'll find someone else." Fran looked up at a crow that had followed her into the office. It perched on top of the mirror-making machines with its claws hooked into the carpet cover. "You want to help, right?"

The crow shook its head. Maybe it had been through one of their previous tests, or perhaps it was smart enough not to walk into a trap.

"Perhaps we could try it on me," Fran said. "I mean, it could be kind of fun to see this from the other side."

"Absolutely not," Gruffbar called.

"It's not you this time."

"No, it's the head of our company and the public face of everything we're doing. If you get hurt by one of our devices, that could be a PR disaster. It doesn't take Elethin's skills to work that one out."

"Then who can we test it on?"

"Well…" Smokey prowled over to the far side of the room, where a dust sheet still hung across the massive mirror running most of the length of the wall. He grabbed the sheet between his teeth and tugged. It fell to the floor.

Seven figures glared out at the Mana Wave team from the revealed mirror: a witch and a wizard with matching features and pale hair, a gnome with two fingers missing, a scarred elf, and three ghostly spirits dressed in ethereal rags. They were the assorted minions of a mysterious enemy who'd come to steal an enchanted mirror and were trapped in one instead.

"I almost forgot they were there," Fran said.

"I didn't." Singar grinned. "It's a constant and satisfying reminder that sometimes jerks get what they deserve."

She raised her middle finger and gestured provocatively at the captives, who glared back at her.

"They're trapped already," Fran pointed out. "Surely you don't want to let them all out?"

"Not all of them," Smokey said. "Only one. Our control software is more sophisticated than it was when we captured them. I can use it to plug into the tech Singar put on the mirror, make a hole in the enchantments, and pick one of them to let out. Can you think of any better target for the new containment units?"

Fran considered the suggestion. She wasn't totally comfortable with turning someone into an involuntary guinea pig, but they needed a test subject, and these guys had attacked them.

"All right," she said. "It'll make for a better test if they struggle."

Singar ran cables over to the mirror while Smokey got his software ready.

"All right, I've picked out one energy signature," Smokey said. "Feeding that one back into the software. Release in three, two, one, now."

The mirror shimmered. One of the spirits that had been pressing against the glass emerged into the open air. It *hissed* at Fran.

"Uh-oh." Smokey tapped rapidly on the keys. "Looks like we might have more than one."

"They're all breaking out?" Fran looked around in alarm.

Another spirit had emerged from the mirror and stood next to its companion.

"Not that bad, but this setup isn't sensitive enough to tell the difference between those three spirits. In letting one out..."

"...we've let the others out too."

The third spirit had emerged, leaving the other prisoners banging futilely on the glass behind it.

Fran raised her hands. She'd been preparing some sound magic that she could use to direct a single spirit into the containment unit, but three was a much bigger issue.

"I don't suppose you'd like to come over here and help with our test, would you?" she asked.

The spirits *hissed* and rushed at her.

Fran flung a blast of sound magic that knocked one of the spirits back against the wall. Smokey leaped onto the back of another. His claws raked its ragged shape, and it twisted around to fight him. That left one more, which grabbed hold of Fran and flung her to the floor. Icy fingers clutched her throat, and a terrible cold ran through her flesh, making it hard to breathe.

"Help!" she gasped.

"I've got you." Singar leaped off the workbench and swung her switchblade. The blade passed through the spirit without doing anything. Singar passed through too and landed face-first on the floor next to Fran.

"Dung and dust," the Willen hissed. "I should get this thing enchanted."

The spirit had made its hands solid to grab hold of Fran, and that gave her something to fight back against. She took hold of them and sent sound waves into them. The trembling ran into her flesh, shaking and disconcerting her, but the spirit's grip weakened.

"Buy me some time." Singar leaped back up onto the workbench. "I have to get the machines going."

Fran pried the spirit's grip off her throat. She drew a couple of big breaths while she had the chance, then thrust a hand into its face and unleashed a blast of bright light. The being's flesh felt insubstantial, but its eyes must have been real enough since it lurched back, clutching its face.

Across the room, Smokey was still grappling with one of the apparitions. He could affect some creatures that were otherwise immune to non-magical effects in his current form, but he was still a house cat fighting against a magical spirit, and frost covered his coat as his opponent unleashed its magic on him.

The third spirit had recovered from being flung back and rushed across the room toward the workbench. Fran flung another blast of sound magic at it a moment before it would've hit Singar, who was frantically operating the controls of one prototype containment unit.

"We should've prepped this in advance," Singar said. "Idiots, getting carried away like this."

"Lesson for next time." Fran shot light at the spirit. It covered its eyes long enough to avoid being blinded, then fell upon her, clawing with icy fingers. "Right now, think of this as extreme testing."

Singar flipped a switch and the sleek black unit with the new mirror hummed into life. The runes around its edges glowed. She scrambled across the workbench, jumped to Smokey's computer seat, and typed in a couple of commands.

"All ready. We only need to get it in."

"Can't the magic grab the spirit?" Fran ducked a blast of freezing wind.

"That was too unstable. Come on. You got this."

The spirit's hands became solid again as it grabbed for Fran. She caught one of the hands and pulled like she was trying to yank the being off its feet. There weren't any feet involved, but it still swung around, and its head thrust through the containment frame.

"Now!" Fran shouted.

Singar hit a key. A sound like a vacuum cleaner sucking up ten tons of Jell-O filled the room as the containment unit pulled the spirit in. The mirror beneath it glowed, the frame shrank, and their opponent was left trapped within a three-foot-tall box.

"One down." Singar tapped the keys. "That's the FBI's

device working. I'm going to switch to the other prototype and make sure they both get tested."

Smokey had gotten up onto the head of the apparition he was fighting and was riding it around the room, using swipes of its claws to send it one way and the other. The spirit *hissed* and swiped at the dark-furred cat but couldn't shake him off although ice crystals covered his coat, his tail stood on end, and he shivered from the cold.

"Incoming!" Smokey shouted as he steered his prey toward the workbench.

Fran jumped clear. The spirit swooped past where she'd been and straight at the white frame. Smokey leaped off a second before his opponent ran into the trap. Singar hit a key, there was another slurping, sucking sound, and the spirit's entire form slipped inside the frame.

One more deadly figure remained. It hovered at the side of the room, claws raised threateningly. It kept glancing toward the stairs and the way out. Fran wondered why it wasn't floating away through the ceiling. Maybe it wasn't that sort of being, or this place had a special ceiling, or...

"Stop it!" Singar shouted as the spirit rushed toward the stairs.

Fran flung a blast of sound at the entity. It was hurled into the wall, momentarily stopping it mere feet from the bottom step. That was long enough for Smokey to race across the room and leap to the attack. He scrambled up its side, claws hooking into it, and planted himself on its face.

The spirit screeched and flailed at the cat. Ice formed across Smokey's body.

"Q-q-quick," he stuttered with shivering breaths. "I can't cling on for long."

Fran ran around to the far side of the spirit and started her sound magic again. This time she formed two beams instead of one focused blast, one from each hand, and crossed them. Then she drew the beams together as though closing a scissor's blades. They pressed against the spirit from two sides, pushing it across the basement, past the meeting room and the office, and into the workshop area.

The entity must've been able to feel the magic of the containment units or perhaps to hear the distress of its trapped siblings. It *hissed* in increasing agitation as she pushed it closer to confinement. After much flailing and scrabbling, it finally grabbed Smokey and flung him to the floor. It looked around in time to see the containment unit inches from its face.

It was too late. Fran gave one last thrust of power, shoving the creature into the trap. The sound of the device sucking it in drowned out its *hiss*. The mirror in the base shuddered as the second spirit joined the first.

"Got 'em all." Singar hit a key. The containment units stopped their magical *hum*. The runes along the edges of their mirrors still glowed as the magic worked overtime to contain their prisoners.

Exhausted, Fran sank to the floor, her back pressed against the workbench. Smokey made his way over, his tail trailing low, and flopped down beside her. She patted his head.

"Good kitty."

He purred.

"Well done." From his seat in the office, Gruffbar clapped. "Good work."

"No thanks to you," Smokey muttered.

Gruffbar shrugged. "I'm a lawyer, not a ghostbuster. Give me a solid enemy, and I'll happily wield my ax, but there was nothing I could do today. Besides, it was fun watching you at work." He looked around. "You know what we need here? A coffee machine to help recover from moments like this."

"I hope there aren't any more moments like this," Fran said.

"I like your optimism."

"I like these results." Singar was looking at readouts from the prototypes as they scrolled across a computer screen. "The fields are holding, the magic is steady, and the power drain is within expected parameters. Not only is our broken prototype up and running, the new one's working too. I think we're ready for a field test."

CHAPTER NINE

Josie sat at her desk, scrolling through the latest messages from around Philgard Industries and deleting most of them. This was something she'd learned within a few days in her new job. A big business produced a lot of committees, clubs, and layers of management, all of whom felt that it was not only their privilege but their responsibility to keep churning out messages to the staff.

Between that, the repetitive updates on projects she was involved in, and the times people clicked on "reply all" to acknowledge that they'd read something, her inbox was constantly full to bursting. Most of the emails were devoid of content or crammed with information she didn't care about. A lot of swift deleting helped keep her from getting overwhelmed or wasting her time on the latest procedures from parts of the company she never dealt with.

She looked up from her computer and realized that everyone else was equally focused on their screens. There was a feverish intensity to their concentration. They hunched so close to their monitors that it seemed like they were trying to crawl into the space behind the screen. She'd never seen the place so quiet at the start of the day, which was usually the time for coffee, gossip, and grumbling about people farther up the corporate ladder.

That was another thing Josie had quickly gotten used to. She loved working at Philgard, playing with all the latest exciting technology. Everyone else said they did too, but many of them seemed grumpy for people doing their dream jobs.

Simon Green, Josie's manager, looked around his monitor and across the low partition between their desks. "We're going to the test lab, Josie."

"Okay."

She got up and followed him out of the office, down the corridor toward their more practical workspace. Simon was never the most relaxed person in the building, but today the middle-aged wizard seemed particularly tense, his shoulders hunched almost around his ears. Whatever was going on, it was contagious. Josie resisted the urge to ask about it until they were in the test lab, with the soundproof door firmly closed behind them and no one else to hear his response.

"What's going on today?" She kept her demeanor calm. She wasn't going to get stressed until she knew for sure that there was something worth getting stressed about.

"Didn't you read your emails?" he asked sharply.

"All the ones that seemed relevant."

"So you saw that they've launched another round of performance reviews?"

"Isn't that something a good business does, checking how its staff is doing at their jobs and working out how to support them?"

"Support them." Simon snorted. "That's not how any of this works, not unless you're safely at the top, or you know the right people to talk to. Performance reviews are a purge."

He made the words sound darkly foreboding like something terrible was bearing down upon them.

"What do you mean, a purge?" Josie sat across the workbench from him. Around them were rows of diagnostic machines and cupboards full of equipment for analyzing the gadgets Philgard was preparing for market.

"I mean that five to ten percent of the people working here right now will be gone by the end of the month." Simon glared at her. "That's how they make space for the bright young things like you—by hacking away the deadwood."

Josie tried to stay calm. She'd only been at Philgard a month. Surely they wouldn't get rid of her so soon? Besides, she was good at her job, and she knew it.

"Why is everyone so worried? Surely if you're good at your job, they'll keep you here."

"So naïve." Simon shook his head. "You think that with everyone's neck on the line, it won't get cutthroat around here? Everyone's looking at their performance stats, at their hours logged, at the objectives they have and haven't fulfilled, and they're working out who they can blame for the bits that don't look perfect."

"You're doing that?"

"Of course. Let me tell you. I've written a very scathing

note this morning about Erin's goal setting and the tools she's supplied us with. You should do the same. If we both say it, then it'll sound more convincing, and that shifts the blame off us."

Erin was Simon's supervisor, who oversaw their work daily. From what little Josie had seen, she was perfectly nice and at least adequate, possibly even good at her job. Josie didn't want to contribute to getting someone like that fired.

"I'll bear it in mind." She had no intention of doing what Simon had suggested, but she wasn't going to pick an argument with him, especially while he was in this state. "If this is about proving that we're doing our jobs well, shouldn't we be focused on doing our jobs right now?"

"Oh yes. Someone's set us a trap."

"A trap?"

Simon unlocked one of the cupboards and took out an object the shape and size of a grapefruit with a smooth black surface and a dial marked around the outside.

"Isn't that the magical detection device we were working on?" Josie asked. "For finding a specific sort of magic?"

"Oh yes, that's what it was for. That's why they've sent this copy down to us. Officially the project never left our team, even though our copy went into the field. Now they want it to detect something different. Do you think it's a coincidence that the specs got changed as they announced the performance review?"

"Probably."

"Ha! No. This is a trap." Simon slammed the device down on the workbench. "Now it looks like we've been working on it for a month without achieving the objective for the device, even though they only set that objective today."

"Can't we explain that?"

Simon gave a bitter laugh. "So naïve."

"Well then." Josie took out her wand. "Let's do what we would've done anyway and get this done as well and as quickly as we can. What do they want it to do now?"

"Let me get this exactly right. I don't want to fall foul of some technicality…" Simon pulled out his phone and scrolled through his emails. "Here. They want it to 'identify sources of light and sound magic, with a particular focus on unusual or anomalous readings.' Seriously, what does that even mean? It's so broad that it could be almost anything."

"Light and sound magic, huh?"

Josie waved her wand above the device and cast an opening spell. The outer shell split open and its pieces settled on the workbench around it, like a peel separating from the fruit underneath. That fruit was a mass of electronics and magical components, tightly packed together to make the most of the available space.

Not for the first time, Josie admired the elegance of Philgard's designs, so much neater than the improvised devices she and Fran botched together at home. This was what happened when you channeled the resources of a vast corporation and hundreds of Mana Valley's most skilled technicians into making the best magitech in the two worlds.

"Do they mean that the magic should begin with a light

or sound casting," she asked, "or is it anything that affects light and sound?"

"What difference does it make?" Simon leaned forward to see what she was doing. "Careful not to break it."

"The difference is in how we set up the sensors. Think about a spell that creates fire. That fire is going to throw out light, right?"

"Yes, obviously."

"The root casting is one of heat or fire, not light. If we're after light and sound powers, we don't want to catch every bit of magic that casts a shred of light, so we set the sensors for source power. If we're after light and sound effects, we need to go much broader, which is also going to cause problems with interpreting the results because there will be so much magical clutter."

"I told you it was a trap. I bet they didn't tell us which it is so whatever we do it will be wrong, and they can...oh." Simon stared at the message he'd been scrolling through. "Actually, they did say. This is supposed to detect magic rooted in light and sound powers."

"I guess someone wants us to do a good job more than they want to prove they're better than us."

"Or their evaluation relies on this working." Simon's cynical sneer had returned. "Well, at least now it's something we can deal with, right?"

Josie hesitated. He was the manager. Shouldn't he tell her what they could and couldn't deal with?

If she'd been the type of person to put her position in the hierarchy before doing the job, she would've been out there sending out catty emails and frantically looking for ways to improve her performance stats. Meanwhile, she'd have torn her hair out about this evaluation business. Instead, she put her faith in the fact that the system could work and focused on the thing she loved, making better magical technology.

"We can do this, I'm sure," she said. "It might take time."

"We don't have time. We have management peering over our shoulders, waiting for us to fail. Did you see where this project originates?"

Josie hadn't seen, and she didn't really care. The challenge was the same no matter who it came from.

"We'll need some time, at least. We need to get the sensors out of this thing or get copies of them from the department that made them and test them against a bunch of different magical sources to see the readings we get. Then we need to change how those readings are filtered in the device so instead of looking for portals it… Hang on, why are we doing this? Shouldn't it be with the design team?"

"The buck has been passed. No way it gets passed back right now. It's every magical for themselves out there."

As ways to run a project went, it didn't make the most sense, but Josie wasn't going to complain. This sort of work, redesigning and rebuilding tech, was exactly the sort of thing she'd hoped to work up to from a lowly testing job. If she got to jump straight to it now, all the better. What made Simon angry was making her happy, but she wouldn't tell him that since it would only make his resentful mood worse.

Josie's phone vibrated.

"Is that about the project?" Simon asked. "It would be

just like Erin to go around me, straight to you, to try to get evidence that I've failed."

Josie pulled out her phone. It was a message from Julia Lacy, PA to the mighty Howard Phillips. Josie had met Julia through her recent work for the company, work which had led up to this.

"If u want any advice on ur evaluation, just ask," the message read. "Been here a while. I know what the bosses r looking for."

Josie smiled. It was nice to have a helpful contact in the business, someone who could show her the ropes in a way that Simon hadn't.

"It's something personal," she said. "From a friend."

She didn't like to lie, but telling Simon that she was receiving messages from Julia seemed like the worst possible idea right now, the sort of thing that would fuel his paranoia.

"Thnx," she messaged back. "Will pick ur brain later."

"Put that thing away," Simon snapped. "No time for personal business. We need to get on top of this."

He brought out his wand and started gathering magic to pull out the sensors from the device.

"Wait!" Josie saw the damage his clumsy approach was about to do. "I can do that. You have far better contacts than I do. Can you rustle up a bunch of different artifacts and devices to test this on? The more types of magic we work with, the better the results we'll get."

"That's exactly what I was thinking." Simon put his wand away. "I want to see those sensors extracted and set up by the time I get back. Remember, my report on you will be part of your evaluation, and I want to see your absolute best work."

"Of course." Josie watched him leave the test lab, then turned back to the device. If they'd wanted a jerk detector, she could've made Simon her sole test subject. For now though, she would have to make do with light and sound. Unlike Simon, those were things someone might want to find.

CHAPTER TEN

Smokey stood beneath a vast and ancient oak tree in one of the small parks preserved as wild space during Mana Valley's rapid urban expansion. Its branches twisted through the air, scarred, tangled, and dotted with distinctive dark green leaves. Nearby, carnivorous plants snapped at the bees trying to reach the more sweet-smelling flowers around them.

The way the plants' traps snapped shut, like jaws full of tiny green teeth, reminded Smokey of his nighttime hunts, pursuing mice through the streets. He seldom bothered to eat them, usually releasing the terrified creatures to catch again another day. It was the pursuit that gave him satisfaction.

He was wearing the harness Singar had made to carry his phone, wallet, and a small tablet while roaming the city in feline form. His small trailer was currently hooked up to it, which he'd loaded up with cheaply printed fliers, tape, and pots of glue, then brought with him from his apartment.

That had involved a few awkward moments in the street when larger magicals hadn't noticed him and almost stepped on the trailer, but hissing and growling always got them to back off. They should be looking where they were going, but until they did, he was happy to teach them a lesson.

Cawing came from the branches of the oak. Half a dozen crows had settled there, peering down at Smokey.

"I don't have any food for you. If you think I'm going to die soon so you can scavenge my corpse, you have the wrong cat. I eat well, and I get plenty of exercise."

One of the crows *croaked*, and the others flapped their wings as if applauding something.

"Stupid birds." Smokey shook his head. He was out here for the magicals, not for the wildlife.

There was a *thump* of broad wings moving through the air, and a shadow crossed the park. A winged lizard, her body human-sized and long tail stretching out behind, landed on the grass close to the tree. Smokey pressed his paws against the posters to stop them from being blown away by the final gust of her wings.

"Good to see you, Vaudrek," he said. "Thanks for coming out here on the weekend."

"These weeks of yours, they mean little to me." Vaudrek's tongue slid out of her mouth, tasting the air. "I enjoy this thing you are creating, this battle against the bipeds. I wish to be part of it, for now at least."

"I like your enthusiasm, but remember, we're not fighting against the bipeds. We're fighting against the system and against the prejudicial attitudes it inculcates in our two-legged peers."

"They're the ones acting this way, yes? So they're the ones we must fight."

"Not fight, persuade. It's fine to talk in combative terms, sometimes necessary, but remember, some of them could be allies."

"Yes, yes, I know, don't go eating the wizards." Vaudrek stuck her tongue out again. "Although they're tasty."

Smokey didn't know how to answer that or feel about it. Was she joking, or had she eaten people? He knew almost nothing about her species, never mind Vaudrek herself. Perhaps she'd been living in Mana Valley for hundreds of years, a life stretching back to conflicts in which monstrous-looking magicals like her might've eaten their opponents. Or maybe this was her idea of funny, playing on popular images of dragon-looking creatures.

"Is anyone else coming?" she asked, scales shifting as she bent her neck to look all around.

"Probably not. It's hard enough getting anyone to come to the meetings. Until we get more recruits, it's only the two of us."

The crows fluttered down from the tree and landed between them. One of the birds pointed its beak at the pile of posters.

"Wait, are you here to help?" Smokey frowned. "Are you the crows that keep hanging around Fran?"

The lead crow *cawed* and nodded.

"I thought you were ordinary birds, not magicals. I mean, not ordinary, you act weird sometimes, but I thought that was about Fran, not you."

The crow *cawed* again and flapped its wings.

"Sorry, didn't understand that," Smokey said. "The

system hasn't prepared me to see the sentience in creatures like you, but awareness is the first step toward overcoming prejudice, and I'm prepared to learn."

The crow looked at Vaudrek and tipped its head on one side, then let out an inquisitive *croak*.

"Yes, he talks like this a lot," Vaudrek said. "I think we're all supposed to. It's part of this activism he talks about."

The crow made a sound that could've been laughter, and the rest of its feathered gang joined in.

"Hey!" Smokey snapped. "This is serious business. The language we use shapes the way we think. That directs the action needed to instigate a radical, even revolutionary change. Equality is grounded in better discourse."

The crows cackled again.

"Right, that's it." Smokey glared at the lead crow. "I don't have to put up with this attitude. How do I even know that you're sentient magicals and not some carefully trained pet, sent here to play a trick on me?"

The crow jabbed at the ground with its beak, drawing something in the dirt: first a stick figure, then a line through it.

"What does that even mean?" Smokey snapped.

"I think I understand this curious creature's meaning," Vaudrek said. "It's suggesting that you would not even have questioned its sentience if it was human-shaped."

Smokey stared at the picture, then at the crow. If he'd been in dwarf form, he would've blushed. As a cat, he didn't look away. Admitting embarrassment was for lesser creatures.

"Fine, I get it. I'm showing my prejudice. I was wrong."

The crow *cawed* and spread its wings triumphantly.

"That doesn't mean you're in, though," Smokey said. "Paws and Claws is a serious campaigning group, and you showed up out of nowhere, laughing at it all. How do I know you're not more troublemakers, like those bipeds who interrupted my meeting the other week?"

"You mean your friends?" Vaudrek asked. "I thought you creatures were supposed to like each other."

"Not them, the ones from the meeting before that."

"Ah, the troll and the greasy young human."

"The 'troll' troll, yes."

"It's an intriguing question, is it not?" Vaudrek stared thoughtfully at the crows. "How can anyone assess the intention of another when we don't share a language?"

The crows gathered in a small circle with their heads pressed close together. They made small *croaking* noises, scuffed the dirt with their claws, and flicked the tips of their wings. It was clear from the energetic back and forth that they were having a serious discussion. Or at least a convincing impression of one.

At last, the crows reached a conclusion. They flew into the air, past Smokey, and grabbed materials off his cart.

"Hey, what are you doing?" Smokey demanded.

The crows fluttered off between the trees, some of them with claws full of fliers, one carrying a tub of glue, another a roll of tape.

"Thieves!" Smokey shouted. "After them!"

He charged after the crows. He wasn't as fast or as agile as usual, thanks to the weight of the trailer he dragged behind him. It bounced over bumps in the ground, scattering fliers into the air, rattling as it went. Smokey felt as though the harness was holding him back, but he wasn't going to abandon it, not when he was carrying all the materials for the day.

"Catch them, Vaudrek," he called.

"I'm trying." Vaudrek ran after him, but her legs were very short compared to her body. She slithered along at what seemed to Smokey almost like a crawl.

"They're flying. Why can't you fly?"

"Because they're under the trees. My wings are too big."

The two of them pursued the crows into a small woodland area. It might once have been wild and magical but was now carefully managed with paths laid out and branches trimmed to make space for the usual bipedal magicals. It made Smokey even angrier and frustrated, but at least the smooth trail meant that his trailer stopped bouncing and rolled better.

Up ahead, the crows were doing something to the trees. One of the birds had hung back to slow the pursuers. It spread its wings wide and *cawed* loudly, as close as it could get to screaming in Smokey's face.

"Get out of my way." He tried to bat it aside with his paw. The crow landed on his head and stretched its wings across his eyes, blocking his view. He stopped running and instead swiped at the crow with one paw while it clung on tight. "Vaudrek, help me."

The lizard scuttled up, her belly trailing in the dirt. She swung her head around on the end of her long neck and caught the crow's body between her teeth. The bird froze in terror as the lizard lifted it off with a gentleness that was surprising for her size and ferocious appearance, then set the bird down on the side of the path. While it stood staring helplessly, Vaudrek and Smokey stalked past.

They reached the other crows at a particularly impressive stand of trees, where there were benches for magicals to sit on and good views out along the paths. One of the birds had tangled itself in sticky tape and was hanging from a branch, swaying back and forth like a feathered pendulum on the end of a sticky string. Another sprawled on the ground with a brush between its claws and its feathers weighed down with glue. Two more were pressing a flier against a sticky spot on one tree while their leader watched from the branches above.

Smokey stopped and looked around. Some of the stolen fliers lay scattered in the dirt, but the crows had glued or taped several more to the trees and benches. They'd done the work in haste with claws that hadn't evolved for this sort of work.

Sheets were crumpled and twisted, gobs of glue dribbled from behind them, and judging by their orientation, it seemed likely that the birds couldn't read. Still, the intention was clear. They'd been putting up the fliers as Smokey had intended.

"Were you trying to help?" he asked.

The lead crow glided down from its branch and landed in front of him. It spread its wings wide, gesturing at what the crows had done.

"Let me guess. This was your way of proving that you're here to help?"

The crow nodded.

"Well…" Smokey's suspicion faded away with his anger. If the crows had wanted to waste his resources, they could've dumped this stuff in the river. Instead, they'd tried to help. Whatever sort of creatures they were, their intentions were good.

"You'll need to learn to stick those up straight," Smokey said. "And not to use so much glue. It doesn't grow on trees, you know."

One of the crows made a sound and the others burst out into their cackling laughter.

"Fine, it's on the trees today, but you know what I mean."

Smokey unhooked himself from the trailer and walked over to the glue-soaked crow, which was struggling to lift itself from the path.

"That can't be good for you," Smokey said. "We'd better get you home and cleaned up before it dries."

He carefully picked up the bird between his teeth, like a mother cat carrying her kitten by the scruff of its neck. The taste of dirt and cheap glue wasn't pleasant, but activism wasn't always going to be fun. Smokey carried the bird to the trailer and laid it down on a stack of fliers.

Vaudrek bit through the tangled thread of sticky tape from which the other trapped crow was hanging from the tree. Two of the crow's companions caught it as it fell and carried it to the trailer.

While he gathered the discarded fliers and hooked himself up to the trailer, Smokey considered his new allies. They certainly seemed determined, and they would be able to reach places he couldn't. That could be invaluable for gathering information and getting their message where no one expected it to be.

Plus, there had to be some attention-grabbing stunts they could pull off with a flock of crows. The day hadn't worked out like he'd wanted it to, sticking up their fliers around town, but perhaps it had led to something better—recruits for the cause.

"Welcome to Paws and Claws," he said. "You seem like the sort of troublemakers we need."

CHAPTER ELEVEN

Fran stared at herself in the mirrored window of an office building. The person looking back at her seemed very strange. It wasn't the first time she'd worn a suit or even owned one, but it still wasn't something she could get used to. She always felt like she was looking at her head stuck on top of someone else's body.

This particular suit was a deep gray, with black shoes and belt, a light blue shirt, and a darker blue tie. Her mom had helped her pick it and had been surprised when Fran chose pants rather than a skirt. While she liked sparkles and pink, Fran's tastes had never been entirely girly. She preferred jeans over skirts, t-shirts over dresses, and boots over high heels. If she was going to dress up for the world of stuffy business people, she might as well go the whole hog.

Thinking of it as dressing up helped a little. Suits were stiff and formal, but costumes were fun. This was a costume, a chance to roleplay being someone she wasn't.

That was a much more relaxing way to think about it rather than behaving like she wasn't herself.

"Are you all right?" Bart asked. He'd walked on a few more paces without her when Fran stopped to stare at the window, but now he came back. "I didn't think you were into model making."

"Huh?" The spell of her reflection broken, Fran noticed the model houses and vehicles, the dioramas, and boxes of unmade kits that filled the window display. "Oh, no, I was checking how I looked."

"Very smart. Perfect for the occasion."

Elethin, standing behind Bart with her arms folded, gave a curt nod.

"He's right. You chose well. The tie is still an unusual choice for a female executive, but it asserts confidence and a willingness to adapt. The choice of colors is good too, more adult than your usual wardrobe. When you said you were buying a suit, I half-expected something bright red or covered in polka dots."

"My mom helped me pick it."

"You should take her shopping more often. She's a good influence. Now, we have an image to assert, and showing up late won't help, so…"

Elethin gestured down the road to a large office block. It was new but built like some traditional warren hills where the smaller local magicals often made their homes. That meant a domed shape, but larger and steeper than a real hill would be, with round windows like tunnel openings instead of whole walls of glass.

As if in concession to the building's natural inspiration,

they'd planted flower beds around its base. Since this was a corporate headquarters, they weren't ordinary plants. Instead, the tendrils of magical creepers waved at passersby. Meanwhile, flowers enchanted to grow at unnatural speeds burst into bloom, wilted, fell away, and bloomed again in new colors on a cycle that lasted only a few minutes.

As they approached the semicircular entrance, there was a *caw*, and a crow landed on Fran's shoulder.

"Hi there," she said. "Have you come to cheer me on?" She stroked the crow's feathered wing. "Wait, are you sticky?" The crow shifted, and she stared in horror at the gluey marks on her new suit. "Am I sticky?"

She shooed the crow off her shoulder and stared in horror at the mess where it had stood.

"Oh, dear." Elethin plucked a tiny black feather from the mess of glue and dirt. "Hold still."

She opened her handbag and took out a small crystal bottle of sparkling liquid.

"What is that?" Fran asked.

"Expensive, so I don't want to waste it. That's why I asked you to hold still."

Elethin depressed the bottle's top, carefully squirting a fine mist of glowing liquid onto Fran's shoulder. The air around the glue stains shimmered. There was a faint smell of lavender and spent magic, and the mess the crow had left evaporated.

"There." Elethin brushed Fran's shoulder. "Almost perfect. Although next time you should go to a better tailor. Frankly, this stitching is cheap."

"I didn't go to a tailor. I bought the suit from a store."

Elethin drew a deep breath as though bracing herself to

endure a shocking revelation. "I see. Clearly, everyone in this business has a lot to learn. Don't worry, once the money starts coming in, I'll take you shopping and sort out a proper executive wardrobe."

Fran wasn't completely sure that was something she wanted, but she also wasn't sure she had a choice.

"I'm not convinced that's what I want to spend my money on," she mumbled.

"It will be on expenses."

"You can't put suits on expenses," Bart said sternly.

"As I said, a lot to learn. Now come on, we have an appointment."

The glass doors of the office burrow *hissed* open as they approached. Inside was a foyer with a tiled floor and a leather sofa to one side. A gnome sat behind the reception desk.

"Welcome to Wibbling, Wibbling, and Spears," the receptionist said. "How can I help you today?"

"We have an appointment with Ms. Wibbling," Bart said. "The younger one."

"Mr. Trumbling, is it?" The receptionist glanced at her computer screen. "And one of you must be Ms. Berryman?"

"Ooh, yes, that's me!" Fran stuck up her hand.

"Elethin Tannerin," Elethin said. "I'm with them."

"That's fine." The receptionist handed them each a badge on a lanyard. "These will let you get to the meeting room. Please wear them at all times while you're in the building. You should go down the left-hand passage, third right, and through the blue door. Have a lovely day."

As they walked past the desk, Fran could see why they needed the left-hand passage. The right-hand one was a height suitable for the gnomes who seemed to work there. They bustled back and forth, carrying laptops, tablets, and bundles of documents, greeting each other cheerfully as they passed. Fran could've gotten down that corridor in a crouch, but Elethin would've had to crawl, and that didn't seem like something the elf would accept.

"Is this, like, the guest part of the office?" Fran asked as they walked down the human-scale corridor.

"That's right," Bart said. "Wibbling, Wibbling, and Spears is a very old gnomish trading house. They have a strict traditionalist approach to hiring, but they've adapted their working practices to the modern world. This custom office, with space for taller visitors, is part of that."

As he talked, he seemed to swell up, and a smile spread across his face.

"Is this where you used to work?" Fran tugged at her shirt collar. She wasn't used to it, and it rubbed uncomfortably against her neck.

"Yes, but I was in the accountancy division, not the investment one. I never worked in this office, but I visited sometimes, and it's good to be back."

They walked through a blue door into a room with a low boardroom table and chairs of assorted sizes down its sides. A suited gnome personal assistant sat to one side with a laptop on his knees. At the end of the room was another gnome, who stood as they came in.

"Bart." She walked down the room to reach them, her hand outstretched. "It's great to see you."

The gnome appeared to be in her early thirties, or whatever the gnome equivalent was: Fran had never been good at understanding comparative aging. She wore a smart blue skirt and matching jacket, a silk blouse, and a string of pearls around her neck. There would've been high heels if she'd been human, but her shoes were expensive flats, the footwear of a gnome who took pride in her height.

"Tilda." Bart shook her hand. "Thank you so much for taking the time to talk to us."

"Think nothing of it. After all your years of service to the firm, it's the very least we could do. I'm sorry that Mama couldn't be here to talk with you in person, but we've started expanding our operations onto Earth, and that makes all sorts of complications with scheduling."

"I understand. She's a busy woman."

"Please, take a seat, tell me all about this new business of yours."

"Not mine, not really. I mean, I'm on the board, but it's very much Fran's creation."

"Of course. Ms. Berryman." Tilda Wibbling flashed Fran a warm smile. "I saw you on television. It's a delight to meet you in person."

"Thank you." Fran straightened her jacket and stifled her first instinct, which was to start talking about how exciting it had been to appear on TV, how she had met Don Karelsky, everything else she had seen there that day. As Elethin had explained several times, the people they were dealing with wouldn't be impressed or interested. Fran needed to sit up straight and stay on topic.

"Shall we start the presentation?" Fran said.

The routine was becoming familiar now. Bart plugged his laptop into one of the cables running from the meeting room table, and the slides appeared on a wall-mounted screen. Fran talked the investor through the fundamentals of the business: who they were, what they made, and the advantages it would bring.

Then Bart came in to talk about the financials—what level of investment they were seeking, what they wanted to spend it on, what they expected to earn in return. Then he turned it back to Fran, who finished the presentation by talking about her vision for the company's future. Not the grand, idealized dream where she was the new Howard Phillips, but the more grounded one that Gruffbar had talked her down to, about building a brilliant magitech company in five years.

Any time Fran got stuck, Elethin would smoothly step in to cover that point and get Fran back on course, but she hardly ever needed that support anymore. In fact, by the end of the presentation, she was smiling excitedly about it all. It would've been better if her new pants had fitted her properly, and she kept having to hoist them up as they threatened to slide off her hips, but she was sure that their host wasn't interested in that. Sure, there was a flicker of something on the gnome's face when Fran finally gave in to the discomfort on her throat and undid her top button, loosening her tie. But no one cared about things like that, did they?

At last, with the presentation over, Fran took her seat.

"Well, thank you very much," Ms. Wibbling said. "That was fascinating. I'll give it some thought and let you know our decision in time."

"Don't take too long." Bart smiled. "We're a hot property right now, and as I explained, we're only after our initial round of funding. If you want to invest in Mana Wave Industries, now is the time to do it."

"Then sadly, we might have to miss out. I wouldn't want to rob a keener investor of this opportunity."

Bart's face fell.

"You were going to say no all along, weren't you?" he asked.

"I don't know, but if there isn't time for a full analysis, then I can't justify the investment."

"Please, Tilda, be straight with me."

The gnome executive's smile had become stiff.

"Perhaps we should talk alone, Bart, for old time's sake."

"Whatever you have to say, you can say in front of Fran and Elethin. This decision is about them as much as it is about me."

"If you insist."

"I do." Bart crossed his arms and gave her a look that was barely short of a glare.

"When you retired—"

"You mean when you forced me out?"

"When you retired, we all understood that you were feeling your age and that it was getting to you. Remember the baseball caps, the desk toys, that unfortunate period where you tried to get into elven hip-hop? That's fine. We all have moments of wanting to recapture our lost youth, and those little novelties are how we do it.

"Some older executives start affairs. Some buy flashy new steam wagons. Others get into modern music. But this, throwing yourself into some ridiculous new startup run by a human who's barely out of school, who dresses like a child that's raided its father's suit rack?"

Wibbling shook her head. "I'm sorry, Bart, but that desperate desire to be young again has clouded your judgment. We're all fond of you, but the company can't throw money at your mistakes."

She turned to Fran.

"My advice for you, Ms. Berryman, is to join an established company, work your way up through the ranks, and prove that you have what it takes. Then, in twenty or thirty years, once you have some executive experience under your belt, we might be ready to invest in what you have to offer."

She stood and smiled sadly at Bart. "I'd say that I'm sorry we can't help, but you asked me to be straight with you, and in all honesty, I think it's best for you that we don't encourage this foolishness. I have another meeting now, but I'm sure you can show yourselves out."

Fran, Bart, and Elethin waited until their host and her assistant were gone, then trudged back down the corridor to the foyer. They dropped their guest badges on the reception desk.

"Have a nice day," the receptionist said brightly.

Fran grunted and headed out the door. A glue-smeared crow fluttered down from the top of the office mound and landed on her shoulder.

"I can't believe I bought a suit for that," Fran said.

CHAPTER TWELVE

Howard Phillips stood in his office, looking out the window across Mana Valley. Usually, looking through it was a matter of pride, a reminder of his power in this place and what he would do with it. This evening was different. This evening, he had a practical purpose.

The sun had almost set, its fiery orb hanging a fraction of the sky above the distant mountains. As Phillips watched, it sank lower, and a mountain ridge blocked a little of its light, a row of dark teeth biting into that warmly glowing fruit.

Phillips turned away from the window and walked to the center of the ritual circle he'd chalked out on the office floor. Many people overlooked sunset as a time of magic. They focused on midnight, that time of darkness and drama when night creatures filled the world with violence. Or they waited for sunrise when the new day was born.

Sunset had a power of its own, a time when the light was fading, and the world was changing. It was particularly potent when hunting a people whose magic lay in light.

That light was being stripped from the world now, as Phillips would wrest the power from these Evermores.

He cast off his clothes, then opened the front of his skin suit and peeled it away, revealing his true form, the Darkness Between Dreams. The Darkness flung the skin away and began a gurgling chant that would've made any mortal listener feel sick. Its tentacles waved, marking out the patterns of mystical incantations.

Power flowed around it and through the cage placed at the circle's edge. The pen was a little thing designed to hold the diminutive birds that miners once carried down into the shafts. That was before technology found less morbid ways to warn of danger.

It wasn't a crucial part of the spell, but it entertained the Darkness Between Dreams to think that the creature it captured now might be a canary in the mine, a warning of terrible things to come. The miners couldn't stop the gas flowing any more than these Evermores could stop the Darkness. All the miners could do was flee. The Evermores wouldn't get that far, whoever and whatever they were.

The cage glowed with power. The Darkness grinned. Perhaps it was the miner, the one extracting a resource from the world. True, that resource was other people or at least the power within them. Still, what were these people, these magicals, if not a resource for greater beings to use, as they transformed this pitiful world into something that mattered?

The Darkness Between Dreams held up the page of Tess's prophecy. It was a tenuous connection to the Evermores but the most powerful one it currently had. This page would do.

The Darkness thrust the narrow tip of a tentacle through the page, directly through the word "Evermore," and cast more magic through that hole. Magic of finding, of summoning, of enclosing. A binding of power, driven by the strength of nightmares. An extension of its darkness reaching into the world.

Magic spread across Mana Valley, a wave of menace looking for the Evermores.

Enfield stood in the doorway of a house in the foothills outside Mana Valley. The sun was setting over the mountain ridge across the vale, light fading from the world. He could do more than see it. He felt it in his magic, the world shifting from a time when he could bend the existing light around him to one when he would have to summon his. Neither time made him more or less powerful as an Evermore, but there was a different experience to each, and that change left him feeling vulnerable around dusk.

"Here you go." The pizza delivery guy handed over a stack of boxes.

"Thank you." Enfield balanced them on one hand and held out the other. "Your tip."

The delivery driver smiled and held out his hand, then looked down in surprise at the handful of tarnished silver coins. "These look old."

"Yes, but they're still valuable. You might want to clean them." Enfield closed the door and headed back into the house.

The rest of the half-dozen Evermores on the expedition

were sitting in the living room, watching a drama about one of the historic elven royal families.

"I don't understand," one of them said. "I thought whoever wore the crown was king."

"No, they wear the crown because they are king," someone else explained. "It's a sign of power, not a source of power."

"I see the distinction, but... Oh good, pizza's here."

The Evermores leaped out of their seats. Pizza had quickly become one of their favorite discoveries since emerging from their hidden lives. Enfield suspected that when the time came to return, the desire for round bread covered with tomato sauce and cheese would be one of the biggest things holding them in the world.

A beam of sunlight shone in through the window, one last moment of the sun's glow before it vanished into the night. As it struck Enfield's face, he felt that sense of sunset vulnerability and something more. It was like hands grabbing hold of him from every direction, trying to wrench him out of the world.

Enfield cried out in panic. The pizzas fell to the floor as he flung out his hands, gathered his magic, and formed a shield of sound around himself. Although the air rippled protectively, it was nowhere near enough. The power still pulled at him, trying to drag him out of the world.

"Back!" Winslow snapped as the other Evermores closed in around Enfield. "Let me see."

Enfield collapsed to his knees. He felt like he was sinking, not through the ground but through reality. The pressure of that feeling was like a vice squeezing his whole body. He grunted in pain through his gritted teeth.

"All of you, put up your wards," Winslow snapped.

"Shouldn't we be helping Enfield?" someone asked.

"This isn't only about him. Can't you feel it? He was merely the first. This is coming for all of us."

They summoned protective magic around themselves, doing what they could with the powers of light and sound. Winslow ignored his advice and focused on Enfield.

Normally, Winslow stayed calm no matter what. Thousands of years had taught him that nothing was ever as urgent as it seemed, that the best option was always to underreact instead of to overreact. Stay calm, and you could take charge of the situation. Panic, and you weren't even in control of yourself.

As he reached into the magic that had hold of Enfield, it was hard not to panic. The weave was darkness and disruption, the deep, instinctive terror that howled through the coldest, bleakest times. It was the magic of nightmares, and it was trying to take Enfield.

Winslow closed his eyes, placed his hands on Enfield, and let the magic flow. His power flowed into Enfield, lending him strength. The dark magic's spell slid off Enfield and up Winslow's arms. It sensed his presence, recognized him as the sort of target it was seeking. The magic gripped hold of Winslow and opened a gap through the world, a passage to carry him away.

Merely touching that magic filled Winslow with terrible visions. A world plunged into darkness, warped hounds howling through the night, malformed monstrosities roaming a broken landscape filled with anguish and despair. It closed in on him like a trap shutting. He wasn't trapped, though. He was calm, he was in control, and he would make this gap through reality his.

He channeled his magic down it, a lining for the tunnel, a beam of light through the darkness. He couldn't tell where it was going, but he sensed something on the other side, something malign, greedy, and oozing power. Something that would turn a world of brightness and hope into one of abject despair.

Winslow's power wasn't hope or goodness or some other emotion that might've burned the enemy's soul. It was light, and that could burn a body. He put all his concentration into narrowing it down, a beam of laser-like tightness and intensity. It shot through the tunnel of dark magic to whoever was trying to take Enfield.

There was a hideous screech, a smell of burning, and the power dragging at Enfield let go. The tunnel snapped shut, and the nightmare visions fled Winslow's mind.

He sank to his knees. The spell might be gone, but memories of those visions remained, terrible things chasing through his mind's eyes. Whatever that thing was, whatever it intended to do, someone had to stop it.

"Master Winslow." One of the younger Evermores placed her hand on his back. "Can you hear me? Are you hurt?"

"I'm fine," Winslow muttered. "Shaken, but well." He looked at Enfield, who had dragged his gaze up from the floor. "You saw it too?"

Enfield nodded. He was pale and trembling, but intensity burned in his eyes, the same determination Winslow felt. If they ever encountered this thing again, they would hit it hard and to hell with asking any questions. Hell was clearly where the thing belonged.

"What should we do?" Enfield croaked.

"Pass me the pizza," Winslow said. "I've never needed comfort food more."

The Darkness Between Dreams crouched in its magical circle, clutching its face. Outside, the sun's last edge disappeared over the mountains, leaving the Darkness Between Dreams in the darkness of night. It shuddered in pain.

Its eye. That blasted Evermore had hit it in the eye with some sort of magical beam. The pain was intense, the smell of burned flesh sickening.

Normally, those were things that the Darkness Between Dreams would've enjoyed, signs of a true nightmare scenario. There was a difference between seeing horrors inflicted on others and experiencing them.

Worse yet, the Evermore had thwarted its goal. The cage lay on the floor, a crumpled and ruined mess, its bars melted by the same blast that had hit the Darkness in its eye. The Darkness had torn down its spell at that moment rather than give its opponent a channel to keep attacking.

That had been a panic move, but the right one. Without it, how many more eyes might the Darkness have lost? Worse, what might its opponents have learned about it?

The Darkness crawled out of the circle and dragged itself to its skin suit. Every nerve ending was tender, its senses intensified by the shock and pain, and it felt every last touch of that suit against its real skin like scraping sandpaper over flesh. Still, the suit was a sort of armor, a protective barrier between the Darkness and this world. It would feel better with the skin in place.

It fastened the suit up to the neck but left the head hanging open. It had so many eyes that losing one would cause no problems with sight, but the wound still felt like it was burning. The Darkness couldn't quite bring itself to pull the skin over it. Instead, it started getting dressed, pulling on underwear, pants, and shirt.

A knock on the door sounded.

"Are you all right?" Julia asked from outside. "I sensed a magical disturbance."

"I am...inconvenienced." The Darkness sat in Howard Phillips' chair and tried its best to summon the man's demeanor. It could have Julia see it like this. She'd seen parts of the Darkness before, but Phillips was how it managed these people, and Phillips was the one it should be now. "Come in."

Julia walked in and closed the door behind her. Phillips hit a switch, and the lights came on, revealing the black mass with its dozens of eyestalks his head should be. The burned-off appendage was readily apparent. Julia stood for a long moment staring.

"You've been hurt. We have some healing potions in the corporate stores. I'll have them sent up."

"Thank you, Julia." Phillips gestured at the flapping skin that was supposed to be his face. "Would you help me with this?"

"Of course."

She walked around to his side of the desk and began pulling the skin up over his head.

"Carefully," Phillips said. "It is uncomfortable."

"Of course."

With steady hands, Julia pulled the skin over her boss's head, moving most carefully over the injured eyestalk. Once it was in place, Phillips sealed the skin shut, and it was as if he was just one more human being, though one who benefited from all the wealth that kept the elite fit and fended off the effects of age.

"I'll go get those potions," Julia said. "Should I summon Handar to talk about improving magical security?"

"Yes, that would be good."

Julia walked out and closed the door behind her. Alone in the space outside the office, she stopped. For a moment, she let the terrible feelings wash over her—the ones she'd felt as she touched the Darkness Between Dreams and pulled a human skin suit over a thing of pure nightmares.

Her body shook. She wanted to puke and howl in horror. However, she was a professional and wouldn't do those things. Instead, she pulled herself together and reached for the phone to do as Phillips had asked.

CHAPTER THIRTEEN

It was getting late in the Blazing Bean. Cameron sat hunched over his laptop, occasionally looking up to ensure he hadn't missed a customer coming in.

When he'd first started at the shop, his boss had been dead set against letting him have his laptop out while he was working behind the counter. Then there'd been the week when almost everyone else came down sick after a staff party, the shifts desperately needed filling, and Cam had a paper to complete.

The manager had reluctantly let him do his academic work while handling the counter, simply to get someone there. He'd proved that he gave better customer service while multi-tasking than half of the other staff did while focused solely on their jobs. It had set a precedent, and everything went from there.

An evening like this one was the perfect sort of shift for Cam. Enough customers to provide him with an occasional distraction, not so many that it got in the way of doing his work. As far as anyone else was concerned, that was the thesis he'd been laboring over for so long. More and more often now, he worked on his other project. The one that truly mattered.

He peered at the fragment of prophecy again. He'd worked out translations and transcriptions of it long ago, but sometimes it paid to go back to the source. It was another chance to look for details he'd missed, things he might've copied incorrectly, and places where the wording might have changed. It would've been easier to do that if he had the original document, but he worked with what he had.

Another thought struck him. Maybe there were other ways he could use the transcription to find out if there was more of this text. It was a long shot, but if he didn't try, he would never know.

The coffee shop's door opened. A pair of Silver Griffins walked in with their official amulets around their necks and their wands in holsters on their hips. Cam had been to a seminar on the evolution of the Griffins as an institution back in his undergrad days. It was interesting how those amulets had changed over time, from a protection a few of the Griffins wore to a piece of regulation uniform in some parts of the force to something they wore openly in areas such as Mana Valley. It was a sign of authority and a piece of magical protection.

There he was getting distracted again from his job and the train of thought he'd hoped to keep.

"What can I get you both?" he asked.

The Griffins got their coffees and donuts, served with a smile and a ten percent discount for public servants. They were laughing about the city's parks and recreation team, who were outraged that someone had stuck fliers to a few of their trees. That didn't seem like much of an issue to get worked up about by Griffins standards, but the parks and rec people cared about their jobs.

"Thanks for these." One of the Griffins waved her coffee at Cam as they headed for the door. "You stay safe now."

"You too."

Cam waved and turned back to his computer. He'd had an idea before they came in, but what was it? This was the problem of juggling research and a day job. Paying the bills got in the way of following pure reason.

That was it. Use the prophecy's transcription to check if anyone else was talking about it.

Cam copied a section from the end of his transcript into a search engine and set it to work. A string of results popped up, most of them irrelevant, completely different texts that happened to use a lot of the same words. He kept reading, just in case, and something on the eighth page of results caught his eye.

The door opened again, and a bunch of skateboarders came in. Cam didn't know their names, but he knew their faces from previous visits, and he knew their regular orders. "The usual?"

"Yeah, bro." The lead skater gave him a dopey grin.

Cam rustled up a round of coffees, then waited patiently while the skaters counted out their change to pay. Once they'd finished at the counter and taken their regular window seats, he returned to his screen.

He'd been doing something, but what? This was the problem with minimizing his windows to hide the work when customers came near. Then he had to remember what he'd been working on. Not the main document, and he didn't have an e-book open... Oh yes, the search results!

He clicked on the link, and sure enough, it took him to a text that included part of the prophecy he was working with. It started partway through his page, continued into new material, then ended.

He followed the text up to its parent page, which was on the website of an academic historian. They'd copied the text from a book in the city archives, a two-hundred-year-old collection of copies of older documents.

The historian didn't seem to understand what they were looking at. They'd misunderstood the prophecy as a garbled account of historical events, possibly a piece of poetry by some obscure writer from nearly a thousand years before. They hadn't made the connection to the Tess prophecies. Maybe the person who compiled that book hadn't realized what they had.

With growing excitement, Cam read the article the academic had written, in which they linked to their transcript of part of the text. The article implied more of it existed, but they weren't interested in the other parts.

Cam was very interested. If there was more prophecy before or after what he had, and if he could find a copy of it, perhaps he could work out who the Evermores were. That would lead to what they were trying to do and how they connected to the coming threat. Maybe he could get more than the faintest shadowy glimpse of what the future held.

The door opened. A couple of witches walked in,

buoyed up by the nervous, excitable energy of an early date.

Cam closed the laptop. He'd finished for the night. He knew what the next step of his research would be, and for once he couldn't do it while working in the shop. It was time for a visit to the city archives.

Howard Phillips laid the sheet of prophecy out on his desk and peered at the ancient parchment. He'd read it many times already, trying to understand what it held for his future and how it could help him.

"When the bell rings silence three times will the darkness peel back and the true one stand exposed."

This was the problem with prophecy. It always seemed so clear and specific after the fact but could read like gibberish until then. Reading it now, was he the darkness it was talking about? Was it something he would create? Was it something else entirely?

Then there was all this stuff about the Evermores, these ancient, powerful magicals who guarded an even greater power and protected the magicals on Earth. That part was clearer, if not helpfully specific, but it didn't seem to be talking about the future. Was it only that he'd passed the time for that part of the prophecy, or was it not concerned with what they would do next? A prophecy that only told him about the past was useless.

He picked up the page and peered at the last few lines. On reading them before, he'd thought they were complete. Now, something seemed odd.

His tentacles were more sensitive than his human fingers, so he made a gap in his skin suit and wriggled one out to run its tip across the page. As he suspected, the space after the last word on the page had been altered. The parchment was rougher and a little paler where words had been rubbed or scraped away.

It wasn't a recent change. The document was too well aged for that. An edit during the writing process, perhaps, as the author realized there was more to say and she needed to move onto another page. He couldn't be sure, but instinct told him not to let this moment slip past.

How to follow up on it though? Back to the Dark Market, where this piece had come from? He didn't know who'd sold it, and the buyer was gone. Turning up and demanding that someone bring him a matching piece would only attract a swarm of forgers intent on taking his money for whatever they could produce.

No, he needed to be smarter about this. He could afford to take his time. He'd waited for centuries to break out into the world, as this prophecy had waited for centuries for its fulfillment. The important thing was to get it right.

This document had existed for centuries. Someone else might've seen it and made a copy or summary of it. There'd been times during the intellectual explosions of previous centuries when publishers would print copies of any old document their researchers found, knowing that it would be of interest to scholars. That eclectic, urgent rush for learning could work to his advantage now. If it didn't, he would try something else. No rush.

The tentacle slid back into his wrist. He picked up the

phone on his desk and called the second number in its contacts.

"My office, now." He set the phone in its cradle.

The parchment stared up at him, a piece of the past that laid out the future. An irony twisted enough to play a part in nightmares—a good omen, perhaps.

The door opened, and Handar Ennis walked in. The Kilomea bodyguard stood stiffly to attention, a habit born from his military experience. He looked from the prophecy to Phillips.

"What's up, boss?"

"Any news from the agents you sent to find the Evermores?"

"Not yet. You want me to give 'em a boot up the ass, get things moving?"

"That won't be necessary. At least not yet." Phillips tapped the prophecy. "We have other channels to pursue on that. Ritual magic. A detection device the technicians are working on downstairs. Feelers through our usual contacts. No need to rush yet. Besides, I have something else that needs doing. I want you to look into it personally."

Handar shifted from one foot to the other.

"Shouldn't I be here with you, boss? Especially after…"

Handar looked straight at Phillips' eyes. He couldn't see the damaged one, but he'd heard from Julia what she'd seen, and that account told him he'd failed. There'd been a danger to the boss, and he hadn't put defenses in place to stop it. He was determined not to let that happen again.

"I'll be fine. I don't intend to leave the building any time soon, and I have the new wards you arranged to protect me. Your witches were very thorough."

"Good. We paid 'em well enough."

"Then you should feel confident in leaving me here and going to find something I can only trust to my closest colleagues."

"All right, boss, if you're sure."

"Very sure. I want you to go to the city archives."

Handar frowned. His face, which had a naturally crumpled look, seemed as if it had been scrunched into a ball by a giant fist.

"Libraries ain't really my thing. You should send Julia. She'll know what she's looking at."

"I need Julia here to keep the business running smoothly. Besides, I'm not sending you to read. I'm sending you to find and retrieve. It might involve convincing someone to let you remove documents that aren't legally allowed out of the building, and I know you have a gift for overcoming people's moral barriers."

"Every magical's got some weakness you can lean on."

"Exactly. I want you to go down there and do some leaning."

Phillips picked up a pen and scribbled a list of books on a sheet of paper. No need to commit this to an electronic record. Sometimes, the old ways were more secure.

"These are indexes of old books, compilations printed in the nineteenth century."

"You want me to get 'em for you?"

"No, I want you to search through them for any reference at all to the word 'Evermore.' Any references you find will lead you to other books. Those are the ones I want."

"You want me to do this now?" Handar took the list.

The flimsy slip of paper seemed absurdly fragile between his thick fingers.

"Start today. The city archive being what it is, it might take a few trips to find what we're after. No rush. No need to lean on people to speed it up. Save the pressure for getting the books out."

"Got it." Handar thrust the paper into his pocket, then marched out of the room.

Phillips sat back. The prophecy lay in front of him. Or part of one. A tentacle snaked out once more, feeling that rough section near the end of the parchment. The patch that promised so much more.

CHAPTER FOURTEEN

Josie sat at the workbench in the test lab, nibbling on an oat bar and contemplating the insides of the magical detection device. It was fascinating to see how they'd constructed it. She'd been comparing how they'd woven the magic with a book on the theory of esoteric resonance, the branch of magical research that discussed how magic in one place could affect other spells in the area.

Philgard's technicians had pushed beyond the bounds of current theoretical understanding, at least as most taught it. Either their practical application of magic had stumbled into something no one had worked out, or someone in the company understood the theoretical framework better than most academic witches and wizards. Possibly both.

Josie wondered how she could meet the people who'd worked out these spells. She would love to learn from them, work with them, even talk with them for ten minutes about the principles at play in their device.

A few crumbs fell from her bar into the device. She

hastily pulled out her wand and summoned a gust of wind to blow them out. This was the downside of working through lunch. The upside was that she could push farther and faster with her work and maybe one day get to meet these designers.

The other advantage was that by staying in the test lab, she could avoid the atmosphere in the rest of the office. Everyone was still tense about their upcoming evaluations. They spent every spare moment polishing their statements, doing unnecessary tasks to push up their performance figures, or writing self-justificatory emails to people above them in the food chain.

They watched each other like hungry jackals waiting for a chance to pounce and steal the weaker beast's food. It was amazing that somewhere as boring as an office could simultaneously be so unpleasant.

She finished her oat bar, put the wrapper in the trash, and closed the book. It was time to turn her full attention back to testing the device to see how the most recent alterations worked.

Josie took a box from the end of the room and laid its contents out around the workbench. They were assorted items from around the business, ranging from ancient artifacts to the latest Philgard tech releases. All of them contained magic in one form or another.

Some used light and sound magic to make them work. Others created light or sound as part of their functions. Some did both, some neither. That was the point of the tests, to see whether the device could find the things it was looking for and if it would pick up others by accident. Too many false positives would make it useless.

With the testing area set up, Josie put the device in the center of the workbench. She also unrolled a couple of leads and used them to connect the device to a laptop.

There was no point in only seeing what the detector did. She needed the extra details that diagnostic software spells could draw out of it, the analysis of what it responded to in each object and how it reacted, of which sensors responded in which ways. That would tell her where improvements should be made, in theory at least.

The door banged open, and Simon Green stomped in. He slammed the door behind him.

"That bitch," he muttered.

"Not me, I hope?" Josie asked.

"Of course not you." Simon rolled his eyes. "It's Erin. She says we can't include incomplete tests in the monthly figures. Can you believe that?"

Josie didn't think the question needed an answer, which was fortunate since she felt Erin was right. If they counted unfinished work in their achievements for each month, it would be counted in multiple months, artificially inflating their figures. Worse yet, it would encourage people like Simon never to finish anything, as a buildup of unfinished work would give them more "achievements" to count.

That wasn't what Simon wanted to hear. For some reason, he assumed that Josie was on his side, and she didn't want to disabuse him of that view. Life was easier while he liked her, or at least didn't dislike her.

"How's it going out there?" Josie nodded at the door.

"Lots of meetings. Lots of reports. Lots of rushing to finish projects. Absolute chaos." Simon looked at the workbench and the items laid out on it. "How are things going in here?"

"You tell me. Am I doing this right?"

She might not think much of Simon as a person, but Josie recognized his skills as a technician and his experience in product testing. If there was a chance to learn from him, she should take it.

Simon paced around the workbench, examining the items on it.

"Switch these two around." He swapped the places of an ancient sacrificial knife and a Manaphone Four. "You'll get better contrast, which is important in the early stages. Don't make it difficult for a device to do its job until you're sure it's doing the basics right."

He pulled out his wand and cast a spell that Josie didn't recognize. A glittering haze filled the air above the workbench, then faded away to nothing.

"What was that?" she asked.

"Clears out any background magic, traces of what's been here before. Most of it, at least. It's not the sort of hardcore cleansing they use to clean up after big accidents or at crime scenes, but it's related, and it's enough for our purposes. It reduces the risk of picking up a signal from something that's not here anymore."

"Could you teach me how it works?"

"Sure, but not right now. We need to prove that we're doing worthwhile work here."

Josie bit back a comment about who was doing all the work. If Simon was finally motivated to focus on the task at hand, that was a good thing.

With the area prepared, she switched the detector on.

For all the buildup, the test itself was incredibly boring. The two of them sat and watched as the green patches that indicated it had detected something appeared on the device's sides. Then Josie went around the workbench and triggered the powers of the items, one at a time, while they watched the changes in the green patches. Once that was done, she switched the device off again, put the video up on a screen on the wall, and compared it with the data in the laptop.

"It's getting closer," she said. "Almost an eighty percent success rate."

"More like seventy," Simon said, tapping a figure on the screen. "This part only looks right because two sensors were wrong at once. But if anyone asks, we can report your eighty percent."

"Won't we get in trouble when they find out the truth?"

"No one cares enough to look that deeply at what we do. Not unless it looks either amazing or terrible, and this is merely fine." Simon glared at the screen. "Fine is not good enough. We need to speed this up."

He switched the device back on and strode around the workbench. As he went, he waved his wand, casting all sorts of spells. Bursts of light and sound, fireballs, freezes, blobs of glue, lengths of chain, sparkling illusions, they all leaped from his wand in a chaotic profusion of power.

As he strode around, he got increasingly carried away. Josie ducked to avoid getting hit by chains, then countered a fireball to stop it from charring the door. The room filled with light, sound, and the smell of magic, while Simon raced faster and faster around the workbench, flinging magic through the air.

At last he stopped and bent over while panting.

"That'll do." He waved. "Switch the detector off."

Josie did as instructed, then shoved a heap of melting snow into one of the waste bins while Simon dispersed the remaining magic hanging in the air.

"All right," he said. "Let's see the results."

Again, they watched the video on one screen while figures crawled up the other. It was harder to make out the results in the video this time because of the sheer volume of magic flying around the detector, but Josie saw enough to work out what had been happening. She realized the value in what Simon had done, even if he hadn't been as careful as she would've liked. The extreme volume of magic had brought out exaggerated results, which made it easier to see the patterns.

"You were right. Seventy percent success rate, at best. The sensors are missing something."

Simon frowned. "What we need is a magical who specializes in light and sound magic so we can study their process."

"If only this device worked, we could use it to find one. Or at least seventy percent of him."

They both laughed and shook their heads, but a real possibility occurred to Josie.

"The funny thing is, I know a witch who loves light and sound magic."

"Somebody here?" Simon asked eagerly.

"Like we're that lucky. No, it's my roommate."

"Can we get her to come in for a few days?"

"She has work."

"We can pay. There's money in the budget for external

specialists." His tone turned bitter. "If Erin will let us spend it, that is."

"It wouldn't matter. She's just got her startup going. She barely has enough hours in the day for that. There's no way we could bring her in anytime soon." Josie sighed. "Sorry, that was a dumb idea. I got carried away before I fully thought it through."

"Maybe..." Simon stroked his chin. "If this is your roommate, you must've spent a lot of time around her, right?"

"Yes, of course."

"So you've seen her casting magic a lot?"

"Quite a bit, sure."

"You're a total nerd for magical theory. You must have paid attention to how she formed the spells."

"Nerd is harsh."

"Really? What were you reading over lunch, a nice entertaining murder mystery or a textbook?"

"Fair point."

"So, you've paid attention."

"Not totally, but I've probably noticed some things." Josie frowned. "The problem is, where to start?"

Simon walked over to the opposite wall, where there was a whiteboard next to a screen. He grabbed a pen and scribbled two diagrams on the board.

"Those are both models for how magic works to produce light," Josie said. "Hey, you're a nerd too."

"No, I merely have an advanced degree."

"Sounds pretty nerdy to me."

"At the time, it sounded like a good way to get employed. Turned out to be mostly a waste of brain space, but I remember a few bits. So…" He tapped the pen against the two diagrams. "Two models, both equally true in theory, but I'm not interested in the theory. What I want to know is which one we should set the sensors to find. So, which one looks closer to what your roommate's magic does?"

"The left-hand one."

"Make a note of that."

Josie pulled up her laptop, opened a document, and noted what the model showed.

"Next one." Simon frowned. "Wish I remembered more of this…" He drew two more diagrams on the board, then shook his head. "That's not quite right."

"No, but I get the idea. Left-hand model again." Josie made another note. "Okay, this could work. I take a bunch of theoretical models, recalibrate the device based on the ones that look most like what I've seen, and test the device again."

She grinned. "This isn't only about building a better device anymore. We could contribute something to magical knowledge. Maybe write a paper on it, get published in the magical journals."

"No, this is all about the device." Simon tapped the table. "We're not here to push forward the boundaries of understanding or build a better world. We're here to make better products for this company to sell, and that's what our evaluations are based on. Don't get distracted from that."

He glanced at the time. "I have a departmental meeting in an hour, and I need to read up again on what everyone's been doing so I don't get caught out by Erin's questions. Can I leave you to get on with this?"

"Sure, of course." Josie smiled at him. "Thanks, Simon. This was really useful."

"Useful will be when it adds something to our stats. So no theorizing, no distractions, no dreaming about your academic paper. Focus on getting the job done."

CHAPTER FIFTEEN

The kemana was in a cave deep under a Mid-west state. It was an echoing chamber with buildings carved from the walls in irregular steps. Trees had been planted around the central crystal, using its glow as a substitute for sunlight, and their roots knotted in intricate patterns around the crystal's base. In many ways, the space reminded Enfield of home.

In other ways, it was completely alien. The shops and cafés with their bright lights and flashy signs would've been out of place on the Evermores' home ground, as would the Willens who managed the space. The short, rat-like people scurried back and forth, some of them tending to the trees, others directing visitors or cleaning the streets. Somehow, it wasn't what Enfield had expected of them.

"Friends of yours?" He nodded toward the nearest Willens.

Singar looked up from the containment unit she was setting up between two of the trees and looked around.

"Huh?"

"The other Willens, do you know them?"

Singar gave him a look of disgust.

"You think that because we're Willens, we must know each other?"

"I'm only asking."

"Do you know all the other Evermores?"

"Most of them, yes. Aside from a few exiles, we all live in the community together."

"That explains a lot."

"What do you mean?"

"I mean that when your creator min-maxed you, he focused on strength, not int."

"I don't understand."

"Of course you don't." She shook her head and turned her attention back to the device.

"So you don't know them?"

"Dung and dirt, you really don't get social cues, do you?"

"How am I supposed to understand something if you won't answer my question?"

Singar pressed her fingers to her eyes and drew a deep breath.

"No, I don't know those other Willen. Happy now?"

"Happier than I was."

"Good. Now shut up and let me do my job."

She positioned the unit's mirror base and assembled the frame that rose from it. Winslow had positioned the other Evermores. Now he walked over to them.

"How are the preparations?" he asked.

"They'd be a lot better if idiots didn't keep interrupting

me," Singar snapped. "If you don't shut up and let me do my job, I swear, I'm going to knife someone."

"Come along, Enfield." Winslow took the younger Evermore by the elbow. "Let Ms. Twitchtail get on with her work."

The Evermores retreated to the shelter of another tree. One of the local Willens watched them with suspicion. Winslow's contacts got them permission to set up here undisturbed, but the locals were still wary of the unknown magicals in their midst.

It didn't take a genius to notice that the Evermores didn't carry wands, so they weren't witches and wizards. That raised the question not only of what they were up to but what they were. Nobody liked to see their space invaded by unknown forces. It amused Winslow to think how much of a shock those Willens would be in for when the Source turned up.

"Are you sure it's coming here?" Enfield asked. "This doesn't fit the initial pattern we mapped out."

"The Source changed its path after our last encounter. It's still a creature of habit, and the new direction of travel is clear. This will be the next place it stops to refuel."

Enfield stared at the brightly glowing crystal in the center of the kemana. The air here was rich with magic, a tingling that sank right through his body, enlivened him, and had a positive effect on the other inhabitants as well. The Willens walked with a sprightly step, while newly arrived magicals always seemed brighter within minutes of arriving. That power was drawing the Source.

"Should we warn them?" Enfield asked. "Let the locals

know what the Source will do, what effect its attacks are going to have?"

"You mean the locals of this kemana, or the locals in the wider sense? The authorities in this country, or across society on Earth?"

"Either. Both. Whichever would be best to help them prepare."

"Either way, the answer is no. They're not prepared for what we know. These are simple minds, ones that don't live long enough to comprehend the moral and magical implications of it all."

"Some of them seem smart." Enfield looked at Singar.

"A dog can seem smart when it's trained. A horse can look like it is counting. Don't conflate outward tricks with inner understanding."

The air rippled and lights around the kemana flickered, drawing the attention of both visitors and Willens.

"It's time." Leaving Enfield beneath the tree, Winslow walked over to the crystal. They would be taking a more direct approach this time.

At her position among the trees, Singar slotted the last part of the containment unit into place, switched the apparatus on, and picked up the adapted Manaphone they were using to control it. The controller contained Smokey's software to manage the unit, as well as some backup programs in case of emergencies. Singar flicked through those, checking that everything was in place, while the runes along the edge of the mirror lit up. She watched the ground around her, expecting the Source to burst out at any moment.

This time, the Source had taken a different route. It

burst through the ceiling above in a shower of falling dirt and dropped to the kemana's floor. Willens ran off, crying out in alarm. Customers of local businesses followed them, leaving only Singar and the Evermores to face the new arrival.

The Source had found yet another new form. This time it was a vast ape. Armored plates protected its broad shoulders. Its face extended into a reptilian snout full of pointed teeth but covered with fur instead of scales. Dragging its hardened knuckles across the ground, it prowled toward where Winslow stood in front of the crystal.

Singar switched to the controller's main software and started a calibration routine. The Source's energy signature had changed since the last time, and it was undoubtedly more powerful, but she, Fran, and Smokey sturdily built the containment unit. It should be able to cope with this.

The Source stopped under one of the trees and ran its fingers through the leaves above. Something like a smile twisted its monstrous face. Then it turned its attention back to Winslow and the crystal, and its fearsome snarl returned.

Singar hit a button on the controller. She'd hoped to have more time to get the containment unit ready. Now she had to run through the warm-up and tests with the target here. Couldn't Winslow have given them more warning that they needed to come out here, today, with whatever prototype they had?

Around the kemana, the Evermores started to chant. The sound became a network of magic, which ran beneath trees, around the crystal, and became a halo of power around Winslow.

That didn't deter the Source. It roared and charged straight at him.

Winslow held out his hands and channeled a burst of magical noise straight at the Source. The power caught it in the chest, hitting it like a battering ram. Even out of the attack's direct path, Singar winced as the sound waves hit her ears like a concentrated roar.

The attack knocked the Source back, flinging it into one of the trees. Leaves filled the air, and there was an agonized *creak* as the trunk cracked, gave way, and crashed to the ground. The Source kept its feet. The damage to the tree enraged it further, and it charged at Winslow. All four limbs pounded the ground, shaking the dirt.

Singar glanced at her screen. Almost ready. Only a few more seconds.

Winslow braced himself. Power flowed to him from the other Evermores, but he'd used so much in that first burst, hoping it would be a knockout blow. Now he had little to hit it with again. Instead of attacking, he turned the power into an intense layer of sound around him, a wall of noise meant to fend off the Source.

The Source screeched and clapped its hands to its ears, but it didn't stop coming. As it approached Winslow and the hazy air around him, it leaped. Powerful legs flung it up and over the protective zone he'd created.

"Singar!" Winslow shouted in alarm.

She ignored him. She was working as fast as she could.

The Source landed on the top of the crystal and clung on with both ape-like hands. The crystal flickered beneath its fingers as power leached away.

Winslow turned in a tai chi-like movement and pressed

his hands together. This time, he flung up a blast of light, straight at the Source's face. The Source swung to one side, putting the crystal between itself and Winslow. The light hit the crystal and fractured, rainbow bursts of color cascading across the kemana, like the output of a super-powered disco ball.

"Quickly, Singar!" Winslow shouted.

"I am going quickly," Singar snapped. "You didn't give me a lot of time."

The containment unit was powered up, synced, and ready to go. However, the energy readings from the Source were changing and growing. Singar frowned.

They'd designed the unit to deal with a lot of power, to take it and turn it back against the creature putting it out. Still, there was only so much it could deal with in the first moment of capture. It could probably deal with the Source, as long as the Source didn't grow any more.

Probably.

The crystal cracked beneath the Source's hand and darkened as it drew power from it.

Winslow flung another futile sound attack. The other Evermores kept channeling their power to him.

Singar hit a button on the controls. The magic in the containment unit triggered.

"Now!" Singar shouted.

The Evermores redirected their power. The magic heading for Winslow suddenly shifted and became a care-fully planned collection of concentrated sound waves. The force of them flung the Source from the top of the crystal and sent it howling through the air, straight at the contain-ment unit.

There was so much power from the Source that the unit was feeding on it already. Its field stretched out. Its rods extended. A cage of energy reached out to catch the Source, and Singar grinned as she saw the device do exactly what it was supposed to do.

Then the Source hit the back of the containment field. The runes on the mirror blazed a fiery orange as they strained to contain it. The battery unit smoked, sparked, and burst into flames. The Source punched through the back of the magical field, which collapsed around it. The mirror cracked, and the Source stepped out of the collapsing framework.

Singar, standing only a few feet from the broken containment unit, stared up in awe and dread at the Source. It stared down at her and flung a piece of the unit aside. It was oozing with raw power, far more than it had held the last time. Behind it, a chunk fell from the cracked kemana crystal and shattered as it hit the floor.

Reaching under her flannel shirt, Singar pulled out her switchblade. If she was going down, she would go down fighting.

The Source reached out. Instead of grabbing Singar, it seized a branch above her head. With surprising delicacy, it plucked a single seed from a twig and held it up in the light.

The Evermores were gathering around, hands raised, summoning their power again. Singar couldn't see the point. The creature had overcome them once. Without a new weapon to bolster their side, wouldn't it do the same thing again? This was the definition of madness.

The Source looked at her. Its face changed and became

more rat-like. Its legs became like those of a kangaroo. Still holding the seed in one hand, it leaped into the air, grabbed hold of the ceiling, and punched its way through into the dirt above.

Winslow had gathered the Evermore magic and flung another spell after it, trying to close the tunnel the Source was digging and trap it there. Either the attack didn't work, or the Source moved faster than Winslow could collapse. With a spray of falling dirt, it disappeared into the earth above.

"I thought this was ready to capture the Source." Enfield pointed at the ruined containment unit.

"It was ready to hold the Source we faced in Texas," Singar said. "Not the one we met here. It's growing more powerful. Is it stealing power from the kemana crystals?"

"Not ex—"

"Yes, that's it," Winslow said. "Or near enough an understanding for our purposes. That's one more reason why we have to stop it soon—before it becomes too powerful for anything you can make."

"Hm." Singar walked past the Evermores and gathered the pieces of the broken device. "Guess it's back to the workshop for me then."

CHAPTER SIXTEEN

Fran and Irene stepped out of the portal into an empty side street between Silicon Valley office buildings. Fran tapped a finger against her handheld mirror, and the portal vanished. A moment later, the mass of electronics and runes on the back of the mirror went to sleep.

"That's very clever, dear, but why not learn to cast a portal?"

"This is safer and more efficient. Less power needed and less chance of something going wrong." Fran grinned as she slid the mirror into her backpack. "Besides, I prefer doing things with tech. It's fun."

Fran straightened her jacket and checked her sensible, black, office-style shoes for dirt. She was all dressed up in her best investor meeting clothes. They might not be comfortable, but at least she was getting used to them, and this was one of the times when they would be important.

"Which way to your friend's office?" she asked.

Irene peered at the map app on her cellphone. "This way."

It was early in the morning, but the streets were already bustling with people, most of them on the way to work. Hundreds of bicycles, electric cars, and a few older vehicles rolled past, including a vintage motorbike that Fran suspected would've made Gruffbar smile.

It was funny being back on Earth when so much of her life was on Oriceran. She'd spent a lot of time here growing up, but Mana Valley was her home now, and she felt a little like a tourist in a place that should've been home.

Of course, a lot of things weren't the way they were supposed to be. Her mother had recently tipped her very identity on its head. Childhood stories turned into the untold tale of her real-life origin, a story that was—for Fran at least—still full of holes.

"Did we ever see other Evermores when I was growing up, Mom? Like, friends of yours who I would've thought were witches but were teachers secretly preparing me to use my powers, that kind of thing?"

"No, dear. Until Winslow gatecrashed your party, I was the only Evermore you ever met."

Fran was surprised by how disappointed she felt. Having discovered that there were big secrets around her, she'd half-expected to find a complex web of deception and tricks, sheltering her from the incredible truth. Instead, there was an absence, a gap where part of her life should've been.

"Why didn't we see them?" she asked.

"Why would we?"

"Because they're the people you grew up with. Some of them must be family, right?"

"Some of them, yes. In a sense, all of them. That's beside the point."

They stopped at a crossing, waiting for the lights to change. Up above, a flight of news drones surveyed the city, looking for signs of disturbance. Across the road, an elf also waited for the traffic lights to change, one of the magicals who now lived openly in the human world.

"Family doesn't seem beside the point," Fran said. "Why didn't we see them?"

"That was the deal." They crossed the street, the green signal man blinking at them as they went. "Evermores don't normally leave the community. To be allowed out into the world, I had to accept many conditions. Those included not telling anyone about the Evermores."

"Not even your daughter?"

"Most especially my daughter."

There was something odd about the way Irene said that, but Fran couldn't work out what she wanted to challenge. She cast around for something else to ask.

"So you didn't explain because if you did, you wouldn't be allowed out into the world?"

"Essentially, yes."

"Then you told me anyway."

Irene sighed, stopped, and turned to look straight at Fran. She took her daughter's hand.

"Francesca, I thought I explained this to you already. With the Source out in the world and Winslow chasing after, it seemed clear that the Evermores would stumble into your path. I wanted to preempt that, to prepare you at least a little for what was coming."

"I didn't feel very prepared."

"Well, it was difficult to deal with. In case you've forgotten, you were under arrest."

Fran laughed. "I guess so."

"Right, now that's out of the way, I should prepare you for today." Irene let go of Fran's hand and strode off down the street. Fran hurried to catch up with her. "What have I told you about Tod so far?"

"Which one's Tod?"

"Tod Anderson, the first of the potential investors I'm introducing you to today."

"Oh, okay, um…"

Fran thought back through what they'd discussed. Her mom had gone through a whole list of contacts she'd made before Fran was born, people who were now influential in Silicon Valley or the American finance system. Fran was hazy on how and why Irene had gotten to know such people, but they seemed to be associated with happy memories, at least judging by her mom's enthusiasm. Today they were meeting with four of them, hoping that they would invest in Mana Wave Industries.

"Is Tod the electric scooter guy?" she asked.

"That's right, dear. He invested in a new sort of electric scooter right before a big craze hit. He invested the profits in a diagnostic instruments company since medicine is usually a good bet. Then a few years ago, he pivoted to drones."

"That's why you think he's our best hope, because flying machines want the best, lightest batteries they can get?"

"Smart as always." Irene looked from her phone screen to the sign on the front of a building. "This is it."

The building was very tall and modern, constructed from one of the new hardened glass substitutes. Fran wondered if it was the one with the flexibility to resist earthquakes. After the recent bout of instability, that would make sense in the Valley.

"We're here to see Tod Anderson," Irene said to a receptionist. "Irene and Francesca Berryman."

"Take a seat, Ms. Berryman. Someone will be with you shortly."

They sat on a large fake leather couch and watched the news on a screen above the receptionist's head. The sound was off with no closed captions, but there was still enough to understand what they were seeing. The headline read **Magical Instability Continues.**

Behind the headline, a reporter talked to a wizard, who waved his wand vigorously and produced only a few disappointing sparks of magic. Then they cut to a small crowd of magicals jostling to be first up the steps to a Silver Griffins station.

"I remember when people would've thought elves and dwarves on the news was a prank," Irene said.

"What's it all about?" Fran asked. "I don't see much Earth news on Oriceran."

"A problem with the kemanas and its follow-on effects." Irene shook her head. "Or, to put it another way, this is the Source at work."

"Oh, wow. Do these people know?"

Irene shook her head again. "You might know our secret, but some discretion is still required."

A man in a sharp suit appeared next to the desk, and the receptionist pointed him their way.

"Ms. Berryman and Ms. Berryman?" he asked. "Come with me, please."

A glass-walled elevator carried them up through the building. Through its transparent walls, they could see the bustle of the entrance area, with people shrinking to tiny dolls, and out the front wall to the Valley beyond.

"This place is so cool," Fran said. "When I have my headquarters, we'll have a glass elevator."

"Whatever you want, dear."

They emerged onto the building's top floor and followed their guide down a corridor to a large private office. Again, glass dominated. Glass door, glass walls, even a glass-topped desk. The man who led them retreated from the room and closed the door behind him.

Another man emerged from behind the desk. He was in his late forties. His hair was turning gray, but he was handsome and in good shape for his age. He looked at Fran's mom with a twinkle in his eye.

"Irene, it's been far too long." The two of them hugged. "This must be Francesca? You've grown!"

"Call me Fran." She held out her hand.

"Pleased to meet you again, Fran." He shook. "I'm Tod."

She didn't remember meeting him before, but that was how it went with her mom's friends. They hadn't meant much to her as a kid, even the ones she'd met more than once or twice, whereas being someone's kid made you memorable.

"I hear you're hunting investors." Tod gestured them to a seat. "Tell me what you have."

Fran didn't have Bart's laptop with its slides, but in a way that made it easier. Instead of working her way stiffly through a pre-written presentation, she talked freely about her business and the parts that excited her. She kept quiet about the containment unit, which was still between her and the FBI, but enthused about the power source and some other devices they were trying to power with it.

Tod listened with interest and an occasional question. He clearly didn't understand much about magic, and he knew it. The same seemed to apply to technology. He was looking for big picture answers, not the minutiae of how it worked.

"...and that's where we're at now," Fran said as she approached an endpoint twenty minutes later. "We have the ideas and we have the beginnings of some really good designs. Now we're looking for the big contracts and the big investors to finance it."

"You think it's venture capital time?"

"That's up to my finance director. As far as I'm concerned, any money will do."

Tod laughed. "So that's what you want from me, huh, an investment?"

Fran shrugged. "Honestly, I'm not sure. Mom said she had some Silicon Valley contacts she thought could be useful, and I'll take anything useful right now. Investment, contracts, advice."

"That's a good attitude. You raised a smart kid, Irene."

"Thank you, Tod."

"I'm sure he'd be—"

"Let's stick to the issue in hand, shall we?"

"Of course. Well then..." Tod leaned back in his seat. "Here's my first piece of advice, and I'm afraid it's going to be disappointing. This isn't a Silicon Valley project. I know that, in principle, several tech firms are talking big about making use of magic. In practice, no one knows what they're looking for yet, never mind what they're doing. That makes investors nervous, which makes boards nervous, which makes the C-suite nervous, which… Well, you get the idea."

"Nobody here will want what I'm offering?" Fran sank into her seat, arms flopping in her lap.

"Not to invest in, no. Not yet. You're better off sticking with Mana Valley. The mood here is too cautious right now, especially with magic acting up at the moment. It makes magitech look too uncertain as an investment."

Fran glanced at Irene. If she could explain about the Source and the Evermores tracking it down, that might be helpful to Tod and might reassure him about investing in magitech. Irene gave a small headshake, and Fran subsided.

"That doesn't mean all is lost." Tod held up a finger. "There are ways we can help each other." He rummaged around in a box of business cards on his desk, then flicked one through the air to Fran.

"That's the guy in charge of sourcing components for my tech division. Tell your equivalent guy to get in contact with him. We have some great deals over here and a line on top-quality components. Once you reach the manufacturing stage, we can help you keep quality up and cost down on the tech parts."

"Thanks, Tod." Fran pocketed the card. "What do you get out of it?"

"We're making plans for a move into Mana Valley farther down the line. Having a contact on your side who knows how to get good magical components will be invaluable. Earth's tech industry might not have fully embraced magic yet, but it's going to. When that happens, I want to be ahead of the pack."

They talked for a little longer. Then the suited assistant showed Fran and Irene back out of the building.

"Well, that was disappointing," Irene said. "I really thought he might invest."

"Are you kidding?" Fran grinned. "That's the most productive meeting I've had all week. Bart will be super jealous. Even if the other three lead to nothing, today is a win."

"All right, then." Irene pulled out her phone. "On to office number two. You might remember Caroline…"

CHAPTER SEVENTEEN

Gruffbar walked cautiously down the stairs into the Mana Wave Industries office, peering at each step before he trod on it. The previous day, Elethin had left marbles on a step just before he came in.

He'd stepped on them, lost his footing, and taken a bruising tumble down the stairs. Fran and Bart had been concerned. Everyone else had laughed, most of all that blasted elf. He didn't think she was trying to break his neck, but she was willing to risk it to get one up on him.

In the old days, he would've started plotting his revenge straight away, and by now she would've been going through some torment. He was still determined to be a better person, whatever that meant, and he was sure that revenge didn't have a place in it.

He stopped and looked around again at the bottom of the stairs, but there was no sign of any other traps. In fact, there was no sign of half the other staff. Fran was on Earth for the day, and Bart and Elethin were out too, presumably in their endless, frustrated pursuit of potential investors.

Only Singar and Smokey were in the building, sitting on a pair of high stools at their biggest workbench.

"About time someone showed up," Singar said. "Come over here."

"I have work of my own to do, you know," Gruffbar said. It was true, although not in a very useful way. He'd written nearly all the procedures he needed to, and until they started signing more contracts, there was little use for his legal skills.

He might feel a little defensive at his colleagues taking his time for granted, but he did have time to spare. Plus, he was genuinely interested in what the tech team was making. So while he went over wearing a scowl, he was smiling on the inside, the place where dwarves were traditionally allowed to smile.

Several devices sat on the workbench with a scatter of components around them. Gruffbar climbed onto a stool across the bench from the others for a better view. "What's all this, then?"

"These are our prototypes." Smokey waved a paw at the assembled objects.

"I thought that was your prototype." Gruffbar pointed at another workbench, where the parts of the containment unit, including the burned-out battery pack, lay spread in battered pieces. The rods were bent, crystals cracked, and the exterior of half the wires looked melted.

"Thanks to Winslow, we have to leave that one for a while," Singar said.

"What did Winslow do?"

"Didn't tell us that this Source of theirs would keep growing so dramatically in power, then took me out into the field to try and catch it. The feedback from its power burned out the battery and shattered some of the rarer crystals in the magical array. We can't even repair it, never mind build an improved version, until a new delivery of crystals arrives."

Gruffbar stroked his beard. "I might know a guy who can speed up the hunt for parts."

Singar shook her head. "Winslow needs to learn that his dumbass actions have dumbass consequences. Besides, it's given us time to work on other things."

"These are our other prototypes," Smokey said. "The ones we've gotten farthest with. We can't sell the containment unit to everyone, so we need some other options if the real point is to get our battery out there. Something with more mass-market appeal. The problem is, we can't decide which one to focus on."

"What are the options?"

"Glad you asked because we were going to tell you either way."

Smokey nodded at Singar, who pressed a button on the first device. It was a box with a pair of mannequin hands protruding from the top. As Gruffbar watched, the hands started to move. It looked like they were dancing.

"This is one I came up with for a competition," Singar said. "You can practice sign language conversations with it. If you want, you could even learn a sign language from scratch by interacting with this device."

Gruffbar watched. He didn't know any sign languages, but it seemed plausible that the device was getting it right.

"That sounds admirable," he said. "Something valuable for its target audience, and probably good PR, though you'd have to check with Elethin about that. But if your aim is for something mass-market, how many people ever learn sign language?"

"Told you," Smokey said.

"I never said you were wrong." Singar switched the device off, and the hands went still. "But like Gruffbar said, it still has value."

"Just not for what we need."

"Perhaps we can find another purpose for it?"

"Like what?"

They both turned to look at Gruffbar expectantly. He shrugged.

"I'm a lawyer, not an inventor. I'm not going to come up with a big idea for what this could do. Why don't you show me what else you've got?"

Smokey jumped from his stool onto the table, took the corner of a cushion between his teeth, and dragged it over to Gruffbar. Aside from a little cat spit on that corner, the cushion had a strange pattern of runes and electrical wires on the underside.

"Sit on it," Smokey said.

"Why would I do that?" Gruffbar asked.

"Because it's a cushion."

"I'm comfortable where I am."

"Just sit on the thing."

Gruffbar reluctantly took the cushion and, with a certain amount of wriggling, got it between his ass and the stool he was sitting on, wires and runes side down.

"What is this?" he asked. "Aside from unnecessarily lumpy?"

"It's a riff on one of Fran's creations." Singar picked up a remote control. "Like a flying carpet, but with more padding for a smoother flight and a softer landing."

She rolled a ball on the remote, and the cushion shifted under Gruffbar. It lifted him into the air. She pushed one of the other controls, and the cushion started moving around the room. Gruffbar clung on tight. One collision with the floor was more than enough for a single week. He still had bruises from the stairs incident.

"Shouldn't I be the one controlling it?" he asked. "People like to drive their own vehicles."

"The controls are counterintuitive at the moment," Singar said. "We need to work on the user experience side of this one. What's it like to ride?"

"You don't know?"

"I haven't tried it."

The cushion shot up, and Gruffbar wished he had his helmet on as his head banged against the ceiling

"Sorry!"

The cushion dropped so fast he felt the bump against the floor through the layer of padding. Before he could climb off, the cushion was on the move again, whizzing him around the office. He hurtled across the computers, almost slammed into the pile of old mirror-making machines, and hit the wall with a *thud*.

"Enough!" he shouted. "Let me down!"

"I've got this." Singar brought the cushion back to the workbench and lowered it onto Gruffbar's stool. "You get that."

"Got it." Smokey tapped a tablet, and a camera on the bench's corner stopped filming. "Got the feed from the controls as well. That should be useful in ironing out the wrinkles."

"I thought I was here to offer opinions, not be a guinea pig." Gruffbar pulled the cushion out from under him and flung it on the floor.

"As a guinea pig, what's your opinion of the cushion?" Singar asked.

"I think I'll stick with my bike."

"Disappointing, but not surprising."

"I guess it has some potential. People could use it to fly over the rush hour traffic, at least until these things become so popular that they *are* the traffic jam. Wouldn't it be easier to fly a carpet? Then you can roll it away at the end."

"Told you." Singar looked at Smokey with a smirk.

"I'm a cat. I like cushions, all right?" Smokey said. "It could have been worse. We could've made it a flying box."

"Huh, you know, that has potential for deliveries…"

"What have you got next?" Gruffbar asked.

Singar picked up a device the size and shape of a cell phone but with a pair of tiny prongs protruding from one end.

"This is another niche market one," she said. "But we think it's a larger niche. Behold, the first magical stun baton."

She pressed a button on the side of the device. A mixture of electricity and magic jumped between the prongs, making a juddering sound.

"You made a magical taser?" Gruffbar asked.

"Exactly."

"How is that better than an ordinary taser?"

"It'll affect creatures that are immune to electricity or that are resistant to non-magical attacks." Singar pressed the button again and watched with a grin as the electricity and magic crackled in the air. "Like our friendly neighborhood spirits."

The three of them all looked over at the wall, where a heavy dust sheet once more covered the long mirror.

"I'll admit, it would've been handy to have that the other day," Gruffbar said. "But how many people get into fights with spirits?"

"I figure we sell it to the authorities. Silver Griffins, police, FBI, private security firms…"

"That's still not mass-market."

"Self-defense enthusiasts?"

"Not many of them carry Tasers."

"They should." Singar pressed the button and grinned again.

"How effective is it?"

Smokey managed to shrug, an impressive gesture from a cat. "We haven't had a chance to test it yet." He eyed the mirror. "Maybe we should let them out again and give it a go."

"After last time?" Gruffbar shook his head. "Terrible idea. We don't have the containment unit to hold them anymore."

"We have the copy we built for the FBI."

"Still a terrible idea."

"Guess we need to find a guinea pig then." Singar pressed the button on the stun baton and grinned at Gruffbar as the electricity emerged.

"By my beard, if you try that on me, I'll use your head to test my new ax blade. Understand?"

"Relax, I wasn't serious." She put the device down. "Well, mostly not serious."

"What else do you have?"

"That's it for now."

They all sat back looking at the selection of prototypes.

"One of these is supposed to convince people of the value of our batteries?"

"That and the value of our company." Smokey rubbed one forepaw across the other. "Investor money, remember?"

Gruffbar stared at the items: a sign language teacher, a magical taser, and a cushion that he wouldn't sit on ever again.

"You have two solutions to problems most people don't have. And a mode of transport that no one except you can currently drive. They all work at least a little, and they're impressive in their way, but that's not the question. The question is, would any of these be useful to a mass market of ordinary people, and the answer's no."

"Have you got a better idea?" Smokey asked sharply. "Because if you have, I'd love to hear it."

"My better idea is that we go to the Blazing Bean."

"Caffeine, that's your whole solution?"

"Caffeine and people. We'll ask Cam if we can run an informal survey of his customers, give them a list of all the things you've been working on, see which ones sound most useful to them and why. We'll run a competition too, offer to buy coffee and cake for whoever comes up with the best everyday problem for us to solve."

"Market research." Smokey licked the back of his paw thoughtfully, then used it to clean his fur behind his ear. "I guess it's what we should be doing in theory."

"We weren't coming up with new ideas sitting here." Singar got out of her seat. "Come on then, let's go."

They grabbed laptops, tablets, and other work notes, then headed out. As they went up the stairs, Gruffbar noticed that Singar was carrying the cushion and its controller.

"What are you doing with that?" he asked.

"Some other market research."

Raulo was sitting behind the counter of Worn Threads as they passed through.

"Here, try this," Singar said, handing him the cushion and the controller. "Flying cushion."

"Cool!" Raulo immediately put the cushion under him and peered at the controls. "How does it work?"

"See if you can work that out for yourself, then let me know how it goes. I want to hear what you did, what worked, what didn't, what you couldn't find, and what sort of advice you would've needed for things to go smoothly. Sound all right to you?"

"Flying a cushion around the store? It sounds like great fun. Thanks, man."

They headed out, leaving Raulo to figure the controls. As the door closed behind them, there was a *thud*, a yelp, and another *thud*.

"Are you sure that's a good idea?" Smokey asked.

"Got to do our user experience research," Singar said. "Better here than in the Blazing Bean. The carpets will give him a nice soft landing."

CHAPTER EIGHTEEN

Smokey sat on his stool at the front of the meeting room. Though he hid it behind a cat's habitual poise of indifference to the world, he was very pleased with what he saw when he looked around. It was only a few weeks since he'd been the only magical at the meetings of Paws and Claws.

Now Vaudrek lounged across a row of chairs. The crows perched on seatbacks behind her. A shifter had turned up for the meeting in tiger form, and even a centaur joined them, although their height had caused some problems coming into the burrow building.

The group was growing. This was the most people who'd ever turned up for a meeting, and they might have to relocate to a more convenient meeting place soon. At last, things were shaping up the way he'd envisioned them.

He'd waited a few minutes after the official start time of the meeting, in case anyone else turned up, but this seemed to be it. He stood, arched his back, stretched his tail, and started to speak.

"Good evening, comrades, and thank you for coming

along today. It's especially pleasing to see some new faces. The movement needs more magicals if we're going to make our voices heard."

Of course, he'd had new faces turn up before, only to turn out to be pranksters who'd come to make fun of his life's work. While he watched the new arrivals with caution born of being hurt in the past, he felt more hopeful about these two. They both clearly and visibly had an interest in the rights of non-bipedal magicals and so were more likely to be there with good intent.

"First up, a big thank you to the crows for all the fliers they've been sticking up around the city," Smokey continued. "You got them to places I wouldn't have thought of, and I expect that's why we have more people here tonight." He twitched his whiskers. "It feels weird calling you 'the crows.' Don't you have names we can use?"

The crows *cawed* and shook their heads. Presumably they had names to tell each other apart, but they couldn't be conveyed to someone without a bird's understanding or said by someone without a bird's vocal cords.

"Guess we'll stick with 'the crows' then. Either way, big thanks for your efforts."

The crows *cawed* in satisfaction and fluttered their wings. One of them still had glue on its wingtip.

"I assume you're all interested to hear about what I've got planned for our first big campaign. As those fliers explained, and as I'm sure you've all discovered from your own experiences, big businesses cause some of the biggest problems. They have the resources to make a world better adapted to everyone's needs, but they don't do it. We singled out a few companies in that flier, and now it's time to start putting some pressure on them."

Somebody cleared their throat, and everybody in the group looked around. A human-looking woman, probably a shifter or a witch, stood in the doorway. She was short and slim, dressed in high heels and a sharply cut suit, with a slender silver necklace around her throat. She'd neatly tied back her blonde hair.

She didn't look like much of a protester or a revolutionary, but she held one of the group's fliers between carefully manicured fingers. "Is this Paws and Claws?"

"It is." Smokey waved a paw in greeting. "Welcome to the revolution. Take a seat."

"Actually, I should probably introduce myself first." The woman walked over to Smokey and held out her hand. "I don't want it to seem like I snuck in somewhere I shouldn't be. My name's Julia Lacy. I'm the personal assistant to Howard Phillips. You mentioned his business in your materials…"

Smokey looked at the outstretched hand, then up at Julia's face.

"Not all of us have hands," he said sternly.

"Sorry, my bad. I'm not very informed on the issues around your campaign, but I hope to change that."

"You want to be radicalized?" Smokey didn't try to hide his cynicism.

"I wouldn't go that far. Surely you want big businesses to listen to your concerns. That's why you mentioned us in this pamphlet, right?"

She held out the flier. It featured spoof versions of the logos of several prominent Mana Valley firms, including

Philgard. It also had a section trying to shame those businesses for being too biped-focused, ignoring the needs of other magicals.

"That's right." Smokey's confidence was faltering. In theory, he very much wanted these businesses to listen, but he hadn't expected it to happen yet. He'd thought there would be months, even years of campaigning before they saw any change. He hadn't prepared for this. He wasn't sure it was for real. It felt a little like a trap.

"Well then." Julia took a seat at one side of the circle, smiled brightly at the other magicals, and pulled a tablet from her handbag. "Why don't you tell me about the problems you have with our products? I'll take notes if that's all right."

The magicals looked at one another uncertainly. Julia looked around again.

"Please," she said. "Start with whatever comes to mind. How could Philgard products be better for you?"

"Your phones are all human-sized and set up for people with fingers." Vaudrek flexed a large, clawed paw. "I've destroyed many of their screens trying to operate them."

"I see. So what would make that better for you?"

"I know the problem. It's your engineers' job to fix it, is it not?"

Julia laughed. "Yes, of course. Sorry, that was ignorant of me."

One of the crows fluttered across the room and landed on the edge of Julia's tablet. If she was alarmed by the bundle of black feathers getting in her face, she didn't show it, remaining composed. The crow tapped the screen with its beak, achieving a grand total of nothing.

"I'm sorry, I don't understand what you're trying to say," Julia said.

"He's not trying to say," the tiger shifter growled. "He's trying to show you. The screen isn't sensitive enough to register him operating it."

"Ah, yes." Julia typed on the screen, which responded fine to her touch. "Thank you."

"I have the opposite problem." The shifter held up a large paw. "If I try to operate your screens in this form, they think that a dozen fingers are touching them at once. It's impossible to get anything done."

"Can't you shift forms to operate the tablet?"

The tiger glared at her.

"I've said something wrong. I'm sorry."

"These are the bodies we're most comfortable in." Smokey gestured at the tiger and himself. "In the modern world, we should be able to go about everyday life in them."

"Of course. It's so obvious when you explain it. I apologize for my ignorance. Now, what other problems have you had with our products?"

She seemed so helpful, so considerate, and eager to learn that even Smokey almost found himself drawn in. They so seldom heard apologies. That was a power move in its way. It hid something else: that her questions were a distraction.

"This isn't a focus group," Smokey said. "We're not here to help you make and sell better devices."

"Surely they'll help you?"

"This isn't about design features. Those aren't the problem. They're a symptom. If you're serious about doing better, that will take real structural change."

"Please, explain that to me." Julia was still smiling and looking at him with what appeared to be genuine curiosity. It was all he could do to remember that she was the enemy, not an ally.

Or was she? Maybe she was genuinely here to help.

"It's not enough to change what you're selling," he said. "You have to address the way your business works. How you represent yourselves and your customers. Who you employ and how."

"Representation, that's a really good point." Julia made more notes. "So that might mean putting more diverse magicals in our advertising?"

"Yeah." The centaur nodded vigorously. "I've never seen anyone like me in one of your adverts or web pages. It's all elves and dwarves, witches and wizards. The rest of us use tech too."

"I hadn't thought about it like that, but I suppose it matters who we show to the world, doesn't it?" Julia looked thoughtful. "This could be our chance to make a real difference, to raise the profile of a wider range of magicals."

"To better advertise to us and sell more products," Smokey said bitterly.

"Which makes it a win-win. That's how capitalism works, right?" She closed the case on her tablet and slid it back into her handbag. "Thank you so much. This has been really helpful. I'll go back to my employer and we'll talk about what changes we can make, for a better world for everyone."

She got up out of her seat.

"Wait," Smokey said. "You haven't answered the big one."

"I haven't? But we talked about structural change, about representation."

"We talked about one structural change, but you're ignoring the bigger one. Employment practices."

Julia smiled, but Smokey could've sworn he saw a tiny flicker of annoyance cross her face.

"How many non-bipedal staff does Philgard employ?" Smokey asked.

"I don't have any data on that. I can try to find the information for another day if you want."

"What adjustments have you made to help people of different shapes work in your business?"

"I don't know the exact policies..."

"Do you even know that they exist?"

"That's an excellent question. I'll look into it."

"What about recruitment? How do you make sure that non-bipeds can get into your business?"

"You know, I've never thought about that. It's something we can look into, though."

"That's a lot of things you're going to look into and none that you're offering to change. What I hear from your answers is that you don't employ people like us and that you've made no effort to change that."

The other magicals were staring at Julia. Moments before, they'd been friendly and talkative, pleased that anyone was listening to them. Now they were glaring.

"Change takes time," she said. "Especially when you're trying to change an organization as large as Philgard. I promise, my presence here is a sign of how seriously Mr.

Phillips takes your concerns. He might be a biped himself, but he appreciates the struggles others face, and he wants to help.

"We will be consulting widely within the company on how we can improve our working practices to take account of everything you've mentioned today, from user experience to advertising to employment. It will take time, but I promise, change is coming."

Her serious expression turned back to the friendly smile. "Now do excuse me. I should get back to Mr. Phillips, and of course, leave you with time to discuss your important work."

She hurried out of the room, and her footsteps faded across the lobby outside.

The members of Paws and Claws looked at each other.

"She seemed nice," the centaur said. "It's good that someone came to talk to us, right?"

"Her words were as hollow as a cave." Vaudrek's tongue flicked out to taste the air. "You can almost smell the evasion. Promises to consider, to consult, to talk, not to act."

One of the crows landed on the seat Julia had occupied and pecked vigorously at the spot where she'd been sitting. Smokey was pleased to see the radicalism emerging among his recruits, the sense of outrage that came when you saw the world fobbing you off again.

"It's going to be like when my building supervisor promised to change the doors," the tiger shifter said. "First they'll be planning something you ask for, then they'll find out that it's more complicated, so they'll delay, and they'll make excuses, and a year later, you still don't have a way to leave the building in a tiger shape. Or, you know, to work at Philgard. Whatever the fix is."

"You're right," Smokey said. "All of you. You've seen the classic corporate response, playing along so they look good, offering empty words to shut us up. It might seem like that's all we'll ever get. But think about this. Would she have come here if they weren't worried about what we might do?"

The others looked at each other. One by one, they shook their heads.

"You're saying we have them scared?" Vaudrek said. "That this Julia Lacy woman is our prey now?"

"Not scared, maybe, but concerned. They've seen that we're mobilizing, that we're drawing recruits and attention, that we could cause the sort of publicity that would damage them. They're trying to avoid that by offering empty promises. Do you think that's good enough?"

"No," the others replied, and the crows joined in with their cawing.

"Are we going to accept this treatment?"

"No!" This time they shouted together, and the crows flung their heads back, croaking more loudly.

"Are we going to let them deter us from our cause?"

"NO!"

"Exactly!" Smokey slammed a paw against his cushion. "So, let's talk about what we do next, how we scare them into taking real action..."

CHAPTER NINETEEN

Josie walked down the length of the test lab, carrying the magic detector with her. Green dots on its surface shifted as she moved past the items laid out on the workbench. Some of them had light and sound magic, some had other powers, and some had no magic at all. At the side of the room, Simon sat with a laptop on his knees.

"That's it," Josie said. "Test fifty-eight is a complete success. Unless you've picked up something I missed?"

"What?" Simon looked up.

"The readings from the diagnostic tools, did you spot anything unexpected?"

"Oh, no." Simon shook his head distractedly.

"Were you watching the readouts, or were you checking your messages again?"

He glared at her. "I'm the manager here, not you, and it's none of your business what I was doing."

Josie sighed. At times during the testing, Simon's experience and technical skills had proved genuinely useful, but he was still far too distracted by these evaluations.

"I'm sorry, mister manager. I just want to finish this job. Then we can report it as a success."

That got his attention, and he snapped the laptop shut.

"Good point. Do you have a plan for the next step?"

Josie switched the detector off and started packing away the test artifacts.

"I was thinking of field testing, taking it out into the Valley to see how well it works in the wild. If you sign off on the authorization, I could take it out this afternoon and get started."

"You want to leave the office? When evaluations are on, and everybody will see that you're absent?"

"Absent doing my work."

"Like they'll see that." Simon snorted. "If you're willing to take the risk, I'll sign it off." He opened the laptop again and typed something. There was a *ping*. "Authorization granted. You are now free to take this prototype out for testing, but make sure to sign it out and back in correctly."

"Of course."

"Provide a thorough log of your results so we can add it to the project record."

"Will do."

"Don't damage it. That's company property."

"Oh, but I was going to go and bounce it off some rocks."

"Ha ha, hilarious. Now go get on with it. I have more report forms to fill out."

Josie walked down the street, the magic detector in her hand, watching the patterns shifting on its surface. They were much more complex out here in the real world, outside the test lab's magical shielding. Instead of picking out the right magic from dozens of discrete items, the device tried to differentiate all the light and sound magic in a city of millions.

There were ten times as many devices as there were people, and a thick layer of background magic hung over the whole place. The result was a mass of swirling patterns that formed more solid points as she approached specific spells and devices, but that could be very hard to interpret even with her experience.

She stopped in the doorway of an empty shop and made a note on her phone. They would either have to simplify the way the device displayed this information or find a way to explain its interpretation to users. Probably both.

It was a shame they couldn't make a more user-friendly design from scratch, based on what they'd learned from this model, but that wasn't the task they'd given her. As Simon kept pointing out, they had to do the job they received. Apparently, that was part of how they would get good evaluations.

With her phone back in her pocket, Josie set off down the street again. Mid-afternoon wasn't one of the busiest times in Mana Valley, but there were still plenty of magicals out on the streets, from shoppers to couriers to off-duty service staff enjoying their free time. A group of gnomes walked past, hands waving as they discussed a story from the news. A pair of skateboarding elves followed, serenely singing as they went.

As Josie passed a park, a distinct point of green stood out on the side of the detector. It was the strongest sign she'd found so far of a powerful piece of light or sound music, so she followed it.

It was a nice day, and there were plenty of people in the park, most of them lying around in the sunshine on well-kept grass. She made her way past them, following the detector's directions, one eye on the green spot and the other on the ground in front of her to make sure she didn't step on a sunbather.

The device led her to the shady cluster of trees in the center of the park, a small patch of woodland that had avoided being cut down to make space for the city. A couple of the trees had fliers stuck to the upper reaches of their trunks, but they were otherwise as nature had made them, with little sign of magic.

As she walked under the trees, the green spot moved, rolling up across the dome of the device. That part of the design was something they should keep if she got to reinvent it. Being able to point out a target above or below, not just left or right, in front or behind, was handy.

Josie looked up. Birds were fluttering between the branches of the trees, but not ordinary birds. They blazed with magical light, shining so brightly that everything else around them seemed darker by comparison. They were so beautiful that for a moment, Josie completely forgot why she was there and stood staring up at the wonder of them.

Then she remembered her work. She took out her

phone, took a photo of the birds, and ensured that the picture had its time and location tags. When she got back to the office, she could compare that with the device's readings to create a record of how its sensors related to reality.

She allowed herself a few more minutes under the trees, watching the birds fly back and forth. Their light changed color, reds, blues, and yellows intertwining. She'd worked through enough lunch breaks recently to earn a few minutes off now. She might not be as evaluation-focused as her colleagues, but she was still a recruit looking to make a good impression, and that meant getting on with the job. She took one more photo for herself, then reluctantly walked away.

Out of the park and down the road, the device found another strong signal. This time it pointed into a parking garage. She followed it down to the basement floor, where an elf crouched by the wall. A bright beam of light shone from her hand.

"Are you all right there?" Josie asked.

The elf looked up. She was frowning. "I dropped my keys down the drain. I can see them down there, but I can't reach them."

"Maybe I can help."

The elf shone her bright, magical light down the drain again, and she and Josie peered into the depths.

"There, see?" the elf said.

Sure enough, a set of keys lay on a ledge halfway down the drain, glinting in the torchlight. They were well out of reach.

Josie set the detector down and took out her wand.

"Subvolo." She pointed the wand at the keys.

The keys shook, rattled, then levitated up the drain, straight into Josie's hand. She passed them to their grateful owner.

"Thank you so much," the elf said. "You're an absolute lifesaver. Is there anything I can do for you?"

"This might sound odd, but could I please get a photo of you casting your light spell?" Josie briefly explained what she was doing, and the elf happily agreed.

"It's the least I can do," she said.

With the photo taken, Josie picked up the orb. The green spot had vanished when the elf stopped her spell.

"Thank you so much," Josie said. "I should get going. Plenty more magic to find."

She left the parking garage and walked down the street. So far, so good. The detector had found two strong sources of light magic. What about sound?

As if on cue, a wail of guitar noise burst from a nearby bar. A bright green dot appeared on the orb's surface, pointing through the bar's doors.

"It's a little early," Josie murmured, "but I'll take the hint."

Inside the building, a barman was putting away glasses while a band tuned their instruments in the corner. Unsurprisingly, the noises were coming from the band. More surprisingly, they had no amplifiers or any other sort of electronic equipment.

"Excuse me." Josie walked up to the wizard who most looked like a lead guitarist. "Are you using magic to amplify your sound?"

"Yeah, man." He nodded, long hair hanging loose

around his face. "It creates this really rich sound, you know? Much better than this electronic stuff from Earth. It's modern but traditional, you know?"

"I don't really. Could you explain it to me?"

"Sure!" He talked eagerly about the magic they were using while Josie made notes and the rest of the band rolled their eyes. They seemed a little happier when Josie asked if she could take a photo of the whole group.

"Are you gonna tell people about our gig on social?" the wizard asked.

"Sure, I can. Mostly though, this is for a work thing." Josie took the photo, then put her phone away. "Thank you so much, and good luck with the gig."

"Maybe we'll see you there?"

"Maybe, if I have time."

"And maybe you'd like to grab a drink with me afterward?"

"Oh!" Josie shook her head. "Thanks for the offer, but no thanks."

She walked out and headed down the street, following the device's signals like a giant dot-to-dot puzzle. Her path brought her toward the part of town where she and Fran lived. Once again, the device was signaling that it had found something. She followed its lead, changing direction with the shifts of the green dot until she arrived at the door of the Blazing Bean. She laughed.

"Well, it would be rude not to," she said to herself, or possibly to the device, which was starting to feel like a companion in its own right. She pushed the door open and walked in.

"Hi, Cam." She briefly turned her attention away from the task in hand. "Can I get a green tea, please?"

"Of course. Always happy to look after one of my best customers."

"I think you're confusing me with Fran."

"Not sure how I could. You're both great, but you're definitely not the same."

"We're both great, or maybe Fran's particularly great?"

She watched his reaction carefully. She'd expected a blush, a smile, maybe even for him to take this opportunity to sound her out about Fran. Instead, he looked away.

"One green tea." He put it on the counter. "Enjoy."

Thwarted in her attempts to help her roommate's love life, Josie turned her attention back to work. Taking her tea with her, she followed the device's signal to the back of the coffee shop, where a familiar figure was sitting at a table, enjoying her e-read and a coffee.

"Hi, Irene," Josie said, looking from Fran's mother to the device. There was no avoiding it. This was where the signal came from.

"Hello, Josie." Irene smiled. "What brings you here in the middle of the afternoon? Do Philgard run meetings here too? I hear it's what all the best companies do."

"Honestly, I'm not sure why I ended up here. I'm testing a device to detect sources of light and sound magic, and it brought me straight to you."

"Really? How curious."

Josie sat and put the device on the table.

"You don't have any spells on you right now, do you?" she asked.

"I don't think so."

"No magical devices?"

"None at all. People keep telling me that I should get one of those new Manaphones, but I'm not convinced."

"That wouldn't have shown up anyway."

"Curiouser and curiouser."

"Do you cast a lot of light and sound magic like Fran does?"

Irene shook her head. "I don't cast much magic at all, dear, if I can avoid it. I've never been very powerful, and I find the effort exhausting."

Irene tapped the device. The green spot glowed intently beneath her finger. Something about her demeanor seemed odd, but Josie figured that might come from being interrupted in her quiet time. With three of them in the apartment, things sometimes got tense, and Irene wouldn't have expected to see Josie now.

"Did you make this?" Irene asked.

"No, I'm only making adjustments. I was supposed to be testing, but then… You know what, office politics isn't very interesting. The important thing is, I have to make this thing work. I refined the inputs it was looking for based on what I'd seen, and… Oh, I'm an idiot!"

Josie laughed, and Irene gave her a quizzical look.

"I based the light and sound detection on magic I'd seen Fran casting," Josie explained. "I must have jumbled in bits of her aura with the auras from the magic. So now the device is looking for magic that appears like light, sound, or Fran."

"As her mother, that includes me?"

"Exactly. It doesn't matter that you don't do light and sound magic. It thinks that's what you are." Josie pulled a device out of her bag. "Do you mind if I take a scan of your aura? Then I can use it to exclude you and Fran from any further searches."

"Of course, dear." Irene smiled and sat still for the scan. "Always happy to help you with your work."

CHAPTER TWENTY

Fran walked carefully down the stairs into the Mana Wave office, carrying a rattling box. A crow perched on her shoulder, watching the box curiously.

"Delivery arrived from Caladir Crystals," she called.

"About time." Singar cleared space on the central workbench. "They said it would be here days ago." She frowned as she noticed the rattling. "Haven't they packed it properly?"

"Something probably came loose in transit."

"Not good enough. I swear, if they sent us cracked crystals again, I'm heading over to their warehouse, and I'm going to kick some heads in."

"I'm sure there's no need for kicking."

Fran set the box down on the workbench, and Singar sliced the tape open with her switchblade. They pulled the top open.

"Hey Smokey, you got a list of what we ordered?" Singar called.

Smokey looked up from his computer. "Right here. Ready when you are."

One by one, they unloaded the packages from the box. All were components for the containment units, some of them quite expensive. As they took them out and inspected them, Smokey checked each one off on a spreadsheet. At the end, he nodded.

"That's it. We've got them all, at last."

"Great." Singar flung the empty box down on the floor. The crow hopped down to poke around inside. "Now maybe we can finally sort this thing out."

From the far end of the workbench, she pulled over a square mirror, a set of extending metal rods, and the remains of the electronic components from the containment unit that the Source had broken. She opened her toolbox, took out two sets of pliers, and started removing the broken crystals from the electronics.

Smokey came over from the computer and perched on the end of the workbench, wielding a screwdriver that Singar had attached to a special mitten the cat could slide his paw into. Fran got her tools, and the three of them set to work rebuilding the unit while the crow watched from the end of the bench.

They were still hard at work an hour later when Winslow and Enfield appeared, stepping out of a portal into the middle of the room. Enfield was carrying two large paper bags.

"Most people use the stairs," Singar said.

"Would you mistake us for most people?" Winslow asked.

"Definitely not."

The Evermores walked over to the workbench and peered at the part-assembled device. The crow stared back at them with its head tipped to one side.

"Is it not finished yet?" Winslow asked.

"It's barely started," Singar said. "Crystals only arrived today."

"Couldn't you have started on the other parts and attached the crystals later?"

"No point starting the job until we could finish it too."

"It might have let you get ahead to have it ready sooner."

"Yeah, well, we had other work too."

"Work other than capturing the magical monster that's running wild through the kemanas of Earth?"

Singar looked up at Winslow, her expression full of disdain. "This might come as a shock to you, but our company's whole existence does not revolve around your interests. Right, Fran?"

Fran, who had been completely distracted by a tangle of wires, looked up in surprise. "What was that? Oh, yeah, business, projects to do…"

"I was saying that we don't only work for these jerk-offs." Singar pointed her pliers at Winslow. "In fact, last time I checked, they weren't paying us, so we don't work for them at all."

"Is that all that matters to you?" Winslow asked. "Money?"

"If you've never had to worry about it, you can't appreciate why it matters."

"Ah, so in my thousands of years of experience, I couldn't possibly have gained any insight into poverty?"

"There's watching, and there's living."

"Well, you don't seem destitute now, and we have a world to save."

"Guys, guys, chill out." Fran waved between them. "There's no need to argue. We're fixing up the device, making it more powerful than before, and that's what matters." She went over to the storage containers against the wall to fetch new wires. "Did you guys come in for anything in particular?"

"To see what progress you'd made on our containment unit," Winslow said. "And to bring supplies."

Enfield set his paper bags down on the workbench and opened them. "Hot drinks for everyone, from the Blazing Bean. Donuts, too. I hope I got the drinks right for everyone."

He handed out the cups and set the box of donuts in the middle of the table. Singar pushed the box out of the way.

"We're working here, remember?" she snapped.

"Working too hard for refreshments?"

"Definitely not." Fran grabbed a donut. "We'll be careful not to get sugar on everything."

A quiet minute followed as they all started on their drinks and donuts. It had been a while since they'd had a break, and even Singar took a moment to sit back and enjoy the refreshments. Enfield had brought lactose-free milk and cat treats, so Smokey could join in without shifting into his dwarf shape.

"These blue crystals are for magic storage?" Enfield looked at some of the components.

"That's right," Fran said. "Those yellow ones regulate the feedback system to ensure we're putting in enough magic to contain the subject, without overwhelming or killing them."

"That's a risk?"

"It would be, but we have a good design."

"She tested it on me once." Smokey paused to lick milk off his nose. "It's fine."

"These are the ones that burned out when the Source punched through the field?"

"Practically everything burned out." Singar prodded a heap of components they'd removed. "Wires, crystals, circuit boards, even the mirror cracked. That was one truckload of power. What is that creature?"

"Ancient," Winslow said. "Very important. We have to make sure we safely contain it."

"Well, that's why we're here." Singar licked sugar from her fingers. "You two can get out of here, and we'll get back to work."

The Evermores didn't move.

"You're welcome to stay and watch if you want," Fran said. "It might not be very interesting."

"I'm curious about how it all works," Enfield said. "I'm used to imbuing magic into potions, but not more complicated objects like this. Could you show me how you do it?"

"I thought you wanted it done quickly," Singar countered.

"Ignore her," Fran said. "Talking won't slow us down much. Take a seat, and I'll explain what I'm doing as we go along."

While the Evermores watched, the Mana Wave team got back to work. Melted wires were stripped out, cracked and burned crystals replaced. Smokey engraved runes onto the edges of a new mirror, carefully copying the symbols from the old version.

For the first half-hour, everything went smoothly. The Evermores were quiet, patient observers, learning from their hosts. Fran talked them through each step in the work she was doing, and the others occasionally joined. She hoped this wasn't breaking their non-disclosure deal with the FBI or endangering their corporate secrets somehow. At least they had Gruffbar to get them out of legal trouble if that happened.

"I thought this was part of the containment system." Enfield contemplated the part Fran was working on.

"It is."

"Then why is the power feeding out into another part of the device?"

"It's about balancing magical and electrical power."

"I see."

There were a few more minutes of quiet before he spoke again.

"Why are you using electricity at all? Surely you could rely on your magical energies."

"Magic doesn't always integrate well with other systems. We get a more reliable, consistent feed from the electricity, and the two combined provide something stronger."

"I struggle to believe that electronics can match the mystical arts."

"Believe it," Singar said. "Or go lick an electrical socket and see how much good your magic does for you then."

Singar flung a broken crystal into a box on the floor,

startling the crow perched there, and reached for a new component.

"What will you do with the damaged crystals?" Enfield asked.

"Send them for recycling," Fran said. "They're no use to us anymore."

"Can't you repair them?"

"Sadly not."

"With your powers, I'm sure you could regenerate the crystals, adding more to your supply."

"Sorry, no, not one of my powers."

Enfield looked at Winslow, who shrugged.

"What about…" Enfield began.

"Listen, keeno," Singar snapped, "this is our job. We've been working on magical devices for years, while you've been living in some out-of-the-way hole doing whatever it is that you do. We know what we're doing here. You don't, so stop interfering."

She tried to shoo him away, but he stayed in his seat next to Fran, looking at the components.

"Why those runes?" he asked.

"Because they work." Smokey put his etching tool down and blew the dust away from the glass. "We tried different combinations, and these are the best."

"Surely, this would be an improvement." Enfield sketched a pattern of runes in the air. His fingertip left a trail of light where it went so the others could read the runes.

"Tried it." Singar gave the runes the briefest glance. "That second one in the top row doesn't bend light the way you think it does."

"I have been wielding light magic for many years, and I assure you, that rune does exactly what I think it does."

"Really?"

Singar grabbed a piece of the cracked mirror, scribbled the rune onto it with a marker pen, and attached wires to either side. The rune lit up brightly, then the air above it started to pulse with unsettling, irregular flashes of light. Enfield stared at it.

"That's not right," he said. "You must have drawn the rune wrong."

Singar pulled the wires off, and the rune went dark. "No. Most people don't understand how that rune does what it does, or what happens when you combine it with even the simplest circuitry."

"In that case, thank you for teaching me a valuable lesson."

"My pleasure," Singar said with absolutely no signs of pleasure.

"What about if—"

"Double dung!" Singar flung her paws in the air. "Will you shut up and let us do our work? Or do you not want your containment unit finished?"

Enfield and Singar glared at each other across the workbench. Winslow, who had been watching proceedings from a few feet away, stepped closer.

"Ms. Twitchtail, we are only trying to help. This work matters to us as well as to you. Doing it as effectively as possible is very important."

"Then let us get on with our damn job." Singar looked at Fran. "Seriously, they're your guests. Can't you do something about them?"

Fran set down what she was working on. Singar was right, in her way. As CEO, it was Fran's job to deal with anything that didn't fit under anyone else's job description. That included managing weird magicals interested in their work. Plus these magicals were her kin, however distantly, so she was probably responsible for their presence.

"Guys, please. I get that you're here with good intentions and you think you understand things about the magic that we don't, but this is our technology. We work with it every day. We've seen the nuances, the interactions, the things that didn't work before. We know the tiny details and the big picture. This device is, like, halfway to being our obsession. Just trust that even if we're younger than you, sometimes we'll know what we're doing, okay?"

For a moment, it almost seemed like it had worked. Then Enfield opened his mouth.

"When I make potions we—"

"La la la, don't care!" Fran exclaimed loudly. "It's not a potion, and it's not your work. This is my company. Scratch that. It's our company." She gestured at her colleagues. "What we say goes, and right now, you have to go. Please. For the sake of my sanity."

Enfield frowned and looked like he was about to speak, but Winslow laid a hand on his shoulder, silencing him. The older Evermore waved, and a portal appeared.

"We'll go now. We'll come back tomorrow to see your progress, if we may."

"That would be fine. Thank you so much for the coffees and donuts. We really did enjoy them."

The Evermores stepped through the portal, and it closed behind them.

"Wow, Fran," Singar said. "For a minute there, it almost seemed like you'd found some backbone, but then—"

"Not now, Sin." Fran stepped away from the work-bench. The pressure of the failed investor meetings had already worn her thin, and now she had to deal with these squabbles. It was too much. "I'm going to go clear my head."

She grabbed her skates and headed up the stairs. The crow pecked Singar's arm, then fluttered away after Fran.

CHAPTER TWENTY-ONE

Bart approached Worn Threads as Fran skated out the door, a crow following her.

"Hi there. How are you doing?"

"Hi, Bart." Fran rolled to a gentle stop. "I'm not great, to be honest. Everything's so stressful right now."

"Sorry to hear that. Are you off to the skate park to blow off steam?"

"That's the idea."

"Is it all right if I join you? I won't be offended if you say no."

Fran smiled. "Of course you can come."

Bart took off his bulging backpack, took out skates and protective gear, and strapped it all on.

"Wow, you came prepared!" Fran said.

"I haven't been in a while, and I don't want to give up yet. You never get good at a thing if you don't persevere, right?"

Once he was ready, they set off along the sidewalk, skating a lot slower than Fran would have done on her own. It wasn't quite the stress-clearing speed she'd hoped for, but it was nice to hang out with Bart for a little. The crow perched on her shoulder, the wind gently ruffling its feathers.

"Tell me, what's bothering you?" Bart asked as they made their way toward the park.

Fran sighed. "A bunch of things. Some of it's about who I am and where I come from and all this weirdness I can't explain, but most of it's about the business. We've been trying so hard to find investors here and in Silicon Valley, and it's not working. It's starting to really stress me out.

"What if I can never find the money? What if I've talked you all into joining my business and now it turns out that the business is terrible? What if it's a complete mess, and we all go broke, and, and, and..."

She stopped skating and stood with her hands pressed to her face. "Bart, what if I can't do this?"

Bart rolled to a stop, then came back to face her. He reached up and drew one of Fran's hands away from her face, forcing her to look down at him. His face was kindly and full of wrinkles, the sort of face that made it hard to stay stressed.

"Fran, relax. You're one of the brightest, most capable young women I've ever met. You have energy, passion, and some excellent ideas. I know it's difficult to navigate the business of Mana Valley, but you'll manage it."

"How?"

"I don't know yet, but it's going to be fun finding out. Now come on, I'll race you to the skate park. Last one there buys the coffees after."

He turned and skated away as fast as he could. Fran

shot after him, grinning, with the crow flying along beside her. Of course, she overtook him in moments. By the time he reached the park, she'd been around the track three times already.

Just like in the days when they'd first met each other, Fran raced around and around the track while Bart made his way slowly along one side. He was a little more stable than when she'd first seen him but still not super confident on his skates. She felt a little guilty for distracting him from all this with her business—a little, but not much.

At last, Fran stopped close to Bart. He was catching his breath after nearly falling over. The crow landed and pecked at something by Bart's feet.

"Feeling better?" Bart asked.

"I should, but it doesn't seem to be working today."

"Well then, what else cheers you up? I'm all for trying something new."

"Milkshakes, I guess, or cocktails with umbrellas and fruit in them, or… Ooh, I know!" A big grin split Fran's face as inspiration struck. "Do you want to go kill some things?"

"That doesn't sound like your sort of entertainment."

"Oh, it is. You'll see."

Bart changed out of his skates, and they headed off through town, keeping to the slightly rundown areas where big tech companies and chain coffee shops hadn't yet taken over. This was where the struggling businesses went.

It was also where the fun, unusual ones found their homes, the quirky places that weren't the natural haunts of business executives, middle managers, and tech bros. Fran led the way to a big black building with "Retro" written in big gold letters across the front.

From the exterior, Bart had expected the inside to be gloomy. While there was no sunlight, there was more than enough artificial light to compensate. Colored lights flashed from arcade machines, game consoles, and old-fashioned monitors. All the signs were second-hand neon lettering, much of it mismatched. At the front was a glass cabinet, its base full of soft toys, with a mechanical grabber that customers could spend small change to operate.

"Isn't it fantastic?" Fran skated over to a box-like machine and tapped her payment card against a sensor. Coins poured out into a cardboard cup. "Most of the machines were imported from Earth. There are dancing games, racing games, quiz games, and most important of all..." She dropped a coin into the slot on a machine. "Shooting games!"

She drew a pair of plastic guns attached to the machine by thick cables and handed one to Bart. Around them, the arcade was full of sounds, from *pings* to engine noises to synthesized screams. A pair of karaoke machines added to the cacophony.

"What do we do?" Bart raised his voice so she could hear him over all the noise.

"Shoot the zombies. Try not to get killed."

Fran hit the start button. Zombies staggered out of a poorly animated jungle on the screen in front of them. Bart opened fire wildly, missing most of them.

"I've run out of bullets!" he exclaimed. "What do I do?"

Fran took careful aim and killed a pair of zombies.

"Look for a crate and shoot that. It'll give you more bullets."

"I don't have anything to shoot it with."

"It'll work."

"Won't shooting the crate make it explode, and I won't get bullets anyway?"

"Bart, stop worrying about logic and play the game."

For the next hour, they battled zombies in a desperate life-or-death struggle. It featured a lot of death since Bart struggled with this new form of entertainment, but Fran kept feeding change into the machine, and the games kept coming. The crow perched on top of the machine, and occasionally hopped down to try to peck the remains of a zombie they'd killed, only to be disappointed by the lack of a real body.

"Look!" Bart exclaimed. "That's my twentieth zombie. That's the most I've got so far. I think I've finally—oh!" Red spattered the screen as a zombie got to him. "No career in monster hunting for me."

"Never mind." Fran put away her gun and picked up her tub of change. "Let's try something else. How are your dancing feet?"

"Depends. Is it formal court dancing or rural traditional?"

"More likely K-pop."

"I didn't know that the Kilomea made much music."

Fran laughed. "You're in for another treat."

Beneath a miniature disco ball, they competed enthusiastically against the challenge of a dancing machine. Bart got the hang of this one more quickly, although his short and aging legs occasionally made it harder to complete a move.

"My word." He wiped the sweat from his brow. "They know how to make dance music on Earth, don't they?"

"You should hear their house music."

"Wouldn't music for around the house be soothing and relaxing? I like the liveliness of these songs."

After dancing, it seemed like time for a rest. They got cans of soda from another machine and sat on giant, brightly colored cushions in the corner of the room, legs splayed out on the floor in front of them. The crow perched on Fran's shoulder and did its impression of their last dance routine.

"Feeling better?" Bart asked.

"Much better, thanks." Fran sighed. "I still need to face up to the problems, but at least I don't feel as though they're, like, the whole world anymore."

Bart sipped his soda. Somehow, the bubbles were tickling his nose even though they were in his mouth. Earth technology could be very strange.

"Why don't we talk about it now?" he said. "If we work out answers to some of the problems, all the better. If we don't, you can take out your frustrations on those poor zombies again."

"I suppose." Fran fiddled with the top of her can. Bart was right, but she still wasn't keen to think about work again. It was a shame because she'd been so enthusiastic about the business when she started it, but now the reality was turning into a struggle. Was this how it felt for anyone who turned their passion into their profession or was it only her?

"Come on," Bart encouraged. "Get it out. You'll feel better after, I promise."

"Fine. It's the investors. I can't convince anyone to give us their money. I've tried everything. I've dressed up, dressed up more, then dressed up the most yet. I practiced my serious, adult voice. I've mostly avoided getting distracted.

"I've practiced that presentation, like, a bazillion times. I even rehearsed it in front of the big mirror in the office, with those trapped thugs and spirits as an audience, so I could get used to people listening. None of it has helped."

"Well, what do you think the problem is?"

"I don't know. You tell me. You've been there for a bunch of my failures." She pulled her knees up, wrapped her arms around them, and rested her head on top while rocking from side to side. "It's me. No one believes I can be a CEO."

"I believe you can."

"You're my friend. You have to believe in me."

"Gruffbar believes in you. Do you think he normally believes in people?"

She sniffed and wiped her eyes. "No, but he's trying to become good. His judgment's all messed up."

"Singar, then. Singar's as tough as a burned pizza crust. There are only two things she believes in: herself and you."

"Okay, fine, you guys believe in me, and that's super sweet. I really value it. That doesn't help us get money, though."

"It proves a point. People can believe in you. So what's going wrong to keep all these investors from believing?"

Fran sipped her drink and stared thoughtfully into the

distance, half-watching a group of teenagers as they wailed into a karaoke machine.

"I guess I'm not good at being serious," she said. "That's what they expect when we go to these meetings, so I try to dress and act the part. Deep down, I don't believe in myself as a serious person, and I think it shows. It's like a crack in the paint on a wall. You can't see what's wrong, but you can see that something underneath isn't solid."

"Hm." Bart leaned back and took another sip of his soda. "So you're trying to convince the investors that you match what they're looking for, that we're a serious business led by serious people."

"I can't do that because I'm not that. Do I need to change myself, to become someone else?"

"Never! I told you. You're one of the best people I know, and we don't want to ruin that."

"So I'll never convince them that I'm serious?"

"No..."

Now Bart's attention was on one of the machines. A dwarf was playing a two-player shooting game on his own with a gun in each hand, grinning madly as he blew the zombies away.

Then Bart looked down at the battered skate pads strapped to his knees. He never tried to pretend that he was good at skating, which was fine. Other skaters could see to give him space or offer advice when he was in trouble. That was how he'd met Fran.

A big grin split his face. "I've got it! Stop trying to be someone you aren't. Instead, convince these people to invest in who you are."

"They're looking for serious!"

"So convince them that they don't need it. Show them that passion, energy, and innovation can come from very unserious people but still be profitable for them."

"Do you really think we can make them see it that way?"

"Not all of them, but maybe enough. Even if it's only one, we'll know that we've got the one investor who suits Mana Wave Industries and the brilliant people working with its fantastic CEO. Isn't that better than getting a hundred investors who don't understand us, who constantly worry and complain about what we're doing?"

Fran thought back to the workshop and the Evermores leaning over Singar's shoulder, driving her nuts as they tried to interfere with her work.

"You're right," she said. "It's a far better plan. Just thinking about it makes me feel better. Thank you, Bart."

"Happy to help. Now, one more game before we head back to the office?"

"Sure. I want to see what this crow thinks of Pac-Man."

CHAPTER TWENTY-TWO

Handar Ennis stood in a side street behind a row of restaurants, leaning against the black body of an SUV. Phillips had imported the vehicle from Earth, a custom armored vehicle with blacked-out windows and reinforced bodywork. It was less a means of transport than a suit of armor, and Handar loved it. He only wished it was useful for more than intimidating the people he worked with.

Today, that was enough. As the freelance lowlifes he'd recruited drifted into the alley, they all stopped to stare at the vehicle and the Kilomea leaning against it. He could practically smell their tension mingling with the stink of kitchen waste from the dumpsters. These were tough magicals, but they knew a tougher one when they saw him.

"What's up, Handar?" Gerta asked. She was a dwarf, dressed in the type of leathers and chains that were popular among a certain group of hardened "back to our roots but still modern" type of dwarves. "You paid enough for this to count as urgent."

Handar surveyed the group she'd brought. There were

half a dozen of them. Aside from Gerta, there were three more dwarves, a human who looked like he spent a lot of time in the gym, and a gnome with an ugly scar across his forehead. They looked like the right types for the day's work.

"We're grabbing someone," Handar said. "I need them alive, so no guns, and careful with the magic." He looked pointedly at the gnome, whose fingers were twitching like an addict.

"Who's the sucker?" Gerta asked.

"Some wizard specializing in light and sound magic. He runs around here most days. He's alone and not carrying much of anything, so it should be easy. Idiot doesn't have the sense to stay in the open around witnesses, so we grab him when he comes down one of these back streets, bundle him up, shove him in the car. Any questions?"

Gerta's gang all shook their heads.

Handar picked up the device sitting beside him on the car's hood. It was a globe about the size of a grapefruit, white with pale green swirls. A green dot was shifting across its surface, becoming brighter as the target came closer. Handar looked carefully at where it was and how it was moving.

"Perfect," he said. "Looks like he's heading for this street. All of you, get out of sight and get ready. Let's make this quick and clean."

Enfield jogged along the busy street, past commuters and people out doing their morning errands. Many runners preferred to find quiet places for their exercise or paths with pretty scenery and clear air.

He preferred these sorts of routes, where he could alternate the challenge of dodging crowds with the occasional back alley. The unseen spaces let him practice vaulting over dumpsters or scrambling up fire escapes to give himself more variety.

Those places smelled lousy, but that was part of the point. In a real crisis, he wouldn't get to pick and choose where he went. He might have to fight in the most noxious atmosphere to protect the kemanas and the magic they represented. Better to be ready than to be caught off-guard and made vulnerable by something as stupid as a smell.

None of the other Evermores were interested in joining Enfield on his runs, and he was perfectly happy with that. After a lifetime lived together within their enclosed community and now weeks of living and working together as they hunted down the Source, he was glad for an opportunity to get time away from them.

The streets might be noisier than the Evermores' retreat in the hills, but they felt quieter somehow. These people weren't ones he knew, and the noises weren't relevant to him. He could let the city wash over him, tune it all out, and simply be by himself.

He'd tuned out so much that he barely noticed anything unusual as he turned down the back street behind a fish restaurant. He'd grown used to accepting and letting go of the rotten fish smell, the slight slipperiness of the ground beneath his feet, and the occasional burst of steam or shouting from one of the nearby kitchens. That was the background of this place. The black SUV wasn't usually there, but it was only a vehicle.

He was halfway down the street before he realized why it seemed out of place. It was an Earth car in Mana Valley. Not unique, but not normal, and a strange place to see such a flashy vehicle.

Something was amiss. Enfield slowed his pace as a pair of dwarves emerged from doorways on either side of him, both of them carrying stun batons with electricity crackling around their tips. He stopped and raised his hands, shifting into a defensive posture.

"No need for trouble." A Kilomea stepped out from behind the SUV. He was six-foot-eight and densely muscled, with tusks that looked like they could tear through a man's arm in a moment. In his hand was a white and green orb. "Come along quietly. My boss wants a word."

"No, thank you," Enfield said. "I don't know your boss, I don't know you, and I have friends waiting for me."

"Your friends will be all right, which is more than can be said for you if you resist." The Kilomea put the orb down on the vehicle's roof and cracked his knuckles. "See, this ain't the sort of situation where you get to say no."

"You mean because you've distracted me from your friend?"

Enfield spun as the dwarf creeping up behind him raised a syringe. His turn became a kick, and she buckled over. The syringe shattered on the ground.

One of the other dwarves lunged at Enfield, who ducked, caught the dwarf's wrist, and twisted it sharply.

Their stun baton fell to the ground, and Enfield kicked it away.

Now they all rushed at him—the Kilomea, the other flanking dwarf, a human, and a fourth dwarf he hadn't noticed before. He still had hold of one dwarf's wrist, so he slammed him into the human and leaped back.

The dwarf on the ground grabbed his foot. He tripped, fell, scrambled halfway to his feet, and rolled aside as they tried to kick him in the ribs. The kick still caught him, and it hurt, but not half as much as if the blow's full force had landed.

Enfield leaped and grabbed hold of the bottom rung of a raised fire escape ladder. The rungs came down as Enfield scrambled up it, heading for the stairs above.

There was a wave of magic. The staircase turned to rust and collapsed under Enfield. He turned as he fell and got his feet under him before he hit the street, but the landing was awkward, and one of his ankles twisted painfully.

Across the alley, a gnome with a scar on his forehead grinned and raised his hands. Magic flew around them.

Enfield pointed. A blast of light shot from his fingertips and struck the gnome in the eyes.

"My eyes!" the gnome screamed. "I'm blind!"

"How'd he do that?" one of the dwarves shouted. "Wizards need wands."

Enfield seized the opportunity their surprise provided. He lunged at the nearest dwarf and punched her in the face. She grunted but grabbed his arm and pulled him down as she slammed her forehead into his.

There was a flash of pain. He tried to pull back, but she had hold of him and brought her leg around to trip him.

He leaped over that sweep, and as the initial shock of pain subsided, brought his other elbow down on her arm. There was a sharp *crack*, the dwarf yelped in pain, and she let go of him.

Still dazed from the head butt, Enfield stepped back and pressed his back against the wall. Two of the dwarves were down and out, and the gnome was still clutching his eyes, but that left two dwarves, the muscular human, and a huge Kilomea closing in on him. Those weren't good odds.

He pointed at the Kilomea and flung another blast of blinding light. The large magical closed his eyes just in time, then opened them again once the magic died. He glared at Enfield.

"You think we're idiots, that a trick like that's gonna work twice?" He cracked his knuckles again. "Gonna make you wish you never tried it."

One of the dwarves—the one without any broken bones—was getting to her feet. Enfield knew the gnome's blindness wouldn't last much longer either. He needed a way out of this.

He flung his hands up and unleashed all his remaining power in a single wild burst. The street filled with lights and sounds. The chaotic mess would only last a few seconds, but everything was intense and bewildering in those moments. As his opponents looked around in confusion, he dashed toward the end of the street.

"After him!" the Kilomea shouted.

Footsteps thundered after Enfield as he ran out into the street and the pedestrian traffic heading in both directions. If he'd been back home and suddenly appeared looking alarmed and disheveled, everyone would've turned to help.

The city was anonymous and isolating, despite the millions of people. They looked away rather than turning to help him.

He ran as fast as he could along the street. Some people stepped out of his way, while others stubbornly stood their ground or didn't see him coming. He almost ran into a dog walker, who shouted something incomprehensible at him.

A glance back over his shoulder confirmed what he'd feared: his attackers were still on his trail. He spotted the Kilomea and at least one of the dwarves, although their height and the people around them made it hard to see if they were all coming.

He turned down another side street. With no one in his way, he picked up speed, sprinting between the dumpsters and abandoned packing crates. Suddenly the air in front of him shimmered, and the gnome appeared. His eyes were bloodshot and his expression furious.

"You think you're so clever?" the gnome hissed. "Let's see how you get out of this." He raised his hands. Magic swirled around them.

Enfield was all out of power, and there were no open doors he could duck into for proper cover. That left only one option. He charged straight at the gnome.

The magic swirled, coalesced, and started taking form.

Enfield pushed himself faster, one step, another.

The magic became something pointed and hard.

Enfield leaped with his foot outstretched and kicked the gnome in the face. The magic evaporated as its caster fell.

Footsteps behind Enfield told him that the others had followed him down the side street, but they were farther behind now, and there were no obstacles in his way. He sprinted out of the end of the alley, turned left, and took another side road right away before his pursuers could see which way he'd gone. He kept running until he was sure he'd lost them, then turned and headed back to the house in the hills.

Someone had come after him, and the only reason he could think of was that he was an Evermore. He had to let Winslow know they were targets.

Handar and his hired thugs regrouped next to the SUV.

"You never told us it was going to be like that," Gerta growled.

"These are the risks you take. Want a safe life? Go work in an office. You'll be bored dead in a week."

"We should get extra pay for the danger."

"You were well-enough paid already."

Handar picked up the detector and looked at the patterns of green across its white surface. The bright dot was fading into the distance. The target got away.

Still, it wasn't a complete waste of time. They knew more now about who they were after. Skilled fighters, or at least this one was, and they could use magic without wands although they looked like wizards and witches. That wouldn't catch him by surprise again.

"If you want to try again, you'll have to pay us again," Gerta said. "We're paid by the gig, not results, especially not when there are nasty surprises."

"We'll leave it for now," Handar said. "I need to report

back and think about what I've learned." He sighed. "Then I've got to go back to a freaking library."

"A library? You?" Gerta laughed. "What, your boss ran out of literate people?"

Handar shrugged and climbed into his SUV. "The job's the job."

"Hey, you're not leaving us here, are you?" Gerta scowled. "We need to get to a healer."

Handar shrugged again. "I paid you well enough. Go hire a cab."

CHAPTER TWENTY-THREE

Fran and Irene stepped out of a portal into a kemana beneath San Jose. The tech valley's influence on the place was immediately obvious. Instead of plants or rock formations around the central crystal, tangles of wires and microchips emerged from the ground. They stretched up its sides, forming irregular, organic shapes like the roots and creepers of a living plant.

The buildings around the outside were tech-focused too. Shops sold magitech devices. Bars advertised their automatic serving machines. Even the magicals wandering around the place were visibly part of tech culture, every one of them wearing some sort of technological clothing, from earbuds to glasses with screens in the corners to t-shirts that showed shifting web pages on their fronts.

"This place really is something," Irene said. "I'm sure it wasn't this extreme back in my day."

Fran closed the portal and put her mirror away in her backpack. She'd agreed to dress nicely again for this latest meeting, but she'd brought some of her regular clothes too, in case it all became too much. That happened a lot at the moment.

"When you say back in your day, do you mean twenty years ago or two hundred?"

Irene chuckled. "I suppose I can't avoid comments like that now you know the truth."

"I know part of it. I still feel like I need to learn more."

"Well, that can wait for another day. Right now, we need to get up to the streets. Honestly, I don't know why you felt a need to bring us in through here, dear."

"It's getting harder to set up a stable portal at the moment, so I thought I'd use this place to reinforce the power."

They followed signs to the kemana's exit, up a long tunnel and a set of spiral stairs that emerged through a tree in a public park. Technically, it was still a concealed exit, set up when magic was secret from the world, but no one made much effort to maintain the deception. The magicals ahead of them strode out with little concern for whether humans would see them, and Fran and Irene followed suit.

It was a sunny day in Silicon Valley. Bright light shone off the glass fronts of a thousand corporate headquarters and as many research labs. The place was buzzing with activity, but not with as much magic as Fran had expected. It still wasn't an everyday thing on Earth, but none of the magicals she saw seemed to be using their powers. A young wizard was stopped by his mother as he pulled out his wand.

"Is it me, or are people afraid to use magic?" Fran asked.

"They're being cautious," Irene said. "Better safe than sorry when the spells have become unreliable. No one wants to be hovering a hundred feet up when their power runs out."

"I guess not."

Fran expected Irene to lead her to an office building for another awkward meeting with an executive who didn't want to invest in Mana Wave but had agreed to give Irene Berryman's kid a chance to shine. Instead, they headed to a restaurant, then took their seats at a pre-booked table.

"Wow, this place is fancy," Fran murmured. She looked around at the suited diners, the classically influenced decorations, the impeccably dressed waitstaff, and the musician playing background jazz on a grand piano in one corner.

"I wanted to put Ali in a good mood," Irene said.

"Really fancy." Fran looked down at the menu. "And really expensive. Mom, I can't afford this."

"Don't worry, dear, it's on me today." Irene patted her daughter's shoulder. "No need to stick with salad and bread. Order what you want."

Fran wanted a more familiar menu with burgers, fries, pizza, maybe even a children's section. At least there were descriptions of the dishes after their exotic names. She picked out one with chicken and potatoes, then practiced saying its name in her head so she would be ready when the waiter came around and not embarrass herself in front of her mom's old friend.

A woman with red hair and a cream suit walked over, her face lit up with one of the brightest smiles Fran had ever seen.

"Irene, darling." The woman air-kissed Fran's mom. "This must be Francesca."

"Hi." Fran waved and smiled.

"Francesca, this is Alison Smith," Irene said. "We go back a little way."

"A little way!" Alison laughed. "So far that I almost wish I could forget. You look so young still, Irene. You must tell me the name of your surgeon."

"No surgeon, only good eating and a moisturizing routine."

"Well, I don't know whose blood you're bathing in, but it's paying off." Alison winked and sat. "Honestly, it's been far too long…"

The two women started catching up, chattering excitedly about people and events that Fran knew nothing about. She zoned out and started thinking about her technology, idly doodling battery ideas on a scrap of paper, only paying attention long enough to order when the waiter came around. Then she went back to her inventing while her mom and Alison talked.

They were halfway through their starters when Alison shifted her attention.

"So, Fran, your mom tells me that you work in tech. Why don't you tell me a bit about that?"

"Sure, well, the company's called Mana Wave Industries, and we're in Mana Valley…"

Fran explained about the company, who they were, what they did, what she hoped they would achieve. It wasn't a formal presentation, but she still steered clear of the less impressive details, like having their headquarters in the basement of a carpet shop or the time their programmer had been arrested naked in the street. Much as she hated giving the sales pitch, she'd done it so many times now that it came smoothly and easily, and ten minutes went by without her even realizing. Then she remembered that this was lunch, not a formal meeting. She stuttered to a halt, smiled awkwardly, and stabbed a fork into what remained of her salad.

"So yeah, that's us," she said. "Mana Wave Industries, getting ready to change the world."

"That's marvelous, Fran," Alison said. "It shows real passion and commitment, which are great qualities to see in an employee. Tell me, do you think that you've gained much leadership experience from this?"

"I guess so. I mean, I've had to make big decisions about which way the company goes, had to get people working together. Oh, and dealing with office disputes or motivating people when they're down. All those kinds of things. My friend Bart, he's our Director of Finance, he's kind of teaching me."

"Well, it sounds a lot less formal than the training structures we provide at my company. Still, it's good to hear that you're getting used to working with these sorts of mentorship programs and that you got such a good experience out of it already. Could you tell me about a time when you've had to go that bit further to manage an employee?"

Fran talked about some times she'd put effort into motivating Smokey when he got down and how they'd all rallied to support his meeting, although she made it seem like something corporate instead of a campaign group. After all, the better she made the company sound, the more likely a woman like Alison would invest in them.

After that, Alison asked her about recruitment, and Fran explained how she'd brought the team together, which made Alison laugh in places, but not in a judgmental way. In fact, she praised Fran for seizing opportunities when she saw them.

"How about technical skills?" Alison asked.

"Oh, Singar and Smokey are amazing. Singar's our hardware lead. She's brilliant at building devices out of whatever components we can get, then working out what would make them better next time around. Smokey's a software wizard, not, like, the magic kind, because he's a shifter, but I mean he's so fast and inventive with his code, and there's hardly any bugs to fix."

"I meant your technical skills. What do you bring to a company?"

It made sense as a question. After all, Fran was part of the team that made the devices. Still, it was weird that Alison was so focused on her. Fran answered, but the whole time, something niggled in the back of her mind, a sense that she was missing part of the picture here.

"I have to say, Irene, you've raised a very accomplished young woman," Alison said. "Fran, I think you'd fit in very well at my company and be a real asset. We're working with mundane technology, nothing magical, but we're still doing some incredibly cutting-edge work, and with your skills, you could make a huge contribution. Of course, the remuneration is a little more substantial than at a startup."

She chuckled and winked.

"I'm sorry, what was that?" Fran asked.

"The job. As well as the pay packet, we have excellent medical coverage, a company vehicle if you want it, and if not then—"

"I'm sorry," Fran said. "Are you trying to recruit me for a job?"

Alison laughed awkwardly. "Well, yes, of course."

"I don't want a job. I'm running my own company."

"Francesca, dear." Irene leaned forward across her plate. "I know that you've been having a lot of fun with this experiment of yours, but I think you can see that it's not going to last. Now that it's starting to stress you out, now that you've seen the hard reality, I thought you might appreciate the opportunity to move on to something more stable and rewarding."

"Mom, this isn't right." Fran pushed her plate away from her.

"Francesca, really!"

"No, I mean it." Fran stood and picked up her backpack. "Ms. Smith, it was nice meeting you. Thanks for your time, but I'm not in the market for a job right now. I have one that I love and no plans to leave it behind."

She strode out through the restaurant, into the street, and headed back toward the park above the kemana with angry, forceful footsteps. She was halfway there when Irene caught up with her.

"Francesca, what are you doing?"

"Going back to work. If I'm not meeting with investors, I ought to be working on the tech."

"That was very rude of you, running out on Alison like that."

"Rude of me? You ambushed me! Walked me into a job interview without telling me. A job interview I didn't even want!"

"There's no need to shout."

"Why not? It's fun! It makes me feel better. Shouting,

shouting, shouting. Shouting about nothing because other-wise, I'll be shouting about you."

"I admit, I could've dealt with that a little better, but I wanted to make sure you came along."

Fran shook her head. "Mom, I can't just give up my job and my life in Mana Valley."

"Why not? There are some amazing opportunities in Silicon Valley. Non-magical technology is very much alive, especially here on Earth."

Fran narrowed her eyes. "Is that what this was all about, getting me back here?"

"I worry about you. Magical technology is more unstable, more dangerous. Spells can go wrong. Dark powers can get involved."

"Ordinary technology can go wrong. Accidents happen, businesses collapse, people get hurt or go broke. Even if I was working for someone else, that could still happen, and I'd have a lot less fun along the way."

"At least you'd be doing it somewhere safer."

There was genuine worry in Irene's eyes. Fran knew it wasn't necessary, but at least she understood all this now. She wouldn't want to see her mom get hurt any more than her mom wanted to see it happen to her. Protecting the people you loved made sense. Being so protected that you never got to grow or have fun, that was no way to live.

"Thanks for looking out for me, Mom." Fran hugged her mother. "I have to do what seems right for me, and that's running my business. It's the most satisfying thing I've ever done, and if it goes wrong, I have good friends around to look after me. That's what happened when those spirits attacked."

"Spirits attacked you?" Irene looked alarmed.

"Oh, yeah, um…" Fran took her mom's arm. "Why don't we go back to the restaurant? We'll eat dessert, I'll apologize to Alison, and I can explain that one to you."

"I'm not going to like this story, am I?"

"You might like the part where we won in the end…"

CHAPTER TWENTY-FOUR

Most of the staff at the city archives were gnomes. They bustled back and forth down tiled corridors, carrying bundles of papers, boxes of microfiche, and heaps of ancient bound books. They spoke only in whispers, even when a pair of them bumped into each other, triggering an angry conversation as they retrieved muddled papers from the floor. Cam almost laughed as he watched the two gnomes try to argue without making noise.

"This way," his guide whispered, leading him down a set of spiral steps into one of the building's many storage basements.

Tunnels and chambers riddled this part of the city, dug using the finest dwarf mining skills to create a hidden repository safely preserved under the ground. Cam had read up about it before coming here, in case he could learn anything useful about how to find the right document or even documents. Maybe there were dozens of pages of prophecy down here, mislabeled and disregarded for centuries, waiting to be discovered. He could hope, couldn't he?

At the bottom of the staircase was a room that stretched out to the size of a warehouse, lit by glowing magical crystals. It was filled with long wooden rows of shelves, with letters and numbers on the end of each row, telling well-informed visitors what the stacks would contain. There was only one problem. They were all pressed together, without space between them. Nothing thicker than a sheet of paper could have gotten into the gaps.

"How do I get to the book once I find it?" Cam shifted his satchel from one shoulder to the other.

"Ah, that's the ingenious part." His gnome guide wore a look of pride. "This way."

She walked down the rows until they reached two shelves with a gap between them, where it would've been possible to browse. She tapped a box fixed onto the end of the set of shelves, roughly the size and shape of a bird box, and a tiny yellow imp poked its head out. The imp looked at the gnome and squeaked.

"Left, please." The gnome pointed.

The imp saluted and disappeared back into the box. *Rattling* drew Cam's attention to the floor, where a chain ran in a recessed track beneath the ends of the shelving units. The chain tightened, then the shelving unit moved, crossing the gap to the next unit over. Now a fresh set of shelves stood revealed.

"Work your way along until the shelves you need are exposed," the gnome said. "The imps won't mind. They enjoy the exercise."

"How does it work?"

"The chains run up into the shelves, over a set of internal wheels and pulleys. The imps are far stronger than they look, and they have help from a set of gear wheels, which they use to pull the shelves along the chains."

"Is that the best way to do this in the modern age?"

"This is the city archive. We're not all that interested in the modern age." She reached up to tap the tin badge they'd given to Cam on the way in, with the word "VISITOR" stamped onto it. It was at least fifty years old, worn smooth on the top and grimy in the recesses. "If you need me, tap on that. I'll be up in the acquisitions section, processing recent releases."

She headed off up the stairs, leaving Cam to his work.

He took out a scrap of paper, on which he'd written the details of the book he was looking for. These included the title, the author, and a code he'd found in the archive's catalogs, which supposedly indicated where they stored it. Follow the code, and he'd find the prophecy, in theory at least.

It took him several minutes of walking amid the rows of shelving units to find the one he was after. It was strange to have such a huge space to himself. His footsteps echoed back from the cavernous ceiling, an unsettlingly hollow sound. He felt like an intruder disturbing the vault's precious silence.

At last, he found the shelf he was after. It took several more minutes to rearrange the shelves so he could access it, tapping on each imp's box in turn and asking them to shift their rows. None complained or went slow, but he still felt weird asking these creatures to do the hard work for him. Were they voluntary employees or bound to those boxes, tiny prisoners serving their bookish masters? Best not to think too deeply about what it meant.

With the shelves he needed open, Cam worked along the row. Like so many codes, the one used to organize the library was perfectly logical to anyone experienced in using it but a complete pain for outsiders. Misremembering how the lettering, numbering, and runic elements went together meant that he wound up in the wrong place twice before he finally found the book he was looking for.

He opened the book and leafed through the index, then from there turned to the section he'd come for: the contents of the prophecy he already had and more of it.

A big grin lit up his face. There were multiple pages of prophecy, several times more than he already had. He flicked through, not reading in-depth, only looking for keywords like Evermore. Sure enough, there they were.

Pages slipped under his thumb, and he found himself a few more pages on. There was the word again. He turned back a page. This was a different document, but talking about the same mysterious powers that interested him.

Footsteps echoed around the vault as someone came down the stairs. Cam glanced around. He was well out of sight of whoever it was.

"How do I get at the books?" a low voice growled.

"Start by tapping on the box." It was the voice of the gnome who'd guided Cam before. She started explaining the whole process, and there was a rattle of chains as a shelving unit moved in the section by the stairs.

Cam glanced at the book in his hands. It was rare, valuable, something no one was allowed to remove from the archive. It contained a prophecy he needed and had to keep out of the hands of people who might misuse it.

The thought of damaging such a rare book hurt, but he'd come to terms with the thought of tearing out the relevant pages, stuffing them in his pocket, and hurrying out. Now he knew more of the book was relevant, possibly all of it. With a mixture of relief and uncertainty, he settled on the only real option. He had to smuggle out the whole book.

The first step would be hiding what he'd been after. He hastily rearranged the shelf to disguise the gap, then hurried down the row and tapped on the box at the end.

"Left, please," he said to the imp, then repeated the instruction to the next imp and the one after that, shuffling shelves across.

The gnome guide's footsteps headed back upstairs while the other visitor strode around the room with heavy steps. They stopped at the far side of the section of shelving where Cam stood motionless, caught in the habit of secrecy. Then there was a low, growled conversation with the imps and rows started to move. They stopped when the shelf Cam had been after was open.

It could be a coincidence, but he was too wary to believe that. He crept along the line and peered cautiously around the corner. Sure enough, a towering Kilomea in a suit stood at one of the shelves where Cam had looked, scouring the same set of books.

Cam ducked back out of sight. Whoever this was, they looked like bad news.

He tapped softly on the imp box. A tiny yellow head appeared.

"Yes?"

"Close the gap, please," Cam whispered.

"Isn't somebody there?"

"They'll be fine."

The imp shrugged. "If a big'un says so."

It disappeared back into its box. Chains rattled, and the shelves started to shift.

Cam grinned and hurried away. That should keep the opposition busy for a while and maybe distract the staff rescuing the Kilomea while Cam slipped out with the book.

"Hey!" the Kilomea roared.

There was a *creak*, a *crunch*, and a more intense rattling of chains that abruptly stopped. When Cam looked back, the shelves had stopped moving. One of them was leaning over with books tumbling out onto the floor and a heap of broken links lying next to it. Heavy footsteps announced that the Kilomea was coming.

Still clutching his book, Cam ran around the edge of a block of shelves, out of sight of where the Kilomea would emerge. He looked around frantically. There was nowhere to hide, only rows of shelves stretching halfway to the ceiling.

The shelves.

Cam stuffed the book into his satchel and scrambled up the shelves, using them as a ladder. At the top, he lay flat, pressing himself against the ancient and dusty wood. He peered over the edge as the Kilomea stormed around the corner with his tusks bared and muscles rippling beneath his suit.

"Whoever you are, I'm gonna mess you up," the Kilomea growled.

Looking left and right but never up, the Kilomea strode past Cam's hiding place and on around a corner. Cam quietly climbed down and looked around. He'd hoped to find a new exit, but there only seemed to be the stairs he'd come down by, and now the Kilomea was in the way of those. He needed some way past. He could've snuck past if only he were as small as the imps, but he didn't have the magic for a trick like that—or any trick.

Perhaps, though, the imps were the answer. Cam rummaged in his satchel and withdrew a multi-tool he used for small maintenance tasks around the coffee shop. He pulled out the sturdiest blade, pushed it in behind one of the imp boxes, and heaved. After a moment of straining, the ancient wood gave way, and the box fell off the shelf.

An imp lay on the floor in the bits of the broken box, looking scared and confused.

"Box," it said, then in a shriller voice. "Box!"

It ran up the nearest shelf and into the box there. Immediately, there were tiny shouts and sounds of a struggle. While the imps battled for control of the shaking box, Cam pried three more off their perches. Then the one with the fighting imps burst open, and they fell to the floor.

Chaos spread as the exposed imps ran off in search of new boxes, starting fights with their neighbors, altercations that smashed apart the very homes they all wanted. Alerted by the noise, the Kilomea came running, but Cam was one step ahead. He scrambled up the shelves, back out of sight, and crept along the top, beneath the magical lights, while the Kilomea ran into the mass of chattering, squirming, grappling imps.

Over by the stairs, Cam climbed back down. He brushed off the thick layer of dust his clothes had swept from the tops of the shelves, then crept up the stairs, followed by the growing chorus of fighting imps.

"What is that noise?" a gnome asked as Cam emerged from the stairs.

"The imps," Cam said. "They've broken out of their boxes. It's anarchy down there."

"The books!" The gnome pulled out a whistle and gave a sharp blast. Other gnomes came running. An alarm sounded, and a red light flashed on the wall.

"All spare hands to vault seventeen," a voice announced over a crackling speaker system. "Code yellow, I repeat, code yellow."

While gnomes ran toward the vault, Cam walked the other way, toward the building's entrance area.

"Everybody out," a senior gnome said as others ushered readers from the building. "We have to get this place under control. No more visits today."

Cam hid his relief under a mask of disappointment as the exodus shoved him into the street. No alarms went off in response to the book in his bag. They were all going off already. He waited around long enough not to look suspicious, then hurried away, clutching his backpack tight. He had a lot of reading to do later.

Handar stood beside the shelves, his arms folded across his chest, staring down at a gnome less than half his height. This ridiculous little creature shouldn't be able to thwart him, but here they were.

"I'm sorry," the gnome said, "but the book you're after simply isn't here."

"You lost it."

"We didn't lose it. Clearly, someone took it."

"Stole it today?"

"Sadly, we can't ascertain that. That book never leaves the archive, and it hasn't had maintenance or reordering in twenty years. Someone could've taken it at any point in that time."

Handar pointed at the cage full of imps waiting to return to their boxes. A team of dwarves was on the task of fixing their homes, *tutting* and shaking their heads as they examined the damage done.

"Could one of them have done something with it?" he asked.

"The imps? Oh no. They're not interested in books. We couldn't use them here if they were. You know imps."

"No, I don't."

"Well, suffice to say, we don't need to worry about that possibility." The gnome shook his head. "I should thank you. We might not have noted that book's absence for another twenty years if you hadn't pointed it out."

Handar grunted. The gnome's thanks meant nothing to him. He'd failed the boss, almost got to his book but lost it. That was all that mattered.

Or was it? Handar hadn't become Phillips' security chief based on muscle alone. He had an instinct for when something was wrong, and it was screaming at him right now.

Surely it wasn't a coincidence that the imps had gone nuts as he was approaching his goal? First slamming shelves against him, then breaking out of their boxes, and now that the book turned out to be missing. Someone else had been after that prophecy, and they'd got it ahead of him. That didn't mean this was over. For now, the book might be out of reach, but he'd find it in the end.

CHAPTER TWENTY-FIVE

Fran rubbed her eyes and looked around the Mana Wave offices. The clock on the wall said ten o'clock, and she was pretty sure it wasn't in the morning. She vaguely recalled the others saying they were leaving and she'd said she would catch up. When had that been? Six, maybe seven? Then she'd gotten back into the work, meaning to take a few more minutes for the power feedback loop, and...

Now she was sitting alone in a basement late at night while the rest of the world had fun.

Not that working on technology wasn't fun. It was precisely the sort of distraction she'd needed after the trip to Earth with her mom, with all the disappointment and frustration that represented. She'd tried her best to make peace with Irene, but she still felt a little betrayed and more than a little disappointed that someone so close to her would try to steer her away from the path she'd chosen for herself. It was one thing for Evermores and prophecies and big magical events to try to deter her, but her mom? That made it personal.

Still, as she looked across the selection of sketches, tools, and components spread out in front of her, she had to admit that it wasn't the sort of distraction most people considered fun. Further, she could do with that sort of break. The trip to the skate park and the arcade with Bart had been good for her mood and weirdly left her feeling more in control of her life.

She got up and stretched. It was probably time to set the alarms and head out. She could watch sitcoms with Josie and come back to this tomorrow.

The air flickered, and the bright magic of a portal appeared. Fran frowned. She wasn't expecting anyone.

Enfield stepped out of the portal, then closed it behind him. "Good evening, Fran."

"Hi, Enfield." She looked at him quizzically. "You know how late it is, right?"

"Yes, I'm aware."

"So what are you doing here?"

"I went to the coffee shop, and your colleagues said you would be here."

"They're still at the Bean?"

"They were a minute ago, yes."

"Cool, let's go join them. I could do with a donut."

"Before we do, I have something to talk to you about."

"Sounds serious." Fran sat at the workbench. "What's up?"

Enfield took the seat next to her. "Something happened this morning, and Winslow thought I should tell you about it."

He told her about the people who'd ambushed him and about his escape. "I believe that they might have targeted me because I'm an Evermore, whether because people somehow know who we are or because they sensed our unusual magic. If that's the case, Winslow believes they might come after you too."

"Oh dear." Fran frowned. "I guess I'd better start being more careful. Thanks for letting me know."

"Winslow further suggests that you join us."

"Join you?"

"You're half Evermore. Joining the Evermore community could be good for you. We can teach you how to use your powers properly, and you can join our great work of protecting the world. Together, we will be safer if someone comes for us, better able to protect ourselves. There's space in the house we rent here, and once we capture the Source, you can return to our true home, where you belong."

"It's a nice offer, Enfield, but my life is here."

"We offer you another life, a better one."

"What is it with everyone wanting to reinvent my life for me?" Fran snapped. She crossed her arms and glared at Enfield.

"I'm sorry if I've offended. We were trying to look out for you. Like it or not, you're one of our own, and we care."

"Thanks, I guess."

They sat in awkward silence, both looking down at their hands. A minute ticked past on the clock, then another.

"You don't want to come to the house then?" Enfield asked.

"No."

"Okay."

He looked at the pieces on the workbench, picked up a crystal, and peered at it.

"I've seen these before."

"They're used in a lot of magitech."

"I don't see a lot of magitech."

"They get used in other places too."

"Okay."

He put the crystal down and looked at the other pieces. There were a lot of small components in the area where Fran had been working. Arrays of tiny crystals, minutely etched circuit boards, wafers of metals and other materials he didn't recognize, miniature runic cards, and slender wires. Next to them all was a sturdy plastic case split into two parts.

"What are you working on?" he asked.

Fran picked up the pieces of the plastic box and held them out for him to see more closely.

"The battery for your containment unit," she said. "Everything about it should fit inside this box."

"I assume there's more to assembling it than shoving it all in a pot and mixing it over heat?"

She laughed. "A bit more, yes."

"Shame. That works for potions."

"Really?"

"Well, no, but it's the general pattern you start from." He looked from the case to the components. "What's the problem?"

"How much do you understand about magico-electrical interface waves?"

"I'm not convinced those are all real words."

"We're going with the simple version, then."

Fran set her components carefully aside and reached across the bench to pull loose offcuts of wire from a plastic tub. She laid them out on the bench in front of her and Enfield.

"Most modern magitech relies on the relationship between magical and electrical energy," she said. "Imagine that these wavy wires are magic and these straight wires are electricity, okay?"

"Okay."

"So, to get magic into the technology, we make the magic behave differently." She straightened one of the curvy wires. "Now it'll go into the circuitry."

"Because it's become electricity."

"No, because it looks like electricity. We still need it to be magic because that lets it do special things, but it's, like, I don't know, magic in disguise, maybe?"

"You've put your magic in a trench coat and a hat."

Fran laughed. "Where did you get that idea from?"

"Old cartoons. We don't have TV back home. I've been catching up on over a hundred years of animation."

"Have you watched the *Flintstones*?"

"I don't think so."

"You should. It's brilliant. They have dinosaurs for machines."

"I'll make sure to find it. Now, this magic in a hat…"

Fran took several of the wavy wires and half-straightened them.

"This the magic transforming, okay? Putting on its hat. It won't do it by itself, so it needs some help. Sometimes it's the machine's structure. Other times it's an enchantment. In our power pack, it's a catalytic crystal."

She took one of her components and laid it on the wires, where they went from curvy to straight. "I've imbued the crystal with some of my light magic. As long as it's in the crystal, it helps the energy to change. We don't totally understand how and why, which is a bit of a problem because having me charge every battery isn't a scalable solution. It works for now. We'll find a way to replicate it once we get past the prototype. All clear?"

"Just about. Your magic changes the other magic."

"Right! Now we get to the problem…" She held up another crystal, bigger than the one she'd been using. "To cope with the energy levels coming out of the Source, we need a larger crystal.

"When we try to fill that crystal with my power, the transformation stops working. We have no idea why because, like I said, we don't really understand my magic. If we can't use a bigger crystal, we can't manage the Source's power, which means we can't contain the Source."

"May I?" Enfield took the two crystals and stared at them, looking from one to the other. When he set them down, his expression had turned thoughtful. "Do you know much about the principles of potion-making?"

"I know that all those words are real."

"Well, sometimes when you want a big batch of a single potion, you have to make it in small batches first. It doesn't sound very efficient, but it overcomes a problem where certain ingredients, in larger quantities, will react in ways you don't want. They'll crystalize out of suspension or maybe explode when you need them to stay dissolved in the liquid. Once they've combined with the other ingredients, the problem goes away. You can have big batches after that, but until then, it all has to be small."

"I wish batteries were that easy to fix."

"Maybe they are." Enfield reached across the table and picked up three more small crystals. "How many of these would it take to deal with the same amount of power as the big one?"

"Six, maybe? Seven to be on the safe side."

"So why not do that? Filter the magic to electricity conversion through seven small crystals instead of one big one."

"Except that we set up the device to work with a single crystal."

"Why?"

"Because…because…because that's what we were using, which is no reason at all…"

Fran grabbed a sheet of paper and a pencil. For several minutes, the only sound was her frantic scribbling as she drew a new diagram for how the device would work. Then she sat back and looked at the results. "It's so obvious, now that I see it. Why couldn't I work it out before?"

"Too obvious for someone on the inside of the problem. Sometimes you need an outsider's perspective."

She raised an eyebrow. "Are you and Winslow going to use this as an excuse to keep interfering in our work?"

Enfield laughed. "Not me, at least. This evening has shown me how little I understand and how much I could mess up if I keep sticking my thoughts in where they're not wanted. Perhaps when you get stuck, or when it relates to Evermore magic, you could ask our opinions."

"That seems fair."

Fran yawned, stretched, and got up. "We have an answer at last. Now isn't the time to build it, though. I'm way too tired. I'll mess it up."

"So you're going home?"

She glanced at the clock. "Coffee shop first, to see if the others are still there. It's open until midnight tonight, and I could do with something approximating fun. You want to come along?"

"If the rest of your team are happy to have me there." Enfield looked uncertain. "I think I might have offended Singar and Smokey."

"Those two will argue with anyone about anything. That doesn't mean they won't hang out with you afterward."

"Your way of living is not what I'm used to."

He followed her up the stairs to the Worn Threads showroom. Fran locked the cellar door and set the various electronic and magical alarms Singar had installed. Then they walked out through the shop, switched off the lights, set Raulo's much simpler alarm, and locked the carpet store's doors behind them. At last, Fran pulled down the shutters and closed a padlock to hold them in place.

"That's a lot of security," Enfield said.

"Don't shops do this where you come from?"

"We don't have problems with theft. No one knows about us, remember. That's part of what makes it safe."

They ambled down the street through the bright pools of light cast by street lamps.

"This place you come from," Fran said. "Is it nice?"

"I like it."

"Other Evermores can go back to visit once they leave?"

"Evermores don't leave."

"My mom did."

"She was an exception."

"I bet there are others. There are always exceptions to everything."

"Maybe."

"So they could've come back?"

"If anyone ever returned in my lifetime, I missed it."

"So you don't know whether an Evermore could leave again once they returned?"

"Why would they want to?"

Fran hesitated. The thought was only half-formed, an impulse she'd barely considered, but it had been bubbling away in the back of her mind since Enfield had talked about her going back with them.

"Curiosity, I suppose. Someday, if I can, I'd like to see where I come from, but I'm never going there if it means I can't leave. I have too much I love out here."

"Like Flintstones cartoons."

"Exactly."

"I understand." Enfield nodded. "You should talk to Winslow or perhaps to your mother. They know more than I ever will. They might not appreciate cartoons or know magico-electrical theory, but they can offer you the wisdom that neither of us would find alone."

CHAPTER TWENTY-SIX

Bart put down the phone and leaned around his computer to look at Gruffbar.

"We might have a small problem," he said.

"What sort of problem?" Gruffbar tapped his chunky metal lighter against the desk.

"The FBI is sending someone over to see our progress on the containment unit."

"The FBI?"

"Yes."

"Sending someone through a portal, to Oriceran, just to chase us up?"

"Um, yes."

Gruffbar looked across the Mana Wave basement at where Smokey, Singar, and Fran worked. Riding high on Fran's new idea, the three had spent the morning disassembling the battery units for all their prototypes, from the containment unit to the sign language hands. Components, casings, and tools littered their workbenches and the floor around them.

"How soon are they coming?" Gruffbar asked.

"A representative is on the way now."

"Oh." Gruffbar stopped tapping the lighter against the desk. "Portaling straight in?"

"They're catching a lift through someone else's portal to the central plaza, then a ride from there."

"Well, that's something, at least. By my beard, we might have time to avoid a disaster."

Elethin, sitting at the desk next to them, cleared her throat.

"If we have visitors coming, don't you think you should be consulting with the Director of Public Relations, Bart, not your resident law monkey?"

"This isn't about image," Gruffbar said, letting only a hint of his annoyance into his voice. "It's about our legal obligations, as set out in our contract with the FBI." He glared at Bart. "A contract that I should've had approval on."

"Sorry, sorry, won't happen again."

"It had better not."

"So what's the problem?" Elethin twitched back the dust sheet on the big wall mirror and started fixing her makeup. An image of an angry Willen battered silently at the glass from the other side, but it was too short to block her view of her face, so she carried on unfazed.

"The contract says that this one prototype for them should take precedence over everything else." Gruffbar got out of his seat. "Any work on any other project could be seen as a breach of contract, which could lose us a lot of money we don't have, not to mention future work from one of the biggest customers for security devices."

"Ah."

"That's right, ah." He pulled the dust sheet back into place. "Also, best not to show law enforcement the prisoners we've been keeping without legal authority."

"They're not the law over here."

"Don't you follow the news? They're in the middle of negotiating a big deal on cooperative work with the Silver Griffins. If there was ever a time for them to snitch on us and win points with the Oriceran authorities, it's now. So, dust sheet in place, and let's get our tech nerds in order."

Bart was already at the workbenches, explaining the situation to the rest of the team.

"I'm sure they'll understand." Fran stroked the beak of the crow that sat on her shoulder. "The FBI man I spoke to on the phone yesterday seemed super friendly."

"They called yesterday?" Gruffbar asked through gritted teeth.

"Oh, yes."

"You talked about your progress so far?"

"Oh, yes."

"Now they've sent someone over on short notice to check what we're doing?"

"Oh… Oh, no."

"Exactly."

"They can't possibly expect us to work on only one thing at a time."

"They can, they will, and they have the contract to enforce it."

"What about when you need a change of projects to refresh your brain and help the creative juices flow?"

"This is the FBI! They don't have creative juices. They

have very strict rules that they enforce because that's their job. Thanks to our contract, they have a chance to enforce a rule on Oriceran for the first time. Do you think they're going to say no to that for the sake of your creative juices?"

"Oh, no."

Fran started frantically sweeping components into a plastic box. The crow fluttered off her shoulder and flapped around the room, a feathered expression of her panic.

"Not that one!" Singar said as she saw what Fran was putting away. "That's for the FBI unit."

"No, it's for the Source. That's why it has the extra crystals." Fran waved a board of crystals and wires.

"No, it's for the FBI because we decided to improve their power output too."

"Why did we do that?"

"I don't know, because we can?"

"Theirs worked before."

"I know."

"Now they're coming to see it."

"I know."

"It won't work because we're doing these changes."

"I know."

"I think I'm starting to panic."

"I know!"

The volume kept rising as they talked over each other and flung components around. Chaos was breaking out around the workbenches.

"Everyone quiet!" Elethin shouted. They all turned to look at her in surprise. She drew a deep breath.

"In one minute, I'm going upstairs. I'll meet these

agents, do my PR thing, show them the limited charms of Worn Threads, and generally delay them as long as I plausibly can before bringing them down here. While I'm gone —and I'm loath to say this, but it's clearly for the best—do whatever Gruffbar says. He understands the contract."

She checked her makeup in the mirror base of a containment unit, nodded in satisfaction, and headed up the stairs.

"Keep both containment units out," Gruffbar said. "We can tell our visitor that the other one's a backup. Singar, make sure the unit does something, even if it's only flashing lights to make them think they see progress.

"Smokey, get the operating software up and running, and three excuses for why it's not quite right today. Fran, work out which things we need them not to see. Bart and I will help you tidy up. Now go, everyone."

With far more calm and quiet, they started rearranging the workspace. Tools went away, components disappeared into boxes, and Singar slotted pieces together into an approximation of the containment unit. By the time Elethin's voice sounded again from the top of the stairs, they were almost ready.

"Be careful on the stairs," she said, a moment after the door creaked open. "We chose this site for the space, not the condition it's in."

"Reckon I'll be fine," a man's voice said. "I've been to far worse in my line of work."

"I'm sure you have. Do you see a lot of action?"

"Not any more. Contracts and acquisitions ain't exactly where the action's at."

Elethin laughed as she stepped off the bottom step into

the basement, leading a man in a sharply cut black suit with a white shirt and black tie. His closely cropped hair was a pleasing mix of black and gray, and he had the sort of genial smile that Fran associated with TV hosts, not law enforcement officers.

"Agent Baldwin, this is our Chief Executive Officer, Francesca Berryman," Elethin said.

"Hi. Hello. I mean, um, yes," Fran blurted, frantically trying to switch mental gears. She'd already gone from hardware work to frantic tidying, and now she needed to remember how to behave for important meetings. She held out her hand. "It's a pleasure to have you here."

"And you, ma'am." Baldwin shook her hand. "Is that a crow on your shoulder?"

Fran looked. It was. Would that count as unprofessional?

"He's, like, a sort of mascot. Less likely to steal our components than a magpie."

"Well, I'll be." Baldwin chuckled. "Crazy old world you folks have over here. This the rest of your team?"

Elethin went around, introducing everyone to the agent.

"We have a new coffee machine," the PR elf added. "Would you care for a cup?"

"No, thank you, ma'am," Baldwin said. "Coffee doesn't agree with my guts."

"I thought it was compulsory at the FBI, along with suits, handguns, and rugged good looks."

Baldwin chuckled and straightened his jacket. "Kind of you to put it like that, ma'am, but we have our share of slobs too. I'll be in trouble with one of them if I don't get this done today, so could you folks show me what you've got?"

"Of course." Elethin nodded at Fran. "Can we manage a demonstration?"

Fran glanced at Singar, who nodded curtly. "Of course. Smokey, could you fire it up?"

The cat hit a button on his keyboard, and one of the devices hummed into life. Runes lit up, crystals shone, and the framework above the mirror extended. It all would have looked impressive if Fran didn't know what it was like at full power. This was nowhere near full power.

"This fragile thing here, it can hold powerful magicals?" Baldwin didn't sound disbelieving, only curious.

"That's right," Fran said. "We've been working on it for months now, and the results are impressive. Just today, we've been improving the battery unit to deal with even more powerful prisoners."

"Can you show it to me in action?"

"Of course." Fran looked around, frantically trying to work out what they could put in there. No releasing the spirits from the mirror this time. That would raise far too many questions, and the field wasn't strong enough anyway. Smokey was too busy checking that the software kept working. This field was too weak for a full-sized magical like Bart or Fran, but...

She grabbed the crow off her shoulder. It *squawked* in protest but couldn't get away before she thrust it through the field. The device gave a low *hum*, and the field reinforced itself off power drawn from the crow. When the bird fluttered up to try and escape, it bounced off a near-invisible magical barrier.

"Not bad." Agent Baldwin took out his phone and took a photo. "You got something a little more intimidating to test it on?"

"Not right now, but perhaps we could arrange something in a few days?"

"Sure, or I could do this."

Baldwin thrust his hand through the containment field and wriggled it around, startling the crow. When he pulled the hand back, it was as though he was dragging it through treacle, but it did come out. He frowned, and Fran tensed.

"Seems to me that I shouldn't have been able to get out of that," Baldwin said.

"It draws on the power of the person contained in it," Fran explained. "That creates a proportional containment field, so perhaps because you're human rather than a magical, it didn't have the power to… Ah."

Baldwin had pulled out a wand and waggled it between his fingers.

"'Fraid that excuse won't cut it, ma'am."

"This is bullshit," Singar said. "Of course it doesn't work right now. You sprang a surprise visit on us. We'd pulled this thing apart to make it better, and we barely had time to reassemble the pieces. Tomorrow, it'll be more powerful than ever."

"I'll tell you what's bullshit, Ms. Twitchtail." Baldwin talked casually, meeting nobody's eye as he put away his phone and camera. "You were supposed to deliver a full working model for our field tests by last week at the latest. You didn't.

"We've given you leeway because this is an unusual project, but there are folks in my division who are starting to suspect you're taking us for a ride. That maybe your device and your company ain't all they're cracked up to be. Or maybe that you've been making some side deal to supply this tech to someone else, hoping we'll forget the details of our agreement."

He looked up at Fran, and his genial expression had become pure steel. He tapped the side of his head. "I don't forget."

"This week," Fran blurted out. "We can give you your working model by the end of this week. I promise. Pinky swear."

"The FBI doesn't run on pinky swears, Ms. Berryman. It runs on force of arms and force of law."

"I know, I'm sorry, we're just trying to make the best version we could for you. We'll arrange a test for the end of this week to show you how well it works."

"Not only a test, a model we can take away."

"Of course. Absolutely. Gruffbar and Elethin can sort out the details while we get on with making this thing just right."

"That's more like it." Baldwin's friendly smile returned. "One more agreement. Break this one, and we'll break you. The FBI doesn't like breaches of contract."

He headed up the stairs with Elethin and Gruffbar hurrying after him.

"The end of the week," Bart said, once the door had closed above. "Can we do that? I mean, with all the changes you've made?"

Singar shrugged. "Guess we're going to have to."

Fran smiled nervously. "Of course we can. I believe in us."

CHAPTER TWENTY-SEVEN

Howard Phillips stared out his office window, enjoying the grand sweep of the urban sprawl. He considered what Mana Valley would be like once he'd sucked its power to unleash a nightmare realm on Earth. Would this be a nightmare zone too, another place where his pets could run free? Or would it be more of a crater, a devastated magical wasteland?

He liked to imagine that it would be a bit of both, a place of ruined buildings, dead plants, and toxic clouds through which nightmare creatures would hunt the survivors or those magicals foolish enough to venture back in. A taste of what lay on the other side of the netherworld.

It was good to have a dream. A motivational consultant had told him that once. He'd hired her so Mana Valley executives would hear about it and see him as more like the rest of them, the same reason he hired psychiatrists and personal trainers.

He hadn't expected to get any other value out of the experience, but there had been something pleasingly haunting about her platitudes and encouragements. They showed how weakly these creatures would stand against him if they considered that motivating.

He ran a finger around the inside of his collar. The skin suit was sitting uncomfortably today. He should return to his home dimension and spend some time free of its constraints. However, he had meetings to attend, business decisions to make, and a presentation in the evening.

The success or failure of his plans depended upon the power he could accrue, which meant pushing this corporate cover for every advantage he could get. Discomfort was fleeting. Nightmares, true nightmares, the sort that seared minds and flayed souls, those were forever.

Figures were moving at the base of his building, like ants around the feet of a giant. He'd ignored them until now, assuming they were employees coming and going. Something was different about the movement today. Were some of them waving signs?

He tapped a button on his desk phone. A moment later, Handar stepped through the door. The Kilomea stood at attention, his jaw thrust out and arms stiff by his sides.

"Yes, boss?"

"What's going on down there by the doors?"

"Protest, boss."

"A protest?"

"Yeah, they don't like that we're not employing the right sort of people, or something like that."

There was conflict in protest and in the resistance it stirred. It often pointed toward other terrible possibilities, bad situations that could be made worse. That was something with potential, something he could perhaps have used. It was also disrupting his business, his power base, and that was something Phillips wouldn't stand.

"Get rid of them," he ordered. "Whatever it takes."

The headquarters of Philgard Industries was a towering, modern office building inspired by human architecture, indicating how much influence Earth had in the valley. While it had a few magical touches, like the enchanted observatory turret and the security wards over the doors, it was mostly glass and concrete, flat and featureless. It was a building designed to look impressive without admitting it was trying.

The protesters couldn't have been more of a contrast. Although only a small group, they were as eclectic in their shapes as in the way they dressed. Smokey's handful of recruits had brought along friends, and while it wasn't a huge gathering, the dozen of them, plus crows, managed to make a lot of noise and fuss.

He was proud of the range of slogans on their placards. Sure, "Philgard = Philbad" wasn't very imaginative, but the centipede shifter with a sign saying "Two Legs Good, All Legs Better" was particularly striking. Next time, he had to remember to come up with slogans that would tell passersby what it was all about.

Some people took the fliers that the centaur was handing out, but more walked past looking confused and disinterested. It wasn't enough to draw attention. They had to make sure they were drawing attention to the issue.

Once again, the crows had proved their worth. They'd

flown up to the third floor and hung a banner demanding jobs for non-bipeds. The company would have someone pull it down, but for now, it was an eye-catching addition to the exterior.

They were starting on a collective chant when a group of stern magicals emerged through the building's front doors. With their dark suits, earpieces, and bulging muscles, their appearance screamed security staff. There was a mix of wizards, witches, Kilomea, and dwarves in the group, but of course, they were all bipeds.

The leader, a towering Kilomea, cracked his knuckles and walked up to the protesters.

"Who's in charge here?" he bellowed.

Smokey ignored him and kept chanting through a bullhorn. The other protesters joined but nervously, except Vaudrek, who flashed the new arrivals a reptilian grin.

"You, loud-mouthed cat." The Kilomea snatched the bullhorn. Their difference in size stopped Smokey from doing anything to stop him.

"Give that back!" he shouted. "That's theft."

"This is private property," the Kilomea said. "You're trespassing."

"This is a public sidewalk. You can't move us on."

"Mr. Phillips had this sidewalk made as part of the building. He lets people use it, but that don't make it a public sidewalk. Now get out of here."

The Kilomea flung the bullhorn on the ground and stomped on it. Pieces of plastic casing and electronic components scattered across the sidewalk and into the street.

"I'm not intimidated by you, Mr...." Smokey craned his

neck to see the guard's ID badge. "...Mr. Handar Ennis, and I'm not going to let you get in the way of our right to peaceful protest. The city has ordinances about public political engagement, and you can't bully us into leaving."

"Last warning, fuzzball. Move it or regret it."

"Help!" Smokey screeched. "Help, I'm being repressed! Come see how the system silences the voice of dissent."

"That's it." Handar grabbed for Smokey, who lithely swerved out of his reach, lashing out with his claws as he went. Handar grunted as the cat left long red scratches down the back of his hand. "Get them!"

As a mass, the security guards pulled extending batons from their pockets and charged in. Vaudrek and the crows took flight while the centipede skittered away. Others stood their ground, waving their signs like weapons, trying to fight off the burly thugs.

Smokey darted through the legs of a bystander, dodged between feet, and got around behind Handar. He leaped and landed in the middle of the security chief's back, claws digging through his jacket. Handar spun, arms flailing, trying to reach behind his back to swat away the cat.

"Someone get this thing off me!"

Another of the security team ran up, swinging a baton. Smokey let go a moment before the blow would've hit. He dropped to the ground, and the baton hit Handar in the back.

"Sorry, boss!" the security guard said.

"Don't waste time on sorry. Get them."

Protesters and security guards grappled with each other around the entrance. The guards had pinned several of Smokey's people to the ground or walls, but others were free. Some had the upper hand on their attackers, tripping and tricking guards, sending them sprawling on the pavement.

Vaudrek swooped down into the melee, wings spread wide, and barreled into Handar from behind, knocking him flat on the ground. The crows fluttered in and pecked him, jabbing with their pointed beaks.

"Flea-riddled vermin," Handar bellowed as he swatted the birds. "Get off me."

He smacked one of the birds against the ground and punched another away in a cloud of feathers. The rest took to the air as he got to his feet.

Smokey was in among the other combatants, darting from one place to the next, biting the ankles of the security guards and clawing their shins. They kicked and stomped, but he was fast on his feet and got clear every time. He was almost starting to enjoy this. What was a protest about if not a fight against the odds?

He was so excited by it all that he didn't see the muscular hands reaching for him until it was too late. Handar hauled him out of the fight and held him up in the air. The Kilomea bared his teeth, his elongated tusks standing out like a pair of white blades from his jaw.

"I'm gonna wring your scrawny neck," he growled.

"Hey, what are you doing to that poor pussycat?" someone called.

Handar looked around. The fight had drawn quite a ring of spectators, some of whom had their phones out and were filming it all. "This isn't a cat. It's a—ow!"

Smokey had taken the opportunity provided by the Kilomea's distraction and clawed him hard. Handar let go,

Smokey dropped to the ground, then darted off into the fight again.

"Power to the people!" Smokey shouted. "Especially the people without two legs!"

Handar charged after the cat shifter, enraged by the pain in his arms. He knocked friends and foes aside in his determination to get him. Smokey ducked around the centaur, who raised his fists, ready to defend Paws and Claws' leader. Handar swung a punch that caught the centaur on the jaw. His hooves *clattered* against the ground as he stumbled and sank to his knees. His hindquarters remained upright.

"No one messes with Mr. Phillips' business." Handar stepped past the centaur and reached out for Smokey.

Vaudrek swept down again.

"All legs better!" she bellowed, grabbed the Kilomea's shoulders between her claws, and hauled him into the air.

Unable to free his shoulders from her grip, Handar brought his hands up to seize hold of her forelegs, then flexed his abdominal muscles and curled his body up. His feet smacked into the underside of her jaw, a kick that sent a shudder through the lizard. Her wings flopped, and the two of them fell into the crowd, still tangled together. People screamed and ran as the lizard and the Kilomea grappled in their midst.

More and more spectators were gathering, some of them blocking the street. Traffic horns blared. Riders and drivers shouted their complaints. Some people cheered on one side or another. Others gasped or cheered for everything.

A magical glow appeared by the doors of Philgard's

headquarters. The glow turned into a portal, and Silver Griffins poured through. There were two dozen of them wearing body armor and protective spells. Their official amulets glowed.

They waved their wands, casting spells to left and right. Two crows fell to the ground, their feathers frozen. A security guard slumped into sleep. Magical chains wrapped around the centaur as he got to his feet. This time, all four legs buckled under him.

Several of the Griffins made for Vaudrek and Handar, the biggest fight of the whole squirming, flailing mess.

"Inretio," two of the Griffins shouted at once. A large net emerged from their wands and enveloped the two combatants. Contained together, they kept punching, kicking, and clawing.

"For goodness' sake," the lead Griffin said. "Split them up, you idiots."

She waved her wand. The net's threads melted, stretched, and split, then reformed as two separate nets. Each one tightened around its target, pinning Vaudrek's wings to her back and Handar's arms to his sides.

"Thank goodness you're here, Griffins," Smokey said. Much as it pained him to praise the Griffins, they were who he needed to see right now. "These thugs have been assaulting us for using our right to free speech."

"These stupid hippies are trespassing," Handar shouted. "They're disrupting our business. You should arrest the lot of them."

The lead Griffin rolled her eyes. "I don't know who started this, but what I do know is that you're causing a public disturbance. We're taking you all in, and we'll sort it out down at the station."

"I knew it!" Smokey exclaimed, forgetting his relief of a moment before. "You're here to stifle our protest again." He raised his voice. "Help, we're being repressed!"

If he'd hoped the crowd might interfere, he was out of luck. They kept watching and filming as the Griffins wrapped up security guards and protesters alike and flung them through the portal.

Smokey took to his paws, running toward the protective legs of the crowd.

"Stupefacio," the lead Griffin shouted.

A bolt of magic hit Smokey. The world went blurry, and his legs gave way under him.

"Subvolo."

He barely heard the Griffin's voice through the fog in his mind as the second spell lifted and levitated him into the portal, away from his protest and off to a jail cell. A random thought occurred. He hoped Fran didn't need him at work today.

CHAPTER TWENTY-EIGHT

Fran emerged from her bedroom in rumpled clothes she'd thrown on when the alarm rang. She yawned, stretched, and tripped over a pair of shoes.

"Ow!"

Using the back of the couch for support, she pulled herself upright and looked around with a frown. Bedding and clothes covered the couch. The coffee table held makeup and chargers. Shoes, coats, and suitcases filled half of the floor. From memory, she knew that toiletries covered every spare surface in the bathroom. She felt like the clutter was closing in on her.

She tried the bathroom door. Locked.

"Your mom's in there." Josie emerged from her room. "Has been for twenty minutes."

"Sorry. I didn't realize she'd be here for so long."

"It's okay."

She was trying to be polite and hospitable, but Josie's tone and the wrinkles on her forehead said it wasn't.

"I'll have a chat with her today and find out when she's planning to leave."

"That would be good." Josie tapped a piece of paper on the fridge door. "I made a list of rental places, but I don't think she's looked at it."

"Today. I promise."

"Thanks." This time it was Josie's turn to trip over the footwear. "Seriously, what are those doing there?" She flung them aside, took her shoes from the rack by the door, and slipped them on. "Got to go. I'm due feedback on my first evaluation today."

"I'm sure it'll be brilliant."

"Maybe." Josie bit her lip. "To be honest, I'm not so sure. I've tried to do the job well, but everyone else is busy trying to look good. What if I've been doing this all wrong, and now I lose this job?"

Fran hugged her friend hard.

"Anywhere that doesn't appreciate you doesn't deserve you."

"Fran, this is Philgard. I might not get an opportunity like it ever again."

"They might not get an opportunity like you again either." Fran took a hat off a hook on the back of the door. "Do you want to wear my unicorn hat? It makes me feel better when I'm stressed."

Josie looked at the hat, a felted creation in pastel blue and pink with a sparkly horn and long flaps over the ears. She burst out laughing.

"It's a kind offer, but I'm good." She patted Fran on the head. "See you later, crazy lady."

Left alone in the apartment, Fran looked around at the scattered debris of her mother's presence. The FBI's deadline was looming. She needed to get to work, but she'd promised Josie that she would deal with this, and if she was honest, she needed to deal with it for herself too. She donned the unicorn hat, the ear flaps enveloping her in soft felt, and took up position by the coffee machine, facing the bathroom door.

A few minutes later, Irene emerged, dressed in yoga pants and a t-shirt, a towel wrapped around her head.

"Good morning, Francesca. My word, are you still wearing that hat?"

"Mother, we need to talk." Fran whipped the hat off and flung it into a corner.

"Mother now, is it?" Irene laughed and lifted a suitcase onto the couch. "What do we need to talk about, dear?" She opened the case and rummaged through the clothes inside.

"How long were you planning to stay here?"

"I don't know. I thought I'd stick around to sort out this mess with Winslow at least. Then maybe you could take a few days off. We could do some tourist things, have some quality family time. After that, well, we'll see, won't we?"

"Mom, you've been here for weeks. Josie and I have been living around you, but it's too much. We need our apartment back."

"Oh. I see." Irene carefully closed the case, then looked up at Fran with one eyebrow raised. "Josie's saying this, is she? Or is this you acting out and using your friend as cover?"

"This is both of us, Mom. It's our home, it's already really crowded, and you're taking up all the spare space."

Fran kicked a pair of shoes on the floor next to the kitchen counter. "Even some space that isn't spare."

"Well, I'm sorry for wanting to spend time with my daughter." Irene wrenched the towel off her head and flung it through the bathroom door. She started picking up clothes and shoving them into her case. "I'll just get out of here, shall I? I'm clearly not wanted."

"That's not fair!"

"Oh, really? I came here to help you out in a difficult time. All I want in return is somewhere to stay, but I'm the one being unfair?"

"Yes, you're being unfair! You know what, you've been unfair for years, not telling me who I was or where I came from, what my powers were or why I have them. You lied to me, Mom."

"I didn't lie to you. I just didn't tell you the whole story."

"That's lying!"

"No, it's not telling the truth. They're different."

"Not when it's about who I am. It's a lie of omission, and it really hurts."

Fran stopped, as surprised by the anger in her voice as by the words she was saying. She hadn't realized how much of this she'd been feeling. It burst out like an angry beast, as if she was a shelter the creature had hidden in, and when it was gone, it left her sad and deflated.

"It's just not fair," she mumbled.

That feeling of deflation was contagious. Now Irene also looked down at her hands, which were crumpling a t-shirt into a wad. "I'm sorry. It's not what I wanted."

She drew a deep breath, dropped the t-shirt into her suitcase, and walked over to Fran. Tentatively, she reached out to take her daughter's hand and squeezed it. Fran didn't resist, but she didn't return the gesture either. She stood waiting, braced to hear what came next.

"Evermores don't leave their home," Irene said quietly. "It's part of who we are. There's an expectation, a commitment that comes from birth.

"To people like Winslow, it's the price we pay for the privileges of our existence—our powers and long lives. The longer my life went on, the less I could accept that deal. What I had back there, it wasn't enough, and there weren't any other options.

"I raged against it all and became a disruption, too much trouble for Winslow and his peaceful existence. Eventually, we reached a compromise. I was allowed to leave, on conditions."

She stopped and stood there, toying with her daughter's fingers like they were something wonderful, an amazing treasure she'd found hidden away.

"What conditions?" Fran asked.

"All sorts. Places I couldn't go. People I couldn't see. Secrets I had to keep. One of the most important was that I couldn't have children."

"But…"

The words froze in Fran's throat as she thought of Winslow, this strange and kindly man with the peaceful air around him, and about Enfield, who'd helped solve her problems with the battery. Was her mother saying that if they'd had their way, Fran wouldn't exist?

Then another thought hit her. "You broke the deal."

"I didn't mean to, but I met your father, and everything with us was so intense, so exciting, so ill-considered." Irene laughed and wiped a tear from the corner of her eye. "It was amazing while it lasted, but when it ended, it left me with my little wonder."

She squeezed Fran's hand again, and Fran squeezed back. She'd long known that she hadn't been part of her mom's original life plan and that Irene loved her all the more for it. What she hadn't realized was that in keeping her, Irene had rebelled against her extended family.

"Why weren't you allowed to have children?"

"Our magic is ancient, a primeval power from before modern magic. Everything that witches and wizards do descends from it. No one knows what would happen if it combined with other powers, and none of the Evermores want to risk finding out. There's danger in what someone could do with that power and in the attention it could draw."

"They think I'm dangerous?"

"They don't know." Irene looked her daughter in the eyes. "Winslow is here to hunt down the Source, but the minute he saw your technology, he realized what you are. Now he's watching you carefully, waiting to see how your power combines with other magic and technology. He can't undo you, so now he's wondering what will happen and whether his fears were right.

"You're the first person in millennia to combine Evermore powers with something else. You were always amazing to me, but that makes you amazing to other people too."

Fran rubbed her eyes. "It's too early for this. I haven't even had coffee yet."

She grabbed two mugs from the cupboard and hit a

button on the coffee machine, which started to rumble and steam. By her feet, a cupboard swung open, and a robot vacuum cleaner peeked out, its googly eyes swiveling.

"Not now, Hoovernator." Fran pushed it back into the cupboard with her foot.

She took the mugs of steaming coffee, handed one to Irene, and went to sit on the sofa with the other. There wasn't much space, and she couldn't bring herself to clear it, so she treated her mother's heaped clothes as one more cushion.

Irene walked around to stand by the window, blowing on her coffee and watching her daughter.

"Why didn't you tell me sooner?" Fran asked.

"All sorts of reasons. Not knowing when to tell you. Not wanting to upset you. Not wanting to reveal things I shouldn't. Hoping that if I kept quiet, none of it would ever be a problem. Wishful thinking is a terrible drug."

Irene's shoulders were tense, and she looked concerned.

"You've told me now. So what's still worrying you?"

"The consequences. I don't know where any of this leads. You know about your powers. Winslow knows about you. The Source got out into the world. I don't want you to get hurt."

"It'll be fine, Mom. I have plans for my life, and my past isn't going to change that. Winslow can want whatever he wants, but I can say no, and I have people around here who will look after me. I don't think he's planning to carry me off to his lair like some storybook princess. If he tries, I have a lawyer on my side, not to mention a Willen with a switchblade and a bad attitude.

"As for the Source, that doesn't have much to do with

me, and it's not going to matter soon. We've almost finished a containment unit that can hold it. Winslow gets his monster, and the world goes back to normal."

"Maybe. Didn't you think your trap would work before?"

"This is different. That was a test version. We've learned from the test." Fran shrugged. "If it fails, we'll make another one."

"It might not be that simple, dear. As for the consequences of giving the Source back to Winslow…"

"Have some faith in me, Mom. I got this." Fran sipped her coffee. She had something else she wanted to ask, and somehow it was more difficult than anything that came before.

"You mentioned my dad earlier. I know you don't like to talk about him, but… Well, I thought you were a witch, and he was a wizard, but now I know at least half of that's not true, so could you maybe tell me more about him? Like, who was he, where did he come from, what were his powers? Things that might help me understand who I am and what I can do."

"I suppose that's fair. Like all these other conversations, it would've come around in the end."

Irene pushed some things around the coffee table and set her mug down on the corner, then shifted her suitcase onto the floor. She took the seat next to Fran.

"Where do I begin? Your father and I met at a difficult time for both of us. I'd gone through a period where people who shouldn't know my identity almost learned it, so I lived on edge and used my powers only in extremes. I suppose birds of a feather flock together." She laughed softly. "Poor choice of words, or perhaps the perfect choice. So, I was at—"

Fran's phone buzzed loudly. She pulled it out of her pocket, intending to turn it off, but seeing Singar's name sent a flash of guilt through her.

"Hang on, Mom. I should take this." She hit the symbol to accept the call. "Hey, Sin. Sorry I'm late. I'll be in soon, I promise. There's been a family thing to deal with."

"We don't have time for family things," Singar said. "We need a finished device for the FBI by Friday, remember?"

"I know, but I thought you and Smokey were—"

"Smokey's been arrested."

"What? Why?"

"Why do you think? Some political nonsense. That cat needs to get his priorities straight."

"Can't Gruffbar—"

"He's on his way there, but in the meantime, the control software needs adjusting so we can test the new array, and unless you think Elethin's secretly a coding genius, that means we need you."

"Can't I just—"

"I'd say it's your company and I'm not telling you what to do, but you made us all shareholders, which means it's our company too. Our time, effort, reputations, and careers. So I'm telling you what to do. Get down here, now."

The phone cut off. Fran stared at the blank screen. Singar was right. Fran wanted to know about her family, but she needed to get to work, not only for herself but for the people relying on her.

"Raincheck on the heart-to-heart, Mom. I have to get to

work." She leaped up off the sofa and ran into her bedroom. Ten seconds later, she ran back out, grabbed a sheet of paper off the refrigerator, and handed it to Irene.

"Leads on places to rent. I love you, Mom, and I love seeing you more, but if you're staying in Mana Valley, you need to get a place of your own. Now I have to dash. The FBI is counting on me."

CHAPTER TWENTY-NINE

The Mana Valley Central station was the most impressive Silver Griffins facility Gruffbar had been in. The observatory in Los Angeles provided a memorable hiding place for a station. It concealed a substantial facility underneath, but that station was starting to show the effects of age and restricted budgets.

Mana Valley Central was what happened when the Griffins worked in public with the financial support of many of the largest companies in the whole of magical technology. Those companies needed to preserve law and order for the sake of their staff and their businesses.

The building itself was less than a decade old, built from reinforced glass and gleaming chrome. Veins of raw magical power flashed down its sides. It could've been mistaken for the offices of a corporation if not for the decorations on the front—a twelve-foot heraldic shield decorated with a stylized griffin clutching a thunderbolt, and underneath it the organization's interlinked rings symbol. The entrance was a wide set of doors that stayed open every day. A spell across the opening kept out the weather and preserved the air-conditioned balance of the hall beyond.

That hall was full of noise as Gruffbar walked in, his heavy boots pounding the tiled floor. Dozens of magicals waited for service at counters at the back of the hall. Griffins hurried back and forth, some heading out on missions, others dealing with the daily admin that occupied the building's collection of gnomes. It wasn't a place to come for calm or quiet.

"Good morning, sir."

A ghostly figure appeared in the air in front of Gruffbar. For a moment, he thought a particularly friendly spirit must haunt the place. Then he noticed the projector points embedded between some of the tiles. He'd heard about intelligently programmed magitech holograms, but this was the first one he'd encountered in person.

"Are you here to report a currently active crime or a civil disturbance?" the hologram continued as she shrank from human size to Gruffbar's height.

"No. I'm a lawyer, and you've arrested one of my clients."

"You seem to be here as a prisoner representative. Please confirm if this is the correct option for you."

"Sure, I guess."

"Please confirm if this—"

"Yes, I'm here to represent a prisoner." Gruffbar shook his head. "By my beard, does every single thing in life have to be driven by a multiple-choice menu now?"

"I'm sorry, I'm not equipped to process that inquiry. If you still want prisoner representation, please proceed to the yellow desk. For complex inquiries, please wait here while I contact a sentient representative."

"It's fine. Sentience is overrated anyway."

Gruffbar strode over to one of the reception desks with a yellow sign above it. Either there weren't many prisoners in the place, or the Griffins dealt with lawyers extra quickly because there was no queue. A plastic crate sat in front and to one side of the desk so shorter magicals could reach the counter. Apparently, no one had considered them at the design stage for this flashy new building. Gruffbar climbed onto the crate and gave the desk officer his most professionally emotionless expression.

"I'm here as legal representation for a cat shifter named Smokey," Gruffbar said. "Might be held under his dwarf name of Smolden Haggerhold."

"Haggerhold...Haggerhold..." The Griffin looked at something on a screen. "Ah yes, here he is."

Next to the reception desk was a doorframe of ancient oak inscribed with mystical runes. The Griffin tapped a key, the runes glowed, and the view through the doorway changed to reveal a concrete corridor with barred cells on each side. It looked like something out of an Earth prison.

"Please step through the doorway," the Griffin said. "Your client is in the first cell on the right. A duty Griffin will come down to speak to you shortly."

Gruffbar followed the instructions. The air changed as he stepped through the doorway, becoming colder and musty. The doorframe vanished behind him, leaving him standing alone in a long corridor.

He looked to his right. Sure enough, Smokey was sitting

in a cell, curled up around himself on a cot built into the wall. His tail twitched as he looked up at Gruffbar.

"This is an outrage," he said. "A violation of my right to peaceful protest."

"Then why don't you leave?" Gruffbar asked. "Slim cat like you, surely you can fit between these bars?"

"The bars are for show." Smokey gracefully jumped down off the cot, prowled across the cell, and pawed at the space between two bars. Magic shone, a powerful field holding his paw back. "Typical Griffins, using magic to oppress the working man, then complaining when other people use magic in ways they don't like."

"Is that why they arrested you, for using magic they didn't like?"

"I got arrested for being assaulted."

"That seems backward."

"Well, I assaulted them back."

"That's more like what I expected."

"The Philgard security guards started it."

"This was all connected to your protest?"

"Of course. Once again, the jackboot of the man stomps on the throat of those of us trying to build a better world."

"This seems to happen to you a lot." Gruffbar tapped a bar and grinned. "Are you sure it's about the man?"

"Typical victim-blaming." Smokey turned his back on the lawyer. "If you're not here to help, stop wasting my time."

"Oh, I'm here to help. Got to get you back to the office, so we can get the containment unit ready for the FBI."

"Of course. You're only here out of self-interest."

"Hey!" Gruffbar snapped. "Maybe this campaign of

yours would go better if you didn't piss off the people trying to help you." He pulled out his phone and scrolled through the notes the Griffins had emailed him. "Fact is, I'm proud of what you're doing here. Standing up for yourself is hard when the whole world seems turned against you."

A door at the end of the corridor opened, and a wizard walked in, wearing the black trousers and t-shirt that seemed standard for the station's staff. As he passed another of the cells, there was a cawing of crows raising their voices in anger.

"Mr. Steelstrike?" The wizard looked at a tablet screen.

"That's right, and I'm here to ensure that you release my client."

"Is that so?" The wizard scrolled down. "According to this, we arrested your client in the commission of a violent affray, which emerged from his act of trespass on the private property of Philgard Industries. I don't see a lot of reason to release him."

Gruffbar snorted. "You can drop the bad cop act. I've seen tougher magicals try and fail to pull it off."

"This isn't about toughness, Mr. Steelstrike. It's about the law."

"That's where I know I'll win." In different circumstances, Gruffbar would've taken out a cigar and lit it, so he could enjoy taking his time over this one. However, there were "No Smoking" signs everywhere, and he didn't think Smokey would appreciate the delay.

"I have someone sending me security and phone footage of the fight now. If you're doing your job, then you already have that footage, and you know as well as I do that it'll show the Philgard security guards starting the fight because that's usually how these things work. That means my client acted in self-defense, which means you have no grounds to hold him."

"Not for the fight, but there's still the question of trespass."

"We were in the street!" Smokey protested. "We have a right to protest in the street. That's free speech."

"You have a right to protest in public streets, but the land in front of Philgard Industries is owned and maintained by that company. The moment they asked you to leave, you were trespassing."

"This is bullshit. Tell him he's wrong, Gruffbar."

"Technically, he's right." Gruffbar stroked his beard. "But that 'technically' is doing a lot of work. You know about the Rubinstein court case, or do you not read about the state of the law until it's settled?"

The wizard tilted his head. "I'm aware of the case. I'm aware that they haven't resolved it yet, so there's no precedent you can use there."

"Ah, but if Rubinstein wins, the court will have confirmed that when corporations create what can reasonably be perceived as public spaces, those spaces acquire public space rights. Hence no trespass."

"If Rubinstein fails, then the trespass stands."

"Do you want to risk my client suing the Griffins if Rubinstein wins?" A glint of triumph entered Gruffbar's eye before he heard the response. He enjoyed what he did. He was good at it. Like a boxer throwing his best punch, he knew when he had a win coming.

The wizard gave a single slow nod and smiled in appreciation.

"You said the magic word, Mr. Steelstrike." He tapped his tablet. The magic between the bars faded and Smokey's cell door swung open. "I'm sorry for any inconvenience, Mr. Haggerhold, and hope you have a nice day."

"My name's Smokey, not Haggerhold." Smokey stalked out of the cell. "You'd better let my comrades go too."

"Most of your fellow protesters have already been released."

"Most?"

"*Caw!*" several voices cried as one.

Smokey and Gruffbar strode down the corridor to another cell. There, the crows of Paws and Claws were gathered, perched in a row on the edge of a cot. They pointed their beaks accusingly at the wizard.

"Why are they still being held?" Gruffbar asked. "Did they peck one of the guards a little too hard, and now you have to prove to Philgard that you'll punish their enemies so they'll pay for your shiny office block?"

"There are some complications about the legal status of these detainees." The wizard looked up at a light that had started blinking on the wall. "We weren't sure what to do with them, but that's about to resolve."

The oak doorframe that had brought Gruffbar to the cells appeared in the air in front of them, and a man stepped through. He wore hard-worn clothes, heavily patched and covered with pockets, along with sturdy boots. Strands of gray laced his long dark hair. The air around him smelled of pine needles.

"Are you Mr. Woodrow?" the duty wizard asked.

"For today at least, yes." The man raised a hand. The crows all rose into the air, then fluttered around their cell, one after another like a feathered conga line. "They're with me."

The wizard opened the cell, and the crows flew out. They landed on Woodrow, several on his outstretched arm, one on each shoulder, and the last one perched on top of his head.

"How do you know these crows?" Smokey asked. "I haven't seen you around our neighborhood.

"They and I share an old connection." Woodrow's voice was deep and rumbling.

Gruffbar examined the man carefully. Something about him wasn't right. He clearly had magic, but it didn't feel like wizard magic, and he didn't carry a wand.

"So they're friends of yours?" Gruffbar asked. "Colleagues, perhaps?"

"Something else."

"Pets?"

Woodrow laughed. "Not so much pets as a part of me."

"So you made them, or you control them maybe?"

Woodrow gave a throaty chuckle. "I'm leaving now."

He turned to the magical door frame.

"You have to sign first." The wizard held out his tablet.

"Make me."

Woodrow stepped through the door frame and vanished. The wizard glared after him. "That's not how this works," he muttered.

"Don't worry. We're going to cooperate." Gruffbar pointed at Smokey. "Where do I have to sign for him?"

"Don't do it!" Smokey hissed. "Don't bow down to the demands of the man!"

"Cooperating on this will make it easier for us next time there's something important." Gruffbar took the tablet and used his finger to sign where the wizard had indicated. "Isn't that right?"

"We certainly take past behavior into account when considering how we detain you and how easily you're released."

Gruffbar looked at Smokey. "Given that you've already been arrested twice in as many months, don't you want better treatment for next time?"

Smokey sighed. "Fine. I'll cooperate."

"Good. Now we need to get out of here. The company has a deadline to meet, and we need you for it." Gruffbar nodded at the duty wizard. "See you next time."

"Or perhaps you could keep your client from breaking the law, so we don't have to do this again?"

Gruffbar grinned. "Like I said, see you next time."

CHAPTER THIRTY

Josie set the latest Manaphone prototype down on the workbench and strolled around it, looking at the device from every angle. This was becoming part of her process, not only handling new devices and examining them up close but taking a step back, studying from a little distance, trying to get a sense of how they were supposed to look and feel.

After all, devices weren't merely practical things. They were design objects and status symbols. Finding the problems wasn't only about functional failures. It was about how function fitted in context.

"God, I love my job," she whispered, then immediately regretted saying it out loud. After all, she hadn't had her evaluation yet, and there was a serious chance she might not have this job for long. Had she jinxed herself?

The door of the sealed testing room opened and Debby, one of the other testers, poked her head in. The sound of someone down the office raising his voice in anger followed her. "Hey Josie, you should come and see this."

It was Debby's tone as much as her words that made Josie look up from the phone. Debby spoke quietly as if she didn't want anyone else to hear, but it wasn't a nervous or hushed instruction. If anything, she sounded amused.

"Did somebody bring in good cakes again?" Josie asked. "Or has another of John's pranks gone wrong? Either way, I'd rather get on with the testing."

"Trust me. You're going to want to see this. It affects you directly."

"Me?"

Josie picked up the phone and took it to a row of lockers at the side of the room.

"Hurry up," Debby urged. "You're going to miss it."

"You know how seriously they take security here." Josie used a key code to open one of the lockers and placed the Manaphone carefully inside. "I don't want to take any risks."

"Evaluations are written. You can relax now."

"It's not about evaluations. It's about doing the job right." Josie locked the safe. "All right, let's go see why you're so excited. Then maybe we can show it to whoever's doing all that shouting, try to cheer them up."

"Oh, that's not going to work." Debby grinned. "Besides, he already knows about it."

They walked out into the corridor, Josie carefully closing the door behind them, then down the corridor to the open-plan office where they had their desks. The sound of shouting grew louder.

"Is that Simon?" Josie whispered.

Debby nodded. "Oh yes. I told you this was good."

They stopped where the corridor opened into the office

space. Simon stood by his desk, which held a prestigious position by the window. A large cardboard box sat in front of him. He was putting his personal effects in one by one under the watchful gazes of a pair of security guards.

He was red-faced and grimacing, and slammed each item down as he put it into the container. Around the room, colleagues carefully pretended not to notice what was happening while they watched him in their peripheral vision.

"After all my years of service, this is what I get?" he shouted. "What happened to loyalty? What happened to rewarding good work?"

He glared at one of the guards, whose only response was to look pointedly from a framed photo at the box.

"All right, all right, I'm doing it," Simon snapped. "Can't you give me space to do this with a bit of dignity?"

It was far too late for that, largely because of Simon's behavior, but if he was aware of the irony, he wasn't going to let it stop him. He glared angrily around the room, daring anyone to catch his eye, and colleagues hurriedly looked away. Then he saw Josie and his mouth fell open.

"You!" he exclaimed. "What the hell did you tell them about me? What lies have you been spreading?"

"I...I haven't." the accusation caught Josie off-guard. She hadn't had many positive things to say about her manager during the evaluation process, but there hadn't been much chance for her to comment. She certainly hadn't shared her negative views of him. That had seemed like a sure way to bring herself trouble, no matter how accurate her opinion was.

"You little bitch," Simon hissed. "You turn up here, poison them against me, steal my job…"

"I haven't taken your job. I'm still testing phones."

"After I helped you, guided you, spent hours showing you how this place works. After all the time and care I put into you, now you stab me in the back."

That was too much. Josie was willing to let him vent, but she wasn't going to put up with lies.

"Helped me? You were hardly there at all! You've been so busy trying to make yourself look good, you've barely taken the time to tell me what this job is about. I've had to ask other people or work it out for myself."

Simon glared at her silently for a moment, and she thought he might've gotten a glimpse of reality. Then he turned to one of the security guards and showed them what he was like.

"See, more lies!" he shouted and gestured at Josie. "Can you believe this, in front of all of you?"

"It's time for you to leave," the guard said.

"I haven't finished packing yet."

"You've had time." The guard tapped his watch.

"I've barely had—"

"I said you're leaving. You want to make that hard?" The guard cracked his knuckles.

Simon hastily swept the last few objects from the desk, picked up his box, and headed for the elevator.

"This isn't over," he called over his shoulder, whether at Josie or the guards following him wasn't clear. "I'm going to find a lawyer, and I'll sue you all for constructive dismissal, you see if I don't."

Flanked by the security guards, he stepped into the elevator, the doors *hissed* shut, and he disappeared from view.

"Wow." Debby grinned and shook her head. "That guy is something special, huh?"

Josie stared at the elevator doors. "Did somebody complain about him in the evaluation feedback?"

"Probably, but it's not only that. Simon's been borderline for years. He's so proud of his degrees and how smart he's supposed to be, but he never puts in the actual effort. Sooner or later, it was bound to catch up with him."

"Poor guy."

"Poor guy? He's been coasting on other people's work for years and trying to pin the blame for anything that goes wrong on other people. Good riddance to a bad manager, that's what I say."

"Still..." Josie had reached the limits of her sympathy. Debby was right. Simon had been more of a problem than a help. She hoped their new manager would be better. "Who's taking over from him?"

"They haven't said yet. HR has been calling people in all day to give them the good or bad news. Word to the wise, if you see security guards outside the room, that means you're getting fired. It's how they make sure you can't steal anything on the way out."

"Have you had your interview yet?"

"Yep. Satisfactory work, small pay raise, same as last year. It's not brilliant, but given the alternatives, I can live with it."

A phone rang, and half the room's occupants jumped in

their seats. Somebody reached across the gap between desks and picked up the handset from Josie's desk. He listened for a moment, nodded, then put the handset down.

"Josie," he called, "you're up. Interview room three."

"Good luck." Debby squeezed Josie's arm.

"I think I'm going to need it."

She caught an elevator up to the HR floor, then followed the signs down the corridor to the interview rooms. As she got near room three, a security guard paced past, and his gaze ran up and down her. Remembering Debby's words, a sense of sadness swept through Josie. The guards didn't have to wait outside, right? They could easily walk up and down the corridor, waiting to escort her out of the building.

She swallowed, forced herself to stand up straight, and knocked on the door. If there was bad news, it was better to get it over with.

"Come in," a familiar voice responded.

Josie opened the door and walked into the room. To her surprise, Julia Lacy was sitting behind an interview desk. She smiled and gestured for Josie to sit.

"I didn't know you were part of HR." Josie sat across from Julia. She liked the PA, but her palms still sweated in nervousness.

"I'm not, but I snuck a peek at your results and asked if I could do this one."

"I guess it's better to get bad news from a friendly face."

"Bad news?" Julia shook her head. "Josie, there's no way you were getting bad news today. You've had one of the most glowingly positive reports in the whole organization."

"Really?" She hardly dared to believe it.

"Really. Everyone says you're a pleasure to work with, that you're great at your job, helpful, smart, exactly the sort of person we need here. Of course, it helps that your file includes a personal recommendation from Howard."

"It does?" Josie grinned, half-disbelieving. "Why?"

"Your work on the detection device. He was really pleased with that."

"I was doing my job."

"No, what you did was to implement smart, practical solutions before anyone else even started thinking about them. The fact that you didn't make a big deal of it only added to how impressed we all were. There are so many pompous idiots in this place that it's a miracle to meet someone smart but not shouting about it."

"So I get to keep my job?"

"No."

Josie sank in her seat. All that praise, and it wasn't worth anything. How cutthroat was this place?

"You get a better job," Julia continued. "If you want it."

"Better?" Josie's mouth hung open.

"Well, it's a promotion, at least. They want you to take over managing your team. Apparently, Simon Green is on his way out."

"I saw him go." Josie paused, taking it all in. "They're offering me his job?"

"Absolutely. You're a perfect choice. You know how the team works, but you don't let old habits constrain you. You're good with technology, good with magic, and good with people. What more could anyone ask for in a candidate for that role?"

"Well, when you put it that way, not much."

"I assume you'll take the job?"

"I… Yes, of course!" Josie laughed. "Sorry, this has all taken me by surprise. It's the opposite of what I expected when I walked in here."

"Really?" Julia laughed. "We need to work on your self-esteem if that's how you see things." She stood and shook Josie's hand. "Welcome to management. Congratulations and commiserations."

"Thanks. What happens now?"

"I let HR know that you said yes, and they sort out the paperwork. They'll send you a new contract and an offer for pay. Word to the wise, always make a counter-offer. Just because they like you enough to promote you doesn't mean they won't try to trim your salary around here."

"Thanks, Julia. I wouldn't have thought of that."

"Happy to help. If you find someone worthwhile in a place like this, it's important to look after them." She opened the door. "Come on, I need to get back to Mr. Phillips, and you should make Simon's old desk yours before someone else grabs it."

"I think I might need to get a coffee first and take a few minutes to steady my nerves. Plus I'm due a celebration."

"Coffee's not much of a celebration. How about cock-tails tonight instead? First one's on me."

"Are you sure?"

"As I said, it's good to meet someone worthwhile around here. Got to make the most of it. Unless you have someone else you want to celebrate with?"

Josie hesitated. None of the guys she'd dated recently had become steady enough to be special occasion material, and Fran would be insanely busy with work until the end of the week. Why not take the opportunity to set the seal on a new friendship?

"I'd love to go for drinks. Thanks. It's great to know that someone around here has my back."

CHAPTER THIRTY-ONE

It was dark in the alleyway. A single streetlight glowed at one end, casting a yellow light across the cracked tarmac and poorly maintained wall. Even with the dumpsters removed and some hasty cleaning, this still wasn't the sort of venue most people would've chosen for a night out. It wasn't even the sort of place most people would opt to sprint through while running for their lives.

"Are you sure this is a good idea?" Bart looked around the alley. "I mean, I understand the principle. I'm just not sure it creates the right impression."

"I'm a lawyer, not a salesman." Gruffbar took a drag on his cigar. "I'll say this for Fran's plan: it's striking. Sometimes that's what you need, something that cuts through the ordinary and makes people pay attention."

"But is it the right sort of attention?"

"It fits our company's style. That makes it a step in the right direction."

"I suppose so, but we're trying to convince people to

give us their money. Does any of this seem like it will do that?"

A gargoyle scrambled down the wall, its stone claws scraping against the brickwork. Something else scurried through the darkness, and there was a brief flash of supernatural power. The light at the end of the alley flickered, then turned bright again as a car pulled up under it.

"I guess we're about to find out," Gruffbar said.

The car door opened and two men in suits stepped out. They looked around uncertainly until Gruffbar waved.

"Here for the Mana Wave Industries presentation?" he asked.

"That's right."

"Then come join us."

The men approached, and the four of them made small talk while other vehicles arrived, dropping off magicals with the types of outfits that said they'd spent big money. Gruffbar counted a dozen of them, most with expensive watches, many with conservatively designed but exquisitely made jewelry. Once Bart had counted off everybody on the list, Gruffbar ground his cigar out under his boot and opened a door.

"This way, ladies and gentlemen," he said.

Bart led the way through the door, down a narrow staircase lit by a bare bulb.

"Are you sure this is right?" one of the investors asked.

"I know it seems unconventional," Bart said, "but I think you'll appreciate what you see."

"I wouldn't do this for anyone less than you, Bart, but the mystery had better end soon."

Bleeps, *pings*, and rattling noises rose to meet them from the room below. They emerged in a basement and into the glow of lights of almost every color. Around the room stood rows of video game machines, no two alike.

There were conventional arcade games, dance mats, and karaoke booths. Other machines invited players to ride plastic bikes, perch on the backs of artificial dragons, or wield guns whose triggers connected to wires instead of ammunition magazines. The investors stopped in a crowd at the bottom of the stairs and looked around. Some laughed while others shook their heads.

Fran emerged between the machines with Elethin on one side of her and Singar on the other. Smokey wound between their feet with typical feline grace. Instead of their usual clothes, all three women wore t-shirts bearing the slogan "Mana Wave Industries: Playing For a Better World." Unlike those of her companions, Elethin's t-shirt perfectly fitted her form.

"Hi there!" Fran exclaimed. "Thanks so much for taking the time to see us today. My name's Fran Berryman, I'm the founder and CEO of Mana Wave Industries, and I'm here to persuade you to invest in us. But it would be rude to take up your evening without offering you some sort of entertainment in return, so here it is. The Mana Wave arcade."

She waved, encompassing the surrounding machines.

"I'm sure some of these will look familiar to those of you who've spent time gaming, but they're here as more than an improvised collection. We've converted every one of these machines to run on Mana Wave's customized power system, using our magitech batteries. They demonstrate how these batteries can power even large devices and keep running as long as you want them to.

"Of course, there's not much point using a magical battery for a mundane machine, so we've adapted a bunch of the games as well. You can cast spells instead of shooting zombies, control your vehicle with the power of your mind, or create illusions through the power of karaoke. I won't spoil the surprises by telling you about everything we've changed, but I like to think there's an option for everyone."

Some sharply dressed visitors drifted toward the machines, but others stood aloof.

"This is all very eye-catching," one of them said, "but I have other places I need to be. Can you cut to the chase?"

"Sorry, but no." Fran shook her head. "We have one rule for tonight. If you want to stay, you have to play. If you'd like to join me for a game of enchanted Pac-Man, we can talk while we play, or you can ask questions afterward if you want to focus on getting a new high score. But there's no shop talk without fun."

"What a ridiculous waste of time."

"Don't be such a jackass Bob," one of the others said. "It's not like she's forcing us to sit through another damn slide show."

"I would rather sit through a slide show than go through this absurdity."

"Then we're not the company for you," Fran said. "Thank you for considering us, and please feel free to stick around as long as you want."

"You can't be serious."

"No, you're the one being serious."

"Apparently the only one here." The man turned and stormed back up the stairs.

Another of the investors, a middle-aged wizard starting to expand around the waist, wore a frown that said he was about to follow suit. Then Elethin swayed up to him with a smile and a plastic cup full of coins in her hand.

"Why don't you stick around for a little while?" She held out the cup. "I'd like someone to play with."

"Well, when you put it like that…" The wizard took the cup and followed Elethin between the machines.

Gruffbar picked up another cup and held one of the coins up in the flashing light. It was the size of a quarter but stamped with the words "Mana Wave" on one side and "Play Like You Mean It" on the other. "Nice touch."

"Thanks." Fran grinned. "They barely arrived in time. That's what happens when you try to make something like this happen at the last minute."

"Something like this? Nothing is like this."

Fran grinned even wider. "I hope you're right."

"You seem pretty sure of yourself."

"Oh, I'm, like, absolutely terrified. Totally clenched up inside. But we're here now, and this is my chance, so…" She waved at the machines. "Got to give it a go, right?"

"You'll be great." Gruffbar reached up to pat her on the shoulder. "Did we sort out that bar?"

"Oh, yes. And it's paid for with these tokens. Elethin said it would help relax the investors and encourage them to like us."

"Never mind the investors. I need a drink."

While Fran went off to play games and talk with their guests, Gruffbar made his way to the bar. An elven waiter dressed in a vest stood behind it, wiping glasses with a cloth.

"Is that really needed?" Gruffbar nodded at the cloth.

"Part of the show," the barman said. "What can I get you?"

"Whiskey, neat. My company's paying for this, so give me the okay stuff. Nothing too expensive and nothing that'll strip the lining from my throat."

A gray-haired witch in a dark suit and pearl necklace emerged between the machines. She set her cup of coins on the bar and caught the barman's eye.

"Give me a dirty martini." She placed a few of the coins on the bar. "Will that cover it?"

"Yes, ma'am."

While the barman got to work with his cocktail shaker, the witch watched Fran move from one machine to the next, excitedly talking with potential investors while they played on the glowing screens.

"Is she for real?" the witch asked.

"Excuse me?" Gruffbar replied.

"Your CEO, is she for real?"

"I'm not sure I get the question, but the answer's almost certainly going to be yes."

"Her whole thing. The bubbling enthusiasm, the talk about tech and magic techniques, forcing fun on people that most CEOs would be bending over backward to treat with conventional deference. Is that who she really is, or did the elf dream it up?"

Elethin walked past, took the elbow of a dwarf who was on the verge of leaving, and steered him toward a karaoke machine.

"Oh, she's for real," Gruffbar said. "I'm not saying that Elethin couldn't have dreamed up tonight, but it was all Fran's idea. Before you ask, yes, she really believes that this is as good a way to show off the tech as if we'd built a phone or an x-ray machine or a flying carpet."

"You don't have a flying carpet?"

"Actually, we do."

"Hm. That I might be interested in."

"But not this?"

"I've never liked games. I had one go on that thing with the guns, for old times' sake, but I won't be heading back out there."

It was disappointing, but Gruffbar had known they would get some responses like this. He was betting that most of these investors didn't get hooked by Fran's approach. They would never win conventional people around by unconventional means, and most finance people were very conventional. The trick was to find the one or two that got on with the occasion and with Fran. Then, maybe, they could get the money they needed.

Not from this witch, though. She was a lost cause.

"Another drink?" Gruffbar asked, seeing that she'd already emptied her martini glass.

"Why not? I seem to have polished that one off a little too quickly."

"Me too." Gruffbar knocked back his whiskey, then signaled for the barman to refill their glasses.

More of the investors were leaving, some shaking their heads, others with smiles on their faces. One was playing with a souvenir coin. Bart stood by the exit, talking to each one before they left. Gruffbar caught his eye and raised an eyebrow. Bart shook his head. No luck so far.

"I like her spirit," the witch said, watching Fran again.

"Shame I can't persuade you to go play with her," Gruffbar said. "I think you'd like what we're producing."

The witch shrugged. "Games won't help me assess that."

More of the investors were leaving. By the door, Bart looked increasingly despondent. Smokey had curled up under one of the machines to take a nap, and Singar was repairing a shooter that had broken down. The empty glasses started to pile up next to Gruffbar and his drinking companion. Soon, only one investor remained on the machines with Elethin and Fran. Gruffbar's heart sank. It had all been a waste of time.

Then the investor turned to shake hands with Fran, and over the tops of their heads, Elethin gave Gruffbar a small nod.

Behind his beard, Gruffbar broke into a grin. It was only one investor, but it was a start.

Fran walked that investor to the door herself then rushed over to the bar.

"Gruffbar, it worked!" she exclaimed. "We got one."

"Actually, you got two," the witch sitting next to him said.

"Huh?" Gruffbar turned in surprise to look at her.

"I don't play games, but I understand their value. More importantly, I understand the value of working with the right people and of avoiding tangling my future with the wrong ones. This evening, you've managed to alienate many of my idiot competitors while still getting someone to invest in your work. You've shown that you have not only the technology but the force of will to make your plans work."

"Don't you want to ask about the batteries?" Fran asked.

"I read the information you sent. It seemed good to me." The witch took a business card from her purse, handed it to Fran, and got down from her bar stool. "Call me in the morning. We can talk about how much you need and the terms I'll provide it on."

Then she stalked away, past the flashing machines and out the door.

"Two!" Fran flung her arms in the air. "We got two! We've got our investors!"

Gruffbar took the card the witch had given her and looked at the name on it. He whistled. "Not just any old investor. Things are looking up for Mana Wave Industries."

CHAPTER THIRTY-TWO

Fran yawned. It was a huge one, the type where she felt like the top of her head had flapped all the way open and exposed the exhausted remnants of her brain to the world.

"Stop that." Singar also yawned, revealing her rows of tiny pointed teeth. She gripped the wheel of the hired steam wagon harder and pulled on the power lever, triggering an extra burst that accelerated them up the hill. "You're going to set us all off."

"Not all of us." Fran pointed with her thumb at the back seat, where Smokey was curled up around himself, sleeping as contentedly as any cat.

"Lucky him." Singar rubbed her eyes with one paw. "If I'd remembered that we were doing this, I would've gone to bed hours earlier."

"And missed out on celebrating our first investors? Or playing on all those machines before we have to return them?"

"We're hanging onto at least one, right?"

"Oh, yeah. They need to be out of that basement by the

end of the week, though. We only got it for a really short lease."

"Why does everything have to be done by the end of this week? Why couldn't we have a few more days, or maybe another month?"

"If we had that time, would we finish anything now, or would it all get pushed to that deadline?"

Singar tapped the wheel. Her whiskers twitched.

"All right, fair point. Still, all this rushing isn't good. What if we've made mistakes with the prototypes?"

"That's why we're testing them now instead of simply handing them over to the clients."

"Clients plural is a stretch. Are the Evermores paying us?"

Fran hesitated. That was a question she really needed to talk about with Winslow. After all, a lot of time and resources had gone into building the containment units. That was the type of thing a business should get paid for.

The Evermores' leader assumed that the Mana Wave crew did it from the goodness of their hearts or to save the world. Those were valid goals and ones that Fran was one hundred percent on board for, but they wouldn't help keep the business running or feed the people who'd made the device.

"The FBI is paying, and once we made one device, we made the other one a lot quicker, so it hasn't added much to our work. The Evermores might still pay us."

"Next time, we get a contract up front, or Winslow can make a machine to save the world."

"That seems very mercenary."

"It's business."

They drove through the foothills, up toward the higher reaches above Mana Valley. To their left, the scenery had a scruffy beauty, with small flowers peeking out from tangled bushes and swaths of low-growing undergrowth running between windswept trees. To their right, the hills gave way to a precipitous drop into the urban sprawl of the valley. Early morning sunlight shone off the windows of tower blocks and the scales of lizards flying overhead.

"Do you think this is going to work?" Fran twirled a paper umbrella between her fingers, a souvenir from the bar the night before.

"Of course it is. I made it."

"We made it."

"Sure, but I'm the one person I have full confidence in." Singar turned off the main road onto a dirt track between the trees. "This should do."

They drove a little farther, then stopped at a break in the trees where a large magical had melted the ground with something acidic, whether spit or blood or sweat. Nothing had grown back on the scoured ground, creating a clearing with a base of half-melted dirt.

Singar stopped in the middle of the clearing and switched off the engine. Pistons on either side of the wagon vented their steam. Then the whole vehicle sank a little lower to the ground. "We should get more cars across from Earth."

"These things are better for the environment." Fran jumped out and patted the wagon's gleaming flank. "Besides, it's kind of fun."

Smokey woke, arched his back, stretched his claws, and

hopped out of the wagon. He watched as the others unloaded equipment from the back seat.

"Stop standing there and help us," Singar said.

"Can't reach." Smokey waved a paw.

"Then shift. And don't start whining about it. We have work to do, and you can do it better with hands."

Smokey glared and muttered, but he jumped back into the wagon and emerged a minute later in his dwarf form, wearing a t-shirt, jeans, and flip-flops.

"Happy now?" He took one of the containment units from the trunk.

"I'll be happy when I can get home and get some sleep, but this will do." Singar started setting up the monitoring equipment around the edge of the clearing. "You two set up the containment units."

Fran and Smokey assembled the containment units halfway between the wagon and the tree line. Fran watched the trees as they worked. There was supposed to be a lot of magical wildlife out here, which was why they'd chosen the foothills for their tests.

Still, what if they'd scared off all the animals with their presence? What if the creatures were too intelligent to come near? What if there weren't many in this part of the hills? This test really mattered. Now that they were doing it, her nervousness increased.

"All set." Smokey tapped one last time on the control pad wired up to one of the units. "Let's do it."

Singar took another device from the back of the wagon. It looked like a trident but with wires dangling from a thick handle and a crystal on the tip of each prong. When she squeezed a button on the side, a blast of energy flew from the crystals.

"Don't worry, it's not lethal." She handed it to Smokey. "Only scary enough to get any sensible creature running."

She took out two more of the devices and offered one to Fran.

"No thanks." Fran waved. "I'm going to use my magic."

"Suit yourself." Singar set aside the spare power prod. "Off we go."

They spread out into the woods, Singar and Smokey carrying the sparking power prods while Fran cupped light magic in her hands. Singar headed one way and Smokey another. Both were soon out of sight.

Fran drew a deep breath. Much as she loved city living, there was something soothing about getting into the woods, the scent of greenery, and the *crunch* of last year's leaves underfoot. The wind through the treetops made a gentle *hiss*, and birds sang to each other. She wondered if her crows would like it here and why none of them had followed her out today. Perhaps she'd gotten up too soon for the early bird.

Once she'd gotten away from the clearing, she found a sheltered place to stand, where the bushes growing between two trees would hide her from most passersby. She waited as patiently as she could, trying hard not to fidget or start singing. It was important not to scare away the local wildlife.

After a while, some creatures appeared. First, a tiny mouse scuttled across the ground. Then a blue squirrel with flaps between its arms glided from tree to tree. A red lizard scurried past, its tail swishing behind it, then turned in alarm as something larger approached. Flames leaped across the lizard's scales, blackening the leaf mulch beneath its belly, and it ran off trailing a small stream of smoke.

These were the things Fran missed when she was on Earth.

At last, something bigger came into view—a wild boar with coarse hair bristling from its muscular flanks. Two rows of short horns ran from above its eyes, crossed the top of its head, and ended before its neck. Tusks like pale knives protruded from the corners of its mouth.

It stopped and sniffed the air, raising its flattened snout and snorting. Then it turned to stare at Fran, and the light of ancient power shone in its eyes.

This was it, the moment she'd been waiting for. A magical creature powerful enough to test the limits of the containment units. Yes, it was scary, with its snarling face and its hoof pawing the ground, but she'd faced worse. She could do this. It was probably more scared of her than she was of it, and it certainly would be once she started with the magic.

She raised her hands and mustered her power. A blast of light shot at the boar, accompanied by a howl of discordant noise.

Fran expected the boar to turn and run from the sudden noise and light, but it stood its ground. As the light reached it, the boar's eyes flashed. The beast sucked in Fran's magic. The light fizzled to nothing, and the noise was silenced, revealing the woodland sounds again. Power crackled across the beast's flanks, and it rumbled as it pawed the ground.

"Oh." Fran stared at the boar in shock. "I didn't know you could do that."

The creature snorted and walked toward her, picking up speed as it went.

Fran ran.

"Help!" she yelled as she dashed through the forest, the boar charging after her. She leaped over fallen logs and shoved through bushes. With every obstacle she faced, the boar gained more ground. "Help!"

She ran in what she hoped was a loop, back toward the clearing. The boar came after her. Its hooves pounded the ground, and half-rotted leaves flew out behind it. Small animals and birds fled from the sound of its approach and Fran's clumsy flight.

"Help!" she wailed again as panic gripped her. "I've found one."

The boar was getting closer. She could almost feel the heat of its breath.

She burst out of the trees into the clearing with the steam wagon in the middle. Devices and cables trailed out around it. On the far side of the clearing, Singar stood with a prod crackling in her hand. Smokey appeared beside her.

The boar was still coming. Fran ran toward the containment units.

"Quick," she yelled. "Catch it, not me!"

Smokey dropped his prod and pulled a phone from his pocket. He urgently stabbed the screen.

Fran sprinted across the clearing. The containment units sat lined up in front of her. First was the one for the FBI, then the one for the Evermores. The glowing runes on the nearest one went out a moment before she reached it. She leaped over and straight onto the second unit.

There was a flash of light and magic. Instead of running out the far side, Fran hit an invisible wall of power. She hammered her fists against it.

"Smokey, I'm trapped!" she yelled.

She turned to look back. The boar had slowed and was strolling toward her. Tiny flickers of fire sprang from its hooves. It stepped onto the deactivated containment unit and stared at her with something almost like a grin. Fran was trapped, and her pursuer knew it.

"Guys," she called again. "Help, please."

Singar approached, tentatively holding the prod out in front of her. The boar stamped its hoof, and a streak of fire ran across the ground. Singar leaped back and almost dropped her weapon.

The boar returned its attention to Fran and raised one leg.

There was a flash of light, the rods on the inactive containment unit shot up, and a wall of magic surrounded the boar. Its hoof slammed against the mirror base, but no fire flew out. It tried to leave, but the magic held it back, and the harder it flung itself against the barrier, the more firmly it held.

Fran sagged in relief. She leaned against the magical wall holding her in. Then the magic gave way, and she fell in the dirt.

She groaned and looked up as her friends approached. Smokey still tapped on the controller's screen.

"That's, like, totally not what I'd planned," Fran said.

"Sorry about the close call there," Smokey said. "I'm a bit clumsy with my dwarf fingers."

"It worked, didn't it?" Singar's whiskers twitched as she read the display on one of the monitoring devices she'd set up around the traps. "Both of them did. Readings are exactly like they should be. We're ready for our customers."

"Brilliant." Fran got to her feet and hugged them both. "Can you believe this? We did it!"

"We did." Singar rolled her eyes and wriggled out of the hug. "Now we need to get this back to the workshop and pack it for delivery."

"One thing, though." Smokey pointed at the enraged boar battering against the containment unit's barriers. "What are we going to do about that beast?"

"Wait for her to tire herself out?" Fran asked.

"She doesn't look like she's going to get tired."

"Hide in the steam wagon, then let her out? If we get lucky, she won't be able to break through the doors."

"And if we get unlucky?"

"Then we're pretty much stuck."

"When you put it that way…" Smokey opened the door of the wagon. "All aboard."

"Wait." Singar waved a handful of cables. "Collect all my devices first. I don't want to leave them behind if we have to make a quick getaway."

CHAPTER THIRTY-THREE

Cam wandered around the Blazing Bean, whistling as he cleared cups and plates and wiped down the tables. The early morning rush was over, and it was turning into a quiet day.

That sometimes happened near the end of the month, when many of the coffee shop's corporate customers focused on meeting their deadlines. They didn't have as much time for informal meetings or to pop out for a coffee. It wasn't great for business, but Cam enjoyed these quiet patches. They gave him time to get the place straightened up and do a little of his work before the lunchtime rush began.

He smiled at the few customers in the shop. They read quietly or simply enjoyed their cup of coffee. The quiet was nice, but he still missed the sense of community the Mana Wave Industries team had brought to the place when they worked there. The excited chatter, the buzz of activity, even the smell of soldering. It hadn't always been great for attracting other customers, but it had its appeal, and they'd bought plenty of coffee.

With one last whistled tune, Cam took his place behind the counter and opened a book. It wasn't the type of story his customers were enjoying. Most of those were thrillers or romances, comfort reading to go with a relaxed morning's coffee.

This was a very different beast and one illicitly acquired. It was almost tempting to hide it under the counter, but that seemed like it would draw more attention than it would dispel. Besides, who would recognize a dusty old leather book as one recently stolen from the city archives? No one who came into his coffee shop, that was who.

Cam poured himself a cup of coffee and started reading. A lot of the book wasn't going to be relevant. He could see that from looking at the contents page. The problem was that the editor who put it together hadn't understood the documents he was working with. If he had, he wouldn't have mislabeled the pages of the Tess prophecies. So while a lot of it might not matter, Cam needed to look through it all, just in case.

He skimmed through the first hundred pages, occasionally stopping when a relevant word caught his eye. As a history student, he'd gotten good at this sort of thing, scouring extensive documents for the relevant passages, wading through page after page of irrelevance to find the parts that mattered, the ones that excited him.

In a way, this whole book excited him. Before, he'd been working with scattered fragments drawn from all over the place. Now he held the possibility of gaining as much information from a single source, or at least a single collection of sources. Everything depended upon what the editor had gathered here. Like a pirate scouring a desert island, he hoped to find treasure amid the dust.

"Excuse me."

Cam looked up. He'd been so distracted by the book that he hadn't noticed a customer come in.

"Sorry about that," he said. "What would you like?"

He made a cappuccino as quickly as he could and skipped over the usual up-sell of persuading the customer that they wanted cake. He had bigger concerns right now. He'd barely finished taking the payment and handing over the cup before he got the book out again and carried on reading.

A moment later, his eyes lit up. There was another fragment of prophecy. This time it was copied out as part of a letter. A few months ago, he wouldn't have paid it any attention, but a single word made it stand out: Evermores.

"Then the darkness will come," the prophecy said. "Those who have stood so long the guardians of the gate will hold it open, and in their arrogance let destruction into the vale. Evermores, ever ready, ever unshifting, but a new world cannot be protected forever by the old. In the age of strings that sing with power, in the age when all is shrunken yet filled with power, in the age when worlds collide, nothing can stand eternal."

Cam kept reading. Whoever had written this letter had been eager to share the contents of a document they'd found because there were pages and pages of the stuff, some of it direct, other parts cryptic. There were kings and merchants, rising seas and falling mountains, all sorts of drama he couldn't quite untangle.

He knew that he would have to go over it again later. That was the other thing history had taught him, the importance of going over the details, of changing context, and working out what you'd missed.

He glanced up in case he'd missed a customer again, but the place was still quiet. Give it another half-hour and people would start coming in for lunch, but that gave him time to skip ahead and read the prophecy that had drawn him to the book.

There it was again, the text he'd already read. It described these Evermores, these magicals protecting a great power on Earth. The pages he'd seen hinted at who they were and what they did, but now he had more. The document continued, advancing into the future.

"Ever powerful, ever standing, ever silent," the prophecy said. "Ever vigilant against their discovery. How can anyone understand a world they've withdrawn from? How can they foresee the dangers of the future when they do not place themselves in the present?

"Ever watching, but never understanding, this shall become their flaw. Those who claim to stand between the world and darkness shall become the ones to unleash its power. The shining towers shall tumble, the beacon of the future shall snuff out, and the hope of a better world shall slide into shadow. But then…"

Cam turned the page. The next one was blank. He frowned as he stared at it, then flicked forward a few more.

The pages were numbered wrong. This part of the book had been misprinted or assembled incorrectly. Was the rest of the document still in here, put into the wrong place, or was it missing, lost, or abandoned to the flow of time?

He gritted his teeth and bit back a shout of frustration. He'd made progress. That was good. Now he knew that these mysterious Evermores would bring some sort of disaster. But what, and where?

Talk of darkness and destruction were standard in prophecies. They didn't tell him anything specific, but some details might. Shining towers. A beacon of the future. Hadn't there been something in the other letter, a reference to a vale? So, a disaster in a valley with shining towers, a place that was all about the future.

The door opened. A couple of wizards walked in, talking excitedly about computer code. The sounds of Mana Valley drifted in with them. Through the window, Cam caught a glimpse of sunlight shining off the glass of an office tower.

Mana Valley. Disaster was coming to the very place he lived, and these Evermores were going to bring it.

Cam half wanted to cheer in triumph, and half wanted to sink into despair. He'd been right, despite everything his family said. The pieces connected. He'd found something that mattered. But that thing was a terrible omen for him.

"Hey, you all right there?" one of the customers asked.

"Sorry, yes." Cam put the book away beneath the counter and put on his best professional smile. "Just got to a bit in my book that was too exciting."

"I know how that is. I keep reading horror stories before bed, and it's practically impossible to clear my head. My boyfriend keeps complaining because I want to sleep with the light on."

"Sounds like you might need decaf," Cam said. "Maybe a donut to go with it, for comfort?"

"Now you're talking."

While he was serving the wizards, a steam wagon pulled up in front of the shop. One door had a large dent, and the steam pipes along that side twisted so steam leaked out even when the conveyance stopped. The door opened and Fran stepped out, then closed the door carefully behind her.

Cam grinned. Fran seemed connected to something weird, but of all the people he knew, she was one he couldn't imagine bringing destruction anywhere. If he'd heard the word "Evermore" at her party, he hadn't heard it from her. They were something bigger, something he needed to hunt down, but nothing that should get between the two of them.

"That's quite a ride you showed up in," he said as she approached the counter.

"Oh, that old thing?" Fran glanced at the steam wagon as it drove away. "Singar hired it. We needed to get up into the hills."

"That explains the leaves." Cam reached out to pluck foliage from Fran's hair. "Was the wagon dented when you hired it?"

"Not exactly." Fran blushed. "We had, like, an incident while we were testing our prototype. But it was totally fine in the end, and Singar says she can fix up the wagon before she returns it, so we almost certainly won't lose our damage deposit." She frowned. "Almost certainly..."

"Doesn't Singar want your help with the repairs?"

"She said she wanted to do it by herself, something

about needing peace and quiet, which, you know, I get it in theory, but…" Fran shrugged. "I'm not a peace and quiet sort of girl."

"No, you aren't."

"What's that supposed to mean?"

"That you're lively, exciting, and always entertaining."

She blushed. "All right, I'll take that as a compliment."

"That's how I meant it. See, you're smart too, to understand where I'm coming from."

Fran laughed and shook her head. "I'm not sure that should be so funny, but I'm, like, super tired right now, and my brain doesn't have the will to resist."

"Maybe a coffee and donut will help?"

"They really would."

"What coffee would you like?"

"Surprise me. Make it strong with plenty of sugar."

"One syrupy cup of caffeine coming up."

Cam worked the grinder while Fran leaned against the counter with her head resting on her hands.

"How's the business going?" Cam asked over the roar of the machine. "I've missed you guys."

"I think we're going to make it. We have to deliver our first proper product tomorrow, and we got it working this morning. Is that unprofessional, leaving it to the last minute?"

"Sounds like you got the schedule just right." Cam put the coffee into the espresso machine and pressed a button. Steam poured through. "Congratulations on your first big win."

"Don't say that. You might jinx it! What if something goes wrong?"

"Then you'll fix it." He grinned and reached for the flavored syrups. "That's what you do."

"Aw, thanks." Fran blinked as she stared at the donut selection. "How about you? How's the research going?"

"Really well. I've made a big breakthrough, I think. Though again, I'm risking a jinx."

"So what did you learn? Something exciting about kings and queens or… Um, this is terrible. I've forgotten which bit of history you're researching."

Cam laughed. "Don't worry about it. Even my family can't remember, and I've been boring them about my thesis for years."

"Still, what's the big breakthrough?"

Cam hesitated, holding a can of squirty cream over an increasingly crowded coffee cup. Should he tell her? He'd long ago stopped talking about the subjects he was researching instead of the ones he was supposed to be working on.

People looked at him like he was crazy when he talked about what he'd found, which wasn't a lot of fun. Worse still, he'd realized that talking about it risked alerting the dark forces that he knew the world faced. For everyone's safety, he had to keep the secret until he worked out what was going on.

Surely there was no risk in telling Fran? With her eccentric interests and kind heart, she wasn't going to mock anyone else's obsessions, and she certainly wasn't going to be on the side of darkness. She had to be as far away from these Evermores and the disaster they were bringing as anyone could be.

He finished assembling the coffee with a sprinkle of silver sugar on the top, then handed it to Fran.

"Okay, so my big breakthrough isn't technically on my thesis," he said. "I've been looking into—"

The door opened, and a noisy band of skateboarders walked in, followed by half a dozen suited executives. The lunch rush had begun.

"You'd better deal with that." Fran took her coffee with her as she backed away from the counter. "Don't want to get in the way of business."

"Thanks. Maybe we can carry this on another time?"

"That would be great."

She headed out, taking her coffee with her. Cam slid his precious book well out of the way, then turned to his next customer with a smile. Prophecies of epic destruction would have to wait. He had coffees to make.

"Welcome to the Blazing Bean. What can I get for you?"

CHAPTER THIRTY-FOUR

There was a knock on the office door.

"Enter," Howard Phillips called, his attention never wavering from his computer screen. The quarterly profits weren't living up to the forecasts. All the managers were falling over each other in their efforts to explain why it wasn't their fault. They'd filled his inbox with thousands of explanations and excuses, their paranoia still cranked into overdrive by evaluation season.

It was exactly the atmosphere of fear he tried to cultivate. Let them all focus on their worst imaginings, even when those were as tedious as losing a job. Let the fear blot out the enjoyment of the here and now. That was how he would weaken the boundary between this world and the nightmare realm, how he would lay the groundwork for his minions to come through.

If they ever had a chance to come through.

He leaned back in his chair and turned to see the new arrivals. Julia had taken a chair across from him, one leg crossed over the other, dangling a spike-heeled shoe. Handar stood at attention, always waiting, always vigilant.

"Do take a seat," Phillips said.

There was a brief flicker in Handar's expression. Then he sat next to Julia. His head twitched from side to side, looking for threats that he felt more vulnerable to now he was seated. Julia shifted a little away from him, made uncomfortable by the Kilomea's sheer muscular presence. A little more misery in the world. That was what Phillips liked to see.

"How's it looking out there?"

"Same as every time we do evaluations," Julia said. "The survivors are caught between triumph and fear, worrying that they'll be the ones to face the ax next time. We've made sure that most of the empty desks stay conspicuously vacant for a few more days to let it sink in."

"Most?"

"There are a few good staff we wanted to give an extra boost to so things would keep moving smoothly in their areas."

"You mean you're playing favorites again."

She looked down, not at her tablet but at her fingernails. "I don't know what you mean."

"It's not a criticism, Julia. Favoritism is part of how business works, as well as fuel for the insecurities I enjoy. You've done doubly well by following that instinct. If it eventually leads to a competent recruit I can let into my inner circle, all the better."

"Thank you, Howard. It's good to know you trust me to do that right."

He decided to let that one slide. Let her have a moment

of stability and faith in her capabilities, in the strength of her relationship with him. He would relish undermining it later.

"Enough with the day-to-day." Phillips leaned forward, his hands clasped on the desk in front of him. "How has the hunt for the Evermores gone?"

"I've done what I could," Julia said. "Some detection spells, some scrying, but you know what the magical currents are like around here. Sometimes, trying to pick out nuance in the magic of Mana Valley is like looking for a specific grain of dirt in a swamp."

"What about your minions?"

Julia frowned. "My best agents are still missing after their last mission. There's no sign that the Silver Griffins have them, so either they're banished, or they escaped my bonds and deserted my service."

"Maybe someone more powerful captured your little toys."

"Not likely." Julia shook her head. "There are only a handful of people in Mana Valley who could've contained them, and I've been checking on those."

"The short version is that you failed?"

There it was, the moment when her wavering confidence collapsed. Her confident smile became a forced mask of calm, so similar that most people wouldn't have seen the difference, but Howard Phillips knew. The Darkness Between Dreams couldn't help but sense such things and relish them.

A tiny black tendril crept out from under the cuff of his shirt. He called it back in.

"I'm still looking for the targets," Julia said.

"I found one of them." Handar's mask of professional calm was different, more fierce, but it was still thin enough for his pleasure to show.

"You did?" Julia flashed a look at him. "Why didn't you tell me?"

Handar shrugged. "Why would I?"

A small smile crept up Phillips' face. There'd been a time when he'd worried that these two would become too close and that together they might become a threat. He needn't have worried. His usual management techniques of fear and division were doing their work.

"Tell me," he commanded.

"We were using that detection device you had made, the one calibrated to light and sound magic. Found a magical running the same route most days, a guy who dripped with light and sound power."

"How did he look?"

"Human-shaped, like a wizard or a shifter, but without their aura."

"Could you be more specific?" Julia asked.

Handar shrugged. "You lot all look pretty much the same to me. Male. Light hair. Some muscle, but not enough that I'd call it a problem."

"Yet you didn't capture him," Phillips stated flatly.

"No, sir," Handar replied. "I set up an ambush to detain the target, using some previously reliable agents, but it turned out that the target was tougher than he looked. He's a skilled fighter, even without weapons, and had more experience than you'd expect from his age."

"Age can be deceptive." Phillips tapped his cheek. "I

have endured for eternities, remember, unlike the one I peeled this disguise from."

"Right, sir. Well then, maybe he's older than he looks. I ain't good at judging that with humans."

"He fought his way clear, that's what you're telling me?"

"Used his magic too, and he didn't need a wand. That's how I know he wasn't only a wizard."

"Hm."

Phillips leaned back in his seat. The enemy was here, as he'd thought they would be, and they were exposed enough to try for a capture. Where did that leave him?

"What about the books I sent you to search out?" he asked.

"Books?" Julia raised an eyebrow. "You?"

"Yeah, me." Handar pulled a piece of paper from inside his jacket.

"You do know that we work for a technology company, right?" Julia said. "We have devices for making notes on."

"I like this way." Handar unfolded the paper and laid it on Phillips' desk. It was a list, and he'd crossed off every item on it—every item except one.

"I checked all of them books you told me to, except for one. The day I went for that one, some weird stuff happened at the archives. Someone else was there first, and they started messing with me. Moving shelves around, stopping the place from working right. They even set off some alarms. When it was all over, the book was gone."

"They stole the book from you?" Phillips asked.

"From the archive. I never saw it."

"Who were they, this mysterious thief?"

Handar shrugged. "I didn't see that either. Someone not tough enough to face me."

"That's almost everyone." Phillips laughed, then frowned as he turned his attention to the list. "So, someone else was after one of the books that might have led me to the remains of my prophecy."

"Prophecy?" Julia leaned forward. "Howard, why didn't you give this task to me? It sounds like something I would've been far better suited to."

Phillips gave her a disdainful look. "Are you questioning my judgment?"

"Of course not, I—"

"You think you know better."

"No, of course not, or at least not better than you, but..." She looked sideways at Handar. "I've worked with occult texts and prophecies before. I might've been able to make more progress with this one."

"You could have stopped someone who robbed me?" Handar snorted. "Yeah, right."

"Not everything is about brawn."

"This was."

"Enough," Phillips said sharply. "What matters is what we're missing. We don't have the book."

Handar shook his head. "Not yet, boss, but I'll find it."

"Could this book thief have been connected to the Evermores?"

"Could be. Although I've got no reason to think they were."

"Well, give it some thought. Someone getting in our way as we reach for them might not be a coincidence."

Phillips felt his mind beginning to strain as he faced

new and unexpected challenges. That strain put pressure on his ability to hold himself together, to stay within the confines of his skin suit, to keep the form of his disguise. He got up and paced the room while pressing his fingers against his temples.

"We need something else," he muttered. "Something I've missed."

His employees sat quietly, waiting for him to address them again. He hadn't dismissed them, and it was risky to preempt the boss's wishes when he might have more for them to do.

Handar's phone buzzed. Seeing that Phillips remained occupied, he pulled out the device and glanced at the screen.

"Small world," he said in a low rumble.

"What is it?" Julia whispered.

"What he wants to hear, I think." Handar raised his voice. "Sir, one of my people has spotted that Evermore again."

Phillips stopped his pacing and turned to face them.

"The one that got away from you before?"

"Yes, sir."

"Where?"

"Hanging out in some coffee shop. She's ninety percent sure it's him."

"Ninety is a very good start."

"Says he was hanging out with a bunch of weirdos from some tech startup, a place called Mana Wave Industries."

"Mana Wave... Should I know that name?"

The others shrugged.

"Hm." Phillips started pacing again. "So, we have two

targets, or perhaps one, a running Evermore and a book thief. By chasing the Evermores, the thief crossed our paths, so if they're relevant, following the Evermores should bring them out again. However, chasing down the Evermores didn't work to capture them before."

"I could try to grab him again. We know what we're facing this time, that he can fight and cast without his wand. I could bring in more guys, make sure he doesn't get away."

Phillips sat and laid his hands on the desk. A slender black tentacle crept out along one finger.

"There's a definition of madness that people keep repeating," he said. "That it's doing the same thing over and over again while expecting different results. Of course, I know that madness is so much more than that, but it's still a useful definition, something to watch out for. It's not a trap I intend to fall into.

"We tried to tackle this directly, and it didn't work. A different approach is needed. No street kidnappings, no trips to the city archives. Something else."

"Like what?"

Phillips grinned and tapped the side of his head. "Something smarter, Handar. Something I need time to plan out in detail. Don't worry. I'll call on both your services soon enough." He gestured dismissively toward the door. "You can both go. I'll call you when I need you again."

Julia and Handar got up and walked out. Julia closed the door behind them, then took her seat behind the desk outside Phillips' office. No one else was there. This was the outer sanctum of the leader of Philgard Industries, and ordinary workers didn't spend their time here. Even managers only came when summoned.

Handar paused for a moment, looking back at the door.

"You ever think that the boss ain't all right?" He tapped the side of his head. "Up here."

"Of course he's not right up there by mere mortal standards. You know what he is. You can't be that and still think like a simple wizard."

"Yeah, but…"

"You're the good soldier. I didn't think you questioned your superiors."

"I know, but…" He frowned like he was straining at some difficult task. "You were right. I was the wrong one of us to send after a book. And the tentacles are showing more. What happens if they show in front of someone else?"

"This is Mana Valley. Do you think we can't explain that away?"

Handar snorted. "Yeah, you're right." He smiled, baring more of his tusks. "Mad or not, I'd rather do this than any other job I've had."

"There's nothing like it, is there?" Julia smiled too. "Go get on with your security sweeps. I'll call you if he needs us."

"When he needs us. You heard him, there's a new plan coming, and we're gonna catch us some Evermores."

CHAPTER THIRTY-FIVE

"Hey, I know this place." Fran followed the Evermores out of their portal and into a kemana. "We're under San Jose, right?"

"That's right," Winslow said. "Although you probably could've guessed from the decor."

They looked around the cavernous space with its tech valley style. Wires and microchips formed knots and tangles around the central crystal, their ends diving into the ground around its base and stretching up its sides. Like the roots and creepers of an electronic plant, they sprawled across the kemana and up the surface of its magical power source. For a moment, Fran felt like an ant that had crawled into a computer, surrounded by wires and circuitry that meant nothing to her.

The buildings in the kemana were also tech-focused. There were magitech salesrooms, bars where automatic machines used artificial intelligence to serve drinks, and three places promising to fix broken machines. The people wore tech in their clothing, not only earbuds but shirts with keyboards woven into their sleeves, piercings that contained Wi-Fi boosters, and dozen of other devices.

Singar had gone straight to the crystal, pulled a tablet from the hefty backpack slung over her shoulders, and was taking photos of the tangled technology around its base. Fran walked over to her.

"Shouldn't we be getting set up?" Fran asked. "Winslow says that the Source is on its way."

"If that thing's coming, all of this could get trashed," Singar said. "Do you want it to be completely lost?"

"I don't know. What is it?"

"The ultimate in magitech. Technology that's grown out of the magic, or maybe grown to meet it. The two great powers of our age, combining in ways we didn't plan for. There have to be things here we can learn from."

"Wow, Sin, that was, like, totally insightful." Fran pulled out her phone and started taking photos too. "I'm really glad you joined the company."

"You're not bad either."

Winslow bustled up to them.

"I don't mean to rush you, ladies, but time is short," he said. "If you'd provided us with a containment unit sooner, we wouldn't have had to wait until the last minute to prepare for the Source's arrival, but now it's almost here."

"Don't you try to make this our fault." Singar turned on him angrily. "You didn't find a way to fix your problem. You should be glad that we're here to help, and you should think about what you're willing to pay for that assistance."

"Excuse me?"

"You heard. We're running a business, and we're not getting enough for this."

"Please, Singar." Fran laid a hand on her friend's arm. "Not now." She looked at Winslow. "We *will* talk about it later."

"Of course." He nodded. "For now, could we deal with the monster coming this way?"

Singar took off her backpack and set it on the ground. Together, she and Fran carefully opened it, then took out the pieces of the containment unit.

"That looks like a good spot." Singar pointed at a flat place in front of the crystal.

"Hang on," Fran said. "Which way will the Source come from?"

Winslow looked around thoughtfully, then pointed at another patch of ground. Fran looked from one place to another, judging the route from that spot to the kemana crystal, then nodded.

"You're right, Sin. Let's go there."

They set up the containment unit, starting with the mirror base and working up. Meanwhile, the Evermores spread out around them, taking their positions in a loose ring around the crystal.

"What's going on?" A Willen had stopped on his way past and was looking with curiosity at what they were constructing.

"Bad magic coming," Singar said. "We're stopping it."

"Shouldn't you call the Silver Griffins?" the other Willen asked. "Bad magic is their job."

Singar made a gesture with her paw that would've been impossible with human fingers.

"Well, really." The other Willen strode away.

"Was that some secret Willen signal?" Fran asked. "Like,

you warned him of the danger, and because of the signal, he knows he has to take it seriously?"

"More like I flipped him the bird."

"Oh!"

"Yeah. The Silver Griffins can go suck on dung for all I care. We're gonna fix this."

"You were complaining about us working for free!"

"Yeah, well, still better us than them." Singar slotted rods into place around the mirror. "Come on. Time's running out, remember?"

As they worked, the magical light from the kemana flickered. The effect grew more intense until it was like standing on a nightclub dance floor.

"Faster," Winslow snapped. "It's nearly here."

"We're going as fast as we can." Fran slid a cable into a socket on the side of the mirror, and its runes faintly glowed. "Almost there."

With a flutter of wings, a crow swept out of the darkness and landed on Fran's shoulder.

"Hey there," she said. "Good to see you. How did you get over here? Or are you one of the crows from this place?" The crow *cawed* urgently. "I'll check if I have food for you in a minute. I need to finish this first."

The crow jabbed her ear with its beak, making it impossible to ignore, then fluttered away to the side of the kemana. It looked back at Fran and waved a wing.

"Hey, that hurt," she said.

The crow flapped its wing again.

The ground shook, and a rumbling emerged.

"It's here." Winslow stepped back from the crystal. "The end of its trail."

The ground burst open, and the Source leaped out, glowing with an inner light. It was shaped like a lion but twice as big as any Fran had ever seen and had rows of spikes down its spine. Eagle-like wings protruded from its shoulders, and when it opened its mouth a long, serpentine tongue rolled out.

"Oh my!" Fran stumbled back, trailing the control wires for the containment unit.

"Back!" Winslow shouted.

Of course, he didn't obey his command. Winslow advanced to stand between the Source and the crystal as Fran and Singar retreated. Around them, the Evermores flung out beams of light, forming a ring of power, while other magicals fled.

"This can end peacefully." Winslow held out his hands. "Come with me back to where you belong. Make the world a safer place for everyone."

The Source threw back its head and howled. The result was a frenzied, horrifying noise that forced Fran to clasp her hands to the sides of her head as pain shot through her brain. Blood ran from Winslow's nose, but he stood his ground and raised his fists.

"Come on, then," he said. "Let's end this."

The Source charged. Winslow leaped to meet it in a flying kick. His foot collided with the side of its head. The creature's tongue lashed out and grabbed him around the waist, then flung him on the ground. A paw slammed down, and Winslow rolled clear just in time to avoid being stamped on.

"Now!" he shouted.

The Evermores had started chanting. Now their voices

rose in volume and their hands raised in front of them. A web of light running between them closed in on the Source.

The Source advanced on the crystal. Before it reached its target, the magical web closed around it. The Evermores raised their voices, and their chanting changed its pitch. The web dragged the Source toward the containment unit a few inches at a time.

The Source howled again, a terrible shrieking noise. One of the Evermores sank to the ground, writhing in pain. The section of the web that had come from her weakened. The Source put a clawed paw against it and pushed. Strands of magic unraveled beneath its concentrated power. It pushed another paw through, then heaved, tearing the web open. It cast the Evermores' spell aside and advanced on the crystal.

Winslow got to his feet. He was chanting now, joining the Evermores' song, reshaping it, redirecting it. Their magic darkened and became thicker strands.

It was too late. The Source had reached the kemana crystal. It pressed its paws against it and let out a low rumble.

Pulses of power ran through the stone. Its exterior strobed with multicolored light as the Source drained it. The creature opened its mouth, and the magic poured from the top of the crystal, running down the Source's throat in a golden stream. Around the base, some of the magical wires melted, while others turned into dust. The Source started to expand as it fed on the raw magical energy.

"We have to stop it." Singar reached for the controller in Fran's hand.

"Not yet," Fran said. "It's not close enough to the unit."

"If we leave it much longer, that thing will be too powerful to contain."

"No, we got it right this time. We can do it."

"Seriously, it's going to fail."

Fran laid a hand on Singar's shoulder. "Trust me. Trust yourself. We've got it."

The Source was bulging with power now. The wires and circuitry around its feet turned into nothing more than a thin, silvery sheen across the floor. It purred with pleasure, a sound loud enough to shake the ceiling above.

The Evermores had finished remaking their spell. Instead of a broad web, it was a single band of dark power. Winslow took hold of it and braced himself, then ran at the Source.

The Source couldn't see him coming, but it sensed his magic. It turned and lashed out with its paw as Winslow leaped at its back. The blow caught him in mid-air and sent him flying. The magical band fell from his hand.

The Source turned back to its feast. Winslow lay on the ground, unconscious. The other Evermores looked at each other, not wanting to abandon any part of their song and the magic they'd forged but unable to do anything with it while they stood there, their leader unconscious. Enfield's chest swelled as he drew a deep breath, bracing himself to take a chance.

"Here." Fran shoved the controller into Singar's hands. "Wait until I give the signal."

"What?" Singar stared at her. "Fine. But be careful."

Fran dashed out across the kemana and grabbed the band of fallen Evermore magic. It felt powerful in her hand, its magic resonating with her whole essence. Every word and note of its summoning song ran through her head, and she understood what she needed to do.

Fran ran at the Source. It turned again to face her and swung a vast paw around. She dodged to the side, like she was ducking around a slower skater at the park, then jumped. She landed on the bent joint of the Source's leg, jumped again, put a hand on its shoulder, and propelled herself up.

Fran stood on the top of the Source's back. It rose onto its hind legs, trying to shake her off, but she grabbed a fistful of its lion-like mane and clung on tight. Its front paws swung around, trying to knock her off, and it buffeted at her with its wings, but she still clung on.

From out of nowhere, a crow swept down and pecked at the tip of the Source's snout. For a moment, the magical creature stood stunned, caught completely by surprise.

Fran flung the magical band over its head and dragged it down across its shoulders.

"Drag it to the trap!" she shouted.

The Evermores waved and shifted their song. The Source staggered and strained, trying to resist, but the band of magic had a powerful hold and was dragging it toward the magical device with its glowing runes. As it stumbled onto the mirror, Fran leaped off its back.

"Now!" she shouted.

Singar tapped a button. The containment unit burst into light. The Source's reflected magic gave it more power than it had ever shown before. Magic rolled up across the

Source, forming a glowing cocoon that snapped shut at the top, its shape made more rigid by the extending poles up the sides and the mirror at the base.

"We got it!" Singar grinned as she scanned the readouts on her controller. "It's trapped."

The Evermores stopped their chanting and instead started shouting in celebration. Fran and Enfield ran over to Winslow, one of them crouching on each side of him. Enfield carefully lifted his master's head.

Winslow opened his eyes and blinked at the light from the containment unit.

"Did we get it?" he croaked.

"Totally!" Fran held her hand out in front of him. Winslow looked at it in confusion, but Enfield understood. He returned her high five.

Beyond the Source, the crystal had stopped flickering. Fran feared that the creature had drained it, but instead it glowed steadily again, more steadily than the power she'd seen in any kemana on Earth recently. The air around her felt different. The power flowing through the world was more certain, more stable.

"We did it," she said with pride.

She only wished that she better understood what it was they'd done.

CHAPTER THIRTY-SIX

The gates of the FBI testing ground opened, and the Mana Wave Industries team walked through. Fran and Bart went first, with Elethin close behind to make sure they didn't say anything inappropriate. Gruffbar and Singar carried a crate between them, while Smokey brought up the rear, tail swishing from side to side.

"I feel like I'm locked up already." Singar looked at the razor wire that ran along the top of the chain-link fence.

"I assure you, ma'am, none of you have anything to worry about." Agent Baldwin, dressed in a black suit and tie, stepped up to meet them. "Not as long as you've fulfilled your contract."

"Oh, we have." Fran pointed at the crate. "I think you're going to like what we've done."

"Let's find out, shall we?"

Baldwin led them past a series of anonymous buildings to a dirt yard surrounded by low huts.

"Y'all can set up here. I'll be back in two shakes."

He disappeared around the corner, leaving them alone with their crate and the empty buildings.

"I bet they're watching us," Singar said.

"Of course we're being watched." Gruffbar pointed at a set of security cameras on top of a pole, then at more on the corners of the buildings. "This is a test and training range. It's all about being watched and judged."

"Then let's make sure they like what they see." Fran opened the lid of the crate. "We'll be, like, the most professional tech people ever."

"How about we just aim for competence?"

Together, the team took the pieces of the containment unit out of the packaging they'd used to transport it, then set it up in the middle of the open space. Using a set of sensors, Smokey measured background magic levels and started calibrating the controls.

"Everything seems a lot more settled now over here," he said. "None of the magical failures people were talking about."

"That's because of what we did, right?" Fran asked. "I mean, with the Source, and, you know…"

Her voice trailed off. She probably shouldn't say any more in front of all these security cameras. After all, the Evermores were still trying to keep themselves secret, and it probably wouldn't be good to let the Earth authorities know what they'd done without their permission.

"Probably." Singar shrugged. "Correlation doesn't always mean causation, but this time it seems pretty clear."

They finished assembling the containment unit, then stepped back.

"Does it always take this much setup?"

They turned to see Agent Baldwin watching them. Five other suited witches and wizards stood behind him.

"We're being extra careful for the test run," Fran said. "Everything should go more quickly once your team is trained to use it. Speaking of which, is this them?"

"No, these are your test targets." Around Baldwin, the witches and wizards pulled out their wands. "You need to get one of them into your magical cage."

Fran exchanged a look of shock and uncertainty with Bart.

"Us?" she said. "We're not law enforcement professionals. Surely the people who use it—"

"I need this thing to be idiot-proof." Baldwin tapped his wand against the side of his head. "I ain't saying you're all idiots, but you ain't exactly trained FBI either, so show me that your device can do what's needed. No need to catch all of us. One will be fine."

"You're ordering us to beat on the feds?" Singar grinned. "Best day ever."

"Sin!" Fran exclaimed, shocked. "This is the FBI. They protect people by upholding the law."

Singar snorted. "We can talk definitions of protection later. For now, let's have fun."

The FBI agents spread out around the open space with their wands ready. Fran gathered her team.

"How should we do this?" she asked.

"Same way we always do." Gruffbar cracked his knuckles. "Get creative, and make a big impression."

He flung aside his leather jacket and charged straight at Baldwin.

The agent raised his wand and shot a spell at the racing

dwarf. Bart had hurried after Gruffbar and countered it with a wave. Gruffbar slammed into Baldwin, knocking him back into the wall of one of the huts. Baldwin grabbed Gruffbar's arm and twisted him around, but then Singar was on them. She scrambled up Baldwin's back and twisted the agent's arm up behind him.

"Cover us!" Gruffbar shouted.

The other five agents were closing in with raised wands, their expressions grim. Fran remembered just in time to pull out the substitute wand she carried to disguise her strange powers. She didn't use it to cast but waved it anyway so the blast of her magical sound seemed to emanate from the wand's tip. The sonic assault hit two agents, who clutched their ears and sank to the ground, groaning. Three more were still coming.

"Help!" Fran called.

Elethin appeared beside her, hands moving as if weaving something invisible between her fingers. Points of light appeared, dancing slowly through the air. Two more of the agents stopped and stared, hypnotized by her powers.

One agent was still loose. He ran at Fran, pulling out an extending baton as he went. This was a wizard more at home with his body than with his magic.

In a gray-black blur, Smokey dashed out between the agent's feet. The agent tripped, fell, and sprawled full length in the dirt, his baton flying from his hand. He rolled over and grabbed Smokey, who shifted, turning from a small cat to a hairy dwarf who grabbed the agent's arms and pinned him to the ground.

"Got him!" Smokey yelled. "Go on, guys, you got it!"

While Fran and Elethin kept their targets down, Gruffbar and Singar wrestled Agent Baldwin toward the containment unit. The agent managed to raise his wand and point it at Gruffbar's face, but before he could cast any magic, Bart launched a spell. A tangle of gooey threads covered Baldwin's mouth, stopping him from chanting spell vocals, and another bundle of them bound his wand hand to his chest.

"Almost there," Gruffbar shouted. "Smokey, the controls."

"I can't." Smokey was rolling in the dirt, grappling with the FBI agent he'd tripped. One moment, the hairy dwarf was on top, the next the suited agent.

"I've got it." Fran gave one last blast of sound, making her targets curl in around their aching heads. Then she lowered her hands and dashed for the containment unit's controls. With a tap of her finger, the containment field sprang into life as Singar and Gruffbar were hauling Baldwin toward it.

Baldwin twisted, got hold of Singar, and flung her at the unit. Fran switched off the field, and Singar flew through it, landing facedown in the dirt. Then Fran switched the power back on.

Baldwin and Gruffbar staggered toward the containment unit, wrestling with each other. It could easily go either way, with the dwarf or the agent pushing the other into the field. As Baldwin swung Gruffbar around, Fran dashed over and raised her hand. She flung a cluster of flashing lights into Baldwin's face. He staggered back and let go of Gruffbar to swat the lights away. Gruffbar took his chance, grabbed the agent around the waist, and threw him into the field.

There was a flash, a *sizzle*, and Baldwin stood trapped on the mirror base, banging his fists against the magic around him. For nearly a minute, he battered against the field with all his strength while Fran and her team fended off the other FBI agents. Then suddenly, Baldwin went still.

"All right, that'll do," Baldwin said with a smile.

The agent wrestling with Smokey went prone. The others took steps back.

"So… You like it?" Fran asked.

"I'm not sure like's the right kind of word for this situation." Baldwin tapped a finger on the field constraining him. "I'm very impressed. Consider the first stage in your contract fulfilled. Now, would you let me out?"

Singar tapped the controls, and the containment unit switched off. Baldwin stepped out and dusted himself down.

"This is quite a team you have here, Ms. Berryman." He nodded respectfully at Fran. "And quite a machine. We'll take it out into the field next for some real-life testing, see how it stands up and what we'd like changed. All being well, we can move on from there to a mass production order."

"Woohoo!" Fran pumped her fist in the air, then remembered that she was supposed to be the calm, professional CEO of a serious tech company. "I mean, that sounds fine. My people will talk to your people."

"What they'll mostly talk about is money," Bart said. "If

you're keeping this device, we need payment. Plus, there's an upfront fee for tech support during the field trials."

"Of course." Baldwin took out his phone and tapped on the screen a few times. "That should cover it. Congratulations, I believe y'all just made your first profit."

"Profit's a strong word," Bart said. "But it's some revenue at least, and that means we can pay our bills."

"Well, that's your business, and this device is mine now. Does it come with a manual?"

"I'll email you instructions," Singar said. "And I'm available if you want in-person support."

"I thought you hated the authorities," Fran whispered.

"Know your enemy," Singar muttered so only Fran could hear.

They helped the agents move the containment unit into one of the buildings and showed them how the controls worked. Then Agent Baldwin walked the Mana Wave team to the front gate.

"Can I call y'all a ride?"

"No, thank you," Fran said as they stepped out between the razor wire-topped fences. She pulled out her portal mirror. "We have this."

"Okay then. See you around." Baldwin headed back into the base.

"What's next?" Elethin asked.

"Time to celebrate," Fran said. "Coffee and cakes at the Blazing Bean, maybe? Or did we earn enough to make it cocktails this time?"

Bart looked up from his phone. "This is cocktail money."

"Brilliant. I'm getting something with a twirly straw and sparklers."

"No one should drink cocktails with a straw, never mind sparklers." Elethin shook her head. "That's not what I meant. I wondered what we'd produce next in terms of technology. We've made the containment units, and we might be making more in the future, but in the meantime, you need another project. Something not tied to this contract, and I need to know what it is so I can start planning publicity."

"Oh, yeah, cool." Fran tapped on the side of her mirror. A portal opened, straight back into their basement office. "Singar and I have a load of prototypes we could work with, but if you've got ideas too, I'd love to hear them. Right now, I feel like we could make anything…"

Get sneak peeks, exclusive giveaways, behind the scenes content, and more. PLUS you'll be notified of special **one day only fan pricing** on new releases.

Sign up today to get free stories.

Visit: https://marthacarr.com/read-free-stories/

AUTHOR NOTES - MARTHA CARR

DECEMBER 5, 2021

Does everyone know the story, A Christmas Carol by Charles Dickens? Let's recreate that but instead of three ghosts that are warnings to Scrooge – I'm going to do three short stories from my own life as a kind of gift of gratitude.

The first one is from five years ago in 2016 when I went to hear Michael Anderle speak at a writer's group. Over ninety people showed up to find out how this new author was making so much money after only being published for six months at the time – and in fiction. That was supposed to be impossible.

I took with me a teenage writer who had already written her first space opera and was hard at work on her next novel. Maybe we could both get at least some interesting marketing tips. I mean, come on, could this Anderle be for real?

About halfway into his chat with us in a small room crammed with people, I realized Michael was onto something that the rest of us in the indie writer's world had

329

missed. He was writing the books he wanted to see that he enjoyed reading and he was a voracious reader. What we call a whale reader. Someone who reads a book a day instead of watching TV. His stories were filled with action and adventure and characters who really liked each other. A great place to escape and have some fun. Turns out, that particular and very large audience didn't have enough books to read, and he gave them a tale that was perfectly suited to them.

At the end of his talk, he finished by saying, "I will stay as long as anyone has a question." I thought I'd have to pass because I had a teenager to get home, but as the other writers streamed past me, they were all muttering to each other that Michael was a fake, a fraud. When I looked back at the podium, only two other writers had gone up to ask him a question. I took my chance and went up there to pepper him with questions and get his contact information.

And I was the only one out of 90 writers who stayed in touch.

Here we are at almost 200 books later and one large universe named, Oriceran and I'm still very grateful for going to that meeting and believing in the possibilities.

The second story would have to be in the present if we're following behind Scrooge's ghosts. The year 2021 for me was filled with doctors and surgeons. I had my 5th bout of cancer and a strenuous round of chemo and a few surgeries. Doesn't sound like the start of a gratitude list but stay with me.

In every large life event, there's always something to learn that could change everything that comes after it – if we're open to it. Frankly, the gifts are always there but most of the time we're so busy with ordinary life, we don't notice.

But chemo will get you to slow down and notice and be present. I didn't have a lot of choice and fortunately knew it and gave it pretty early. Let's just take this ride and be a passenger for a while.

What I learned was there are people around me who have my back. They showed up and made sure everything still ran smoothly and that I was never alone. Charley showed up from Idaho for a week, on loan from his wife, to fix things around the house and make a lot of soup. Sue showed up to sit on the back porch with me and talk about whatever came up. Marissa, Kyle and Janine arrived from Chicago to help celebrate different events and handle all the details. Michael made sure the business kept going and called, often. And those are just a few of the stories. Is there a better gift than being able to see there's a loving community right around me?

Even better, the medical maelstrom is over at least for now and I can head into the new year grateful to have survived all of it and focus on getting stronger. All good news.

Now for the last story. What does the future hold?

Without a ghost to lead the way, there's no way to actually know. Asking 'what if' is like asking a magical question. However, I can instead ask myself if I'm doing my part to stay healthy, to nourish those connections with the people in my life, to stay present and let go of the past or the future. In other words, to keep believing in the possibilities of this very good life, without dictating what it has to look like. Sure, there will be bumps in the road along the way. That's part of life and I've had my share. But what I do with the experience and where I put my focus is up to me. That makes all the difference. Happy Holidays everyone. More adventures to follow

AUTHOR NOTES - MICHAEL ANDERLE

DECEMBER 5, 2021

Thank you for not only reading this story but these author notes as well.

Martha has had a very hard year, but it's finally turning around for her.

One of the items I missed this year was just how much the medicines were taking from her. (Martha, your ability to hide that is amazing. I apologize that I didn't clue in!)

On the other side, it means that she is coming out of the fog her thinking process has been in and the monster is back!

OH CRAP, IS SHE BACK!

In hindsight, it's obvious now how much the medicine was taking from her, but it happened over time, and I didn't catch on.

Trust me, she is making up for lost time.

Together, we will be coming up with two (2) new series in the next thirty to forty-five days and planning 2022 like two sugar fiends just finding out that chocolate is a thing.

One we have been batting around for a couple of

months, during the challenging time we decided on a new type of Urban Fantasy that both of us are excited to push forward, and I'm looking forward to deciding if we will move forward with another Goth Drow set of books.

If you are a Goth Drow fan (and if you don't know the series, by all means go check it out!) let us know if you would like more books, ok? It would certainly help me with the ammunition I need to convince her it's a good idea, ok?

(Editor's note: <waves hand>. Loved that series!)

I'm presently in New York City for a dinner (unexpected invite) and I hope to see the famous Christmas Tree while we are here. Down in Cabo San Lucas, Christmas decorations aren't a huge thing (more tourist-based) than I'm accustomed, so it feels a little like the North Pole when the snow has melted.

Huh, considering it's nearer the equator, maybe that isn't a bad example.

Have a fantastic week or weekend. and I look forward to talking to you in the next book!

Ad Aeternitatem,

Michael Anderle

BOOKS BY MARTHA CARR

Other Series in the Oriceran Universe:

THE LEIRA CHRONICLES
CASE FILES OF AN URBAN WITCH
SOUL STONE MAGE
THE KACY CHRONICLES
MIDWEST MAGIC CHRONICLES
THE FAIRHAVEN CHRONICLES
I FEAR NO EVIL
THE DANIEL CODEX SERIES
SCHOOL OF NECESSARY MAGIC
SCHOOL OF NECESSARY MAGIC: RAINE CAMPBELL
ALISON BROWNSTONE
FEDERAL AGENTS OF MAGIC
SCIONS OF MAGIC
THE UNBELIEVABLE MR. BROWNSTONE
DWARF BOUNTY HUNTER
ACADEMY OF NECESSARY MAGIC
MAGIC CITY CHRONICLES
ROGUE AGENTS OF MAGIC

OTHER BOOKS BY JUDITH BERENS

OTHER BOOKS BY MARTHA CARR

JOIN THE ORICERAN UNIVERSE FAN GROUP ON FACEBOOK!

CONNECT WITH THE AUTHORS

Martha Carr Social

Website: http://www.marthacarr.com

Facebook: https://www.facebook.com/
groups/MarthaCarrFans/

Michael Anderle Social

Website: http://lmbpn.com

Email List: http://lmbpn.com/email/

https://www.facebook.com/LMBPNPublishing

https://twitter.com/MichaelAnderle

https://www.instagram.com/lmbpn_publishing/

https://www.bookbub.com/authors/michael-anderle